I NEVER GET LOST IN THE WOODS

I NEVER GET LOST IN THE WOODS

Aaron Jepson

Waterside Productions

ISBN-13: 978-1-960583-01-7 print edition
ISBN-13: 978-1-960583-02-4 e-book edition

Waterside Productions
2055 Oxford Ave
Cardiff, CA 92007
www.waterside.com

To my parents, who have never given up on helping me find my voice.

CHAPTER ONE

The woods were silent and growing darker as the sun began its descent below the distant horizon. Sandra Lewis was usually not afraid of the dark and had spent countless hours exploring these woods behind her condo complex, so she had no concern about getting lost. She knew exactly where she was and had all her familiar landmarks mapped out in her mind.

But today, something felt different. She could feel it from deep inside, where she imagined that her soul resided. She had never doubted that she had a soul—some other part of her being that couldn't be measured or quantified but was as important a part of her as her body and blood and the parts that had been damaged or just hadn't turned out right. Her soul was not damaged, and it had never lied to her. So, when it told her that something was wrong, she believed it.

· · ·

She needed to get back to her condo soon, or her mother was going to panic and would likely call the police. Every evening at the exact same time—eight o'clock—she called her mother on the telephone, not for the conversation because Sandra couldn't have one, but as a signal to her mother that she was home, and that all was well.

That phone call was on the list of conditions expertly nego-tiated, not by herself—she didn't have the verbal skills for a debate—but by her father, acting on her behalf. Not in a court or anything. No, her parents were still together then and had always made a great team, but Sandra knew which parent to work on when she really wanted something big, and moving out on her own was the biggest thing she could have ever imagined.

Sandra was twenty-five years old at the time and had never spent a single night away from her parents since she was born. She knew that wasn't normal and that most people her age had started careers or families of their own. Sandra's disability had stolen those options from her. But her inner voice, her soul's voice, would not be silenced.

Do it, Sandra. Now is the time. Now while your parents are close by, holding a light up for you. Would you rather start this journey in complete darkness? Do it now! Find your courage! It is right there within you. You are strong. You will succeed.

That voice was familiar, friendly. It had been there as long as she could remember, giving comfort, encouragement, and pushing her gently toward new heights. But there was another voice inside, too, an even louder and more persistent voice. She imagined that it was coming directly from her brain, the organ they say causes autism. It reminded her of her limitations and held her back, constantly telling her that she was slow, damaged, disabled.

Sandra knew that she couldn't keep putting off this decision. Her parents, Tony and Susan Lewis, were getting older. Susan had become pregnant with Sandra in her late forties. They were now both in their seventies. She loved them with all her heart. They had always been there for her, through it all, as difficult as that must have been. But they could not be there forever. She didn't want to be helpless and dependent if something happened to them. She was afraid that she would end up in some group home with rules that she didn't agree to, in a place that was unfamiliar.

She had lived in the same house in Whitefish, Montana, for the last ten years, ever since her father had retired from his job as an investment banker in Chicago. She loved it here. She loved the quiet pace of the Montana lifestyle. She loved the seasons. She loved the clear skies. Mostly she loved hiking in the nearby woods. The woods were the one place on earth where she didn't feel the weight of her disability, dragging her down, telling her that she was incapable.

The woods gave her the energy to face each day. She could feel it just being nearby, inside her home that sat adjacent. Or, maybe, her parents carried the same energy, and it was only because of them that she was able to get out of bed each morning. Sandra didn't know, but her nature craved the answer.

Independence. She thought about it constantly. It enticed her, tempted her. Like a young bird with newly formed feathers, she was desperate to feel the wind buoy her up and to see if she could fly. Of course, the risk was a hard fall from the safety of her parents' nest.

Would her parents let her try? Did they understand that she was ready, that she had to spread her wings? Or would they, also, focus on the things that made her different and would put her at risk of getting snatched up by a fox or a bird of prey? Would her instinct to leave her parents' protection be a major error that could damage her forever and result in a cage with a tether? At least now, she still lived in the comfort of the wild with caregivers that provided everything she needed. Would she wither and die when they were no longer there?

She was afraid of the future either way, so she had to at least try to gain some control over it. But how was she, a girl with such limited language, supposed to find the words that would help her parents understand? Her parents were the only two people in the world that she knew she could rely on. Could they hear her soul speak? If so, they would know her intent. It was not to get away from them but to honor them by showing how far she had come. She also needed to prove to herself that the many years of hard work had been worth it. She knew that if her freedom was ever taken away by some well-meaning social worker, her soul would forever be silenced.

Her brain would cheer that moment, that loss of freedom. Her selfish brain kept her locked in a castle with rock walls and a moat filled with anxiety. Her brain, the merciless guard who held the only key, decided what was allowed through the gate. The thoughts that enjoyed complete freedom within the walls would never see the other side of the bridge. The only time that she felt free from her prison was when she was out in the woods. There she could see the cracks in the wall and the moat began to drain. There, she didn't have to listen to her brain because the woods demanded it be still.

She had discovered the power of the woods during her daily hikes with her father. They had made that part of their routine shortly after moving to Montana. Their house backed to the forest and connected them to the foothills and the mountains beyond. They had spent hours exploring the trails until she had learned every meadow and ravine. Her dad tested her by making her lead the way home, and when she had gained his trust, he let her spend time alone, as long as she wore a tracking watch and carried a phone. They practiced getting lost or injured so that she would know what to do. Over the years, she had earned more time, and now she was allowed hours on her own—in the woods.

The woods had become part of her, or she part of it. It was like a living organism, not just a collection of trees and rocks. Below the surface of its soil, the forest was intimately connected, the roots acting like neurons that could sense danger, assess health, and send signals to distant parts. She could feel its life, could hear it breathe, could feel its heart beating, and her soul becoming one with it.

The life blood of the forest was the stream which flowed year-round through a circulatory system of rivulets and springs. The snow melt swelled it beyond its borders in the spring, but most of the year its flow was gentle and welcoming. The babble of its waters traversing the rocks and fallen trees spoke a language that her soul could hear and understand. The stream invited her daily to come and sit and chat awhile.

Sandra could see the condos from one of her favorite places next to the stream, where a small waterfall had created a deep pool of circular rather than directional flow. She loved to sit on the large flat rock that hung over the pool and soak her feet in the cool water. That spot felt energized to Sandra. She wasn't sure if it was the change in the water or something else, but it felt like this was where the stream had a purpose. Here, she could see trout swimming in the clear water, waiting for food to get trapped in the pool. Sandra was fed here, too. She felt different here, full of energy and courage.

She sat at that spot on the rock, next to the stream, and her soul allowed her to dream. *What would it be like to live on my own—in the condos by the woods?* She knew that she had the basic skills. Her mother had taught her all those things. She had enough money. Her father had made sure of that long ago. She could still go to her favorite places every day. Forest access was non-negotiable. She would be only blocks from her parents and could see them every day. The spot was perfect. More than once, she committed to figure out how to tell her parents but lost her resolve when she stepped from the woods.

Finally, she decided she couldn't wait any longer and woke determined to start the discussion. She knew that it would have to be with her dad; she would get nowhere with her mom by herself. She had to first convince her dad and then partner up with him if she stood any chance of getting her wish.

After lunch, instead of grabbing her watch and phone and heading out the door, she hung around in his office until he took notice.

"No hike today, Sandy?" he asked, surprised to see her.

She went over to the desk, grabbed his arm, and pulled him out of the chair.

"You want me to come with you today?"

"Yes, dad," she smiled.

"Well, okay, I could use some fresh air. Let me grab my jacket," her dad said, happy to be invited.

As they walked down the porch steps, Tony turned toward the woods, but Sandra again grabbed his arm and pulled him toward the street.

"No woods today?" he questioned. "Where are we going then? The park? We haven't been there for a while."

"Yes, Dad. Park." Sandra replied.

Sandra and Tony walked along the road that headed to the park. It was autumn, and the maple trees had turned a bright shade of orange, creating a colorful tunnel where they walked. The crisp fall air was invigorating and boosted Sandra's courage. As they approached the park, Sandra once again grabbed her father's arm and pulled him off course.

"What is it, Sandy?" her dad asked. "Did you forget something?"

She pointed at the condo complex and pulled her dad toward the building.

"Do you need to go to the bathroom?"

"No, Dad."

"Okay?" he said, confused. "A drink of water?"

"No."

She pointed at the units and stood her ground.

"Ahh!" her dad said, after a brief pause. "I think I know what you want. You want to look inside one of these condos, don't you! You want your own place! Am I right, Sandy?"

Sandra smiled and nodded shyly. Now she *was* nervous. She felt that familiar sense of darkness starting to gather around her.

What are you thinking, stupid girl? Her brain began its protest. *You are not ready for this!*

Stop! her soul commanded. *She is ready.*

Tony went into the building and came out with the manager. "It looks like they have a couple of empty units that he could show us. You want to go look?"

Sandra's squeal was a clear reply.

"Okay," the manager said, "right this way."

Tony led Sandra up the stairs to the third floor and down the hall. The manager opened the unit and let them inside. It was not big but was comfortable and updated. There were two bedrooms, a small kitchen/dining area, and a living room—more than enough for Sandra. She could see herself already moving in boxes and furniture. But her dad had a frown on his face. *He didn't like it?*

"Well, Sandy, I can tell that you like it, don't you?" he said quietly.

Sandra nodded and smiled.

"You know that this will be a tough sell to your mother, right?"

Sandra looked down at the floor. There was a prolonged silence between them before she looked up again at her father's face. He was smiling and looking at her with what seemed like pride on his countenance. "I'll take care of it," he said with a wink.

...

Susan Lewis had dedicated her entire life to Sandra. She had studied everything there was to know about her disability, had taken her to the best therapists, the best doctors. She was demanding of all of them. She had spent hours a day working with Sandra on her own, teaching, explaining, drilling. As Sandra got older, the therapies had stopped, but Susan was still always there, making sure that her needs were met, doing her best to read her mind and to give what she could. It had been an exhausting journey but one they had traveled together every step. Sandra knew that a step back would be the most difficult one for her mother to take.

Tony sat down with Susan later that night. "Susie, I need to talk to you about Sandy. She communicated something to me today, and I think we need to consider it."

"Communicated? What do you mean, Tony?" Susan had replied.

"In her way, Susan. In her way."

"What? And how exactly?"

"She took me by the hand and led me to those condos on Forest View Street on our way to the park. She wanted to look inside. She wants her own place, Susan."

"Her own place? Are you kidding? She can't live on her own."

"Susie, we don't know that unless she tries. Letting her try it now, when we are both right here to help her, is the perfect way to see if she can ever have any level of independence. Sandra can prepare her own food, she can wash her own clothes, she keeps her room immaculate. You have taught her all those things. She can respond verbally with simple words, enough to get by at a store or a movie theater. Again, those are skills that you have drilled with her for years."

"Yeah, but it's not safe for her to be alone, Tony!" Susan argued.

Tony countered gently. "She can recognize danger, can dial 911, can report her name and address, and she knows our phone number. We could practice calling home. You can spend as much time there as you want, but for Sandra to have her own space and her own responsibility would be a major breakthrough for her. If it doesn't work, she can move right back home."

"But, what for? She has her own space here. She can do all of that here," Susan objected.

"True. But what will happen when we aren't here anymore? We are no longer young, Suz. We have to help her be ready for the inevitability of us not being around. Who do you trust to take care of her? Truly care for her and not just package her up and put her away?"

Susan was silent. She knew that Tony had a point, though she didn't want to admit it. She was no longer close to her family. She hadn't seen them for years. They didn't know Sandra. They wouldn't know what was best for her. She needed to start planning for Sandra's future without them.

It took weeks before Susan would even go look at the condo. She knew that she should, but the thought of Sandra there by herself was still too painful for her to wrap her head around. Eventually, she conceded to Tony's reasoning and told him to set up an appointment.

After looking through it, she had to admit that the condo was nice. Quiet. Sandra would love that. And the parking lot was adjacent to the woods, immediate access to the one place on earth where Sandra truly felt at peace.

"Okay," Susan said, barely above a whisper.

"What was that?" Tony asked, his hand cupped behind his ear and a smile on his face.

"I said okay. She can try it, but ... "

Sandra jumped up and down with excitement and gave her mom a quick-release hug.

"Are you sure about this, Sandy?" her mother asked her with a worried expression on her face.

Actually, Mom, I'm scared to death about it, but I know that I've got to try it. I need to start gaining control over my own destiny, or my destiny will be decided for me. I can't let people who don't know me tell me what they think is best. Now is the time. Thank you for giving me a chance. Sandra thought this response out in her mind, but what came out of her mouth was a simple, "Yes, Mom."

...

Sandra heard a twig snap close by which quickly brought her back to the present—out in the woods, darkness emerging, and her soul sending a warning.

She had planned on going home earlier tonight as the autumn days were getting shorter, and the night temperatures were starting to feel like the approaching winter. But as she stood from her spot by the stream and started walking home, a large buck crossed the trail in front of her. She had always had a particular fascination with the animals in the forest, almost a kinship. They relied on the woods just like she did, and they didn't seem to be afraid of her. She loved to follow them and watch how they ate, how they listened for danger, how they moved quietly through the trees.

She looked up at the sky. It was a bright orange sunset with a deep blue backdrop. *I have about twenty minutes*, she reasoned. *I'll just follow you for a little bit and see where you are headed.*

The deer moved slowly toward the stream, choosing its steps wisely and pausing frequently to look around and then to take a bite of grass. Sandra loved the grace of its movement, the strength in its hind quarters that were always on alert, ready to bound off at a moment's notice. Its antlers were fully developed and polished to magnificence. Its coat had changed into the dusty color that would carry it through the winter. Its neck was thickening from the hormones preparing it for the rut.

She followed it downstream and watched it refresh itself from the crisp spring water, but then, without warning, the buck quickly raised its head with ears standing alert and pointing down the hill. With a sudden majestic leap, the deer was gone, and Sandra was left standing alone, her skin tingling, and the hair on her arms erect.

She turned her head to face down the hill to see if she, too, could hear the danger to which the deer was so attuned. Was it a predator? A mountain lion or a bear? Sandra had seen them before, and they had never bothered her. She just stayed still until they caught her scent, and then they diverted away from her on their own. It was never at night, though, when they were hunting.

Could it be another human? That was possible but seemed unlikely, at this hour especially. Sandra was always amazed about how infrequently she saw other people in the woods, despite all the houses that bordered them. She mostly avoided the occasional hiker, as they wandered past her on the network of trails. They were loud and unaware of even their immediate environment most of the time. They were outsiders, invaders. She would usually just sit quietly and wait for them to pass.

As she ran through these possible explanations in her mind, she heard a sound from down the hill, a sound that was very out-of-place. It was the unmistakable sound of shovel hitting dirt. *Why would someone be digging in the forest at this hour, with the sun setting and dark rapidly approaching?*

She felt the woods signaling that its surface was being violated. She couldn't explain how she could feel the woods speak to her. It was like a sensation that rose from her feet as they contacted the forest floor.

Humans were causing destruction again. It was her job to stop them. She had always felt personally responsible for all the man-made scars in the woods and did everything she could to reverse them, whether it was picking up trash, scattering rocks and ashes from a fire ring, or clearing a campsite of evidence of human activity. She restored the forest. She cherished that role and felt pride in giving back to the woods that gave her so much.

Now the woods, her woods, were being injured again. She must find a way to put an end to it now before it got worse. She crept slowly toward the sound, staying under the cover of the trees, and letting the stream disguise her footfall.

As she approached, she could hear voices, male voices. They sounded young, maybe teenagers. One voice, the most prominent, sounded angry. No ... *Mean. Threatening.* The other voices sounded scared.

"Hurry up, idiots! How long does it take to dig a freaking hole in the ground?"

"It's not that easy! There are roots and stuff!"

"Just shut up and keep digging! I'll give you five more minutes, and if it's not finished, I'll shoot one of you, and the other one gets to dig a second grave."

"Jeez, man. What's the matter with you, all of a sudden?"

"Dig!"

Sandra inched closer until she could see their shadows through the trees. There were three of them, and one, the one with the deepest voice was pointing at the other two, who were busy digging in the space nearby, just on the edge of a small clearing in the trees. The standing figure shifted slightly, and she saw a flash of metal reflect the rising moon from his hand. *A gun! He was holding the other two at gunpoint!*

"That's good enough!" the deep voice said. "Just throw him in, and let's get out of here."

The others stepped up out of where they had been digging, and with some effort, rolled a large object wrapped in a tarp to the edge of the hole. With another push, the object disappeared with a thud as it hit the bottom of the hole. *Not a hole, a grave.*

Sandra began to panic inside as she gained full realization about what she was witnessing.

Just back away! her brain told her. *Let the police handle it.*

But what if the police never find out?

Well, how are you going to report it? her brain argued. *You can't talk, remember?*

I remember! I will find another way. I will do the right thing.

You are putting your life at risk, her brain said. *They have a gun.*

Yes, but I know the woods.

She took a few steps into the clearing, unnoticed by the group in front of her. She removed the phone from her pocket, let out a high whistle, and when the three looked up, FLASH!

CHAPTER TWO

Tanner Andrews sat alone in his navy-blue Subaru, a relic that showed its miles with rust patches on the paint and more than a few reminders of the minor run-ins with trees and mailboxes from he and his four older siblings learning to drive.

Tanner kept checking his watch compulsively. "Something happened," he said to himself. "They were supposed to be here over a half-hour ago. At 7:30." The digital readout of his watch said 8:07. "What should I do?" He drummed his hands against the steering wheel nervously.

The whole evening, Tanner had fought off a sinking feeling in the pit of his stomach, a feeling that tonight, something was going to go wrong.

Ever since school had started up again, Quinn had been acting different—reckless, almost maniacal. He kept putting the rest of them in compromising situations, and Tanner was convinced that if they kept hanging out with him, they would all soon find trouble.

At the same time, being around Quinn at school was a rush. He was the most popular kid at Whitefish High School ever since he had led the football team to a state championship last year.

He and his dad had just moved to Whitefish the previous summer, but he won the starting quarterback role soon thereafter. Being a starting quarterback by itself brought some fame, but winning the championship elevated him to celebrity status. He had his pick of the prettiest girls and drove a vintage red Ford Mustang convertible that his dad bought him after the win. What more could a high school kid ever dream of?

Everyone wanted to be friends with Quinn Madison. Tanner still couldn't figure out why Quinn had wanted to hang around him and his two friends, Adam Bend and Mark Christiansen. School was now a completely different experience.

Before the three of them had met Quinn, they were nobodies, literally nobodies. Tanner was tall and lanky with skin covered in acne. His clothes were secondhand and perpetually too short for his ever-growing limbs. His black hair was bushy and impossible to style, not that he had ever really tried. He was an average student at best. Even his teachers didn't know much about him. High school teachers know best the students on the extremes, those that are smart and motivated and those that refuse to do their work and like making trouble. Tanner didn't fall into either of those camps, so he was largely ignored. He came to school every day, sat quietly through class, paid enough attention to muddle through the assignments and then spent the rest of his day playing video games.

He was the youngest of five children in his family, and it felt to him like his parents had given up raising kids after number four. None of his siblings had amounted to much, despite their parents' efforts, so they just let him do what he wanted, which most of the time was nothing.

Adam Bend was different from Tanner in most ways. He was short, neat, and quick-witted. Although he only stood five foot six, he usually filled the room with his overgrown confidence and sharp tongue. Tanner was an easy target for Adam but didn't seem to mind being the butt of many a joke. They had been friends since the fourth grade and hung out together every day.

Their friendship started one day on the playground when a fifth-grade bully was picking on Tanner for his mismatched wardrobe. Tanner was trying to ignore it, but Adam, who had been playing on the monkey bars nearby, could see that he was struggling to hold back tears.

"Hey! Dillon!" Adam yelled at Tanner's abuser. "Why don't you pick on somebody your own size! Oh, that's right, there's nobody in our school your own size. Did you get held back another year? What are you, like, sixteen now? Did you get your driver's license yet?"

Dillon turned all his attention with that comment away from Tanner and onto Adam. "Oh yeah? How about coming over here and learning what it feels like to have a grown man hit your ugly little child face?"

"An interesting offer, Dillon. I bet it would feel a lot like having a big sister give me a love tap on the cheek. You're big, but you don't look very tough. Just saying."

"Come find out, you little midget. I didn't know they let elves leave the North Pole after Christmas."

"Ha, ha, ha. You should have known that. You are a spitting image of your father, Santa, without the beard or the niceness, of course. Is Santa embarrassed that his son is always top of the naughty list?"

As Adam was coming over to continue the verbal sparring, Tanner tripped Dillon from behind, causing him to fall onto the asphalt and break his arm.

Dillon rolled on the ground in pain until the teacher who was assigned to recess duty noticed and wandered over. By then,

Adam and Tanner were long gone, and from that moment on, were inseparable.

Their feud with Dillon didn't end there, however. It turns out that Dillon's fist felt nothing like a love tap. They didn't back down to his bullying though. They figured that they just needed to even the sides—and size advantage.

So, they found the biggest kid in their grade, Mark Christiansen, who at the time was just slightly smaller than Dillon. They had to pay him for their protection, at first, with all their lunch desserts for the rest of the year, but after a while, the three of them became best friends.

Mark reached his full growth in the ninth grade, and soon, plenty of boys towered over him. He went from the biggest in their class to just an average-height, pudgy kid that nobody paid attention to anymore.

With his drop in size status, so went his confidence. He became shy and unassuming and faded into the high school crowd of kids that didn't stand out for anything special. He grew his hair long and rarely combed it with anything other than his fingers. He wore sweatpants that were cut off at the knees and paired with an assortment of black concert t-shirts from eighties hair bands. He never went anywhere without his Air Jordans, with colorful shoelaces left untied. He had three pair—red, black, and white—the colors of the Chicago Bulls, his favorite team. On special occasions, he wore his Jordan jersey on top of KISS or Def Leppard. Mark's only real talents were air guitar and the latest version of NBA 2K.

As unlikely a trio that was ever assembled, Adam, Mark. and Tanner had stayed the closest of friends. Adam was the ring-leader, but Mark and Tanner held their own with him, at least in the confines of Tanner's basement where they spent most of the time that they weren't in school.

The day that they met Quinn, Tanner's mom had kicked them out to "fumigate" their space. They hadn't noticed the smell—maybe they were drunk on Cheetos and Dr. Pepper at the time. They looked at each other, shrugged, and went outside, squinting at the sunlight like moles coming to the surface for the first time in their lives.

"What are we supposed to do now?" Mark asked irritably.

"I was just about to beat you with the Pistons, Mark. You should be counting your lucky stars. Do you have some arrangement with Tanner's mom to break things up if it looks like you might get beat? What's your signal? It can't be your incredibly loud farts because you do that every day. Does wearing cut-offs make them louder? Kind of like a megaphone?" Adam teased him with a wry smile. "Hey, what's that on the grass? It's round and orange, and I think it bounces. I've heard that they made those in real life, but I didn't know if I could believe it. Should we try it? Mark, I have no doubt that I can beat you out here. You wouldn't have the advantage of your secret weapon, Cheeto gas, which stuns us and then confuses our minds."

"You forget that you still come up to my belly button, Adam. I don't think you will even see the rim from down that low. But, okay, if you want to humiliate yourself. You will never beat me with the paddle, and you have no chance with a ball," Mark retorted.

"How about you, Tanner? Are you in, or do you just want to stand there with your arms in a ring and confuse us about which pole to shoot at?" Adam laughed.

"You two forget. It's my court, my ball, my rules," Tanner replied, as he leaned down to pick up the ball. "The first rule is that Tanner wins no matter what. The second and final rule is that the losers buy the winner a chocolate shake."

As the three of them started their game, a red Mustang pulled up next to the curb, and Quinn Madison got out and closed the door. Tanner, Mark, and Adam stopped playing, and watched as the basketball rolled down the driveway toward him. Quinn scooped it up with a smooth kick from his foot and started bouncing it effortlessly as he made his way closer.

"Hey," he said. "You boys mind if I join your game? I could use the fresh air."

The other three looked at each other and then back at Quinn, who was spinning the ball on his finger.

Adam spoke first. "Do you think that any of us can do that with the ball?" he pointed, while Quinn kept the ball spinning. "We can barely dribble it without it hitting our feet. Why would you want to play with us? You feeling short on confidence all of a sudden and just needing to remind yourself that you are still a god?"

Quinn stopped spinning the ball and looked hard at Adam. He wasn't sure how to respond to that comment and could feel the heat rising in his face, but he forced it down and smiled. "Very funny. But no, I'm not trying to prove anything to myself or to you. I just want to shoot around and hang out with you guys for a little while. Is that a problem?"

"Shut up, Adam," Mark said. "It's fine with me if you want to play. Your name is Quinn, right?"

"That's right. How did you know my name?" Quinn asked and slapped Mark's hand in a friendly greeting.

"Dude, everyone knows your name," Tanner added.

"Okay, yeah, maybe," Quinn said.

"So, you're really here to just hang out with us?" Adam piped in again. "C'mon, what's your motive? It's not like we are going to up your status with the ladies. And what other motivation is there?"

"A fair point," Quinn said. "But seriously. I'm not the guy that everyone thinks I am. I don't have to be Quinn Madison, football star, all the time. Under the surface, I'm just a regular guy."

The other three looked at him standing there, tan and muscular, and raised their eyebrows at that "regular guy" comment.

"Seriously! Let's just play HORSE. I'll go first," Quinn said.

"And shoot with your left hand!" Adam added.

"Deal," Quinn said and sunk a left-handed jumper from twelve feet.

"It's your turn, Mark," Adam said quickly.

"Great," Mark said sarcastically.

CHAPTER THREE

As soon as Sandra snapped the picture, she turned and disappeared quickly into the trees. She knew that she only had a few seconds before the men registered what had happened and came after her.

She counted on her familiarity with the woods to give her a sufficient head start. She had watched how prey animals escape from danger and would do the same. Making a lot of noise, she ran through the trees away from the clearing until she could hear the men giving chase behind her, then she snuck quietly toward the river, perpendicular to her original path.

She knew of a place by the river where the spring run-off had carved a space in the embankment, creating a small cove that was completely hidden from the trail above. She would just need to hide there until her pursuers got tired of looking, and then she could work her way back home with little risk of being found.

She moved quietly, paying attention to each step. She could hear the men trailing off in the wrong direction and saw the occasional beam of a flashlight highlighting the forest canopy. As she approached the stream, she picked up her pace until she tucked herself unseen into the carved rock of the riverbed. Then she waited.

Thoughts filled her mind as she calmed her breathing and consciously slowed her heart rate. The soothing sound of the water brought her down from near panic-level anxiety. What was she going to do now? She had evidence on her phone of a heinous crime, but how could she explain why she had it without becoming a suspect herself? Anybody else could just walk into a police station and simply explain the whole thing. She, however, could not. Autism had, once again, compromised her very safety. Those men would not stop looking for her now. Every time she stepped out of her condo, she would have to be on high alert until they were caught. Yet, she knew that staying cooped up inside would eat at her soul.

Her soul started speaking to her then. *Sandra, you are brave. You did the right thing. We will find our way through this.*

After an hour by the stream, Sandra knew she needed to try and make it home. Her mom was likely in a frenzy, and once she remembered that Sandra's phone was a tracking device, the woods would be filled with police and first responders. She wasn't yet prepared to explain what they might see if they looked on her phone.

Fortunately, it was her dad who had always been the one to follow her position in the woods on his laptop. Her mom relied on him to be sure that Sandra made it home every evening. Sandra had never had an issue during the many years of solo hikes in the woods, so after her dad died a year and a half ago, her mom did not keep up the daily tracking. She just waited for the evening phone call from Sandra's landline to know that she was safely at home.

Sandra knew that her mom would find her soon enough though, so she had to get moving. She crawled out of her hiding space and looked around carefully for any flashes of light. The moon was full, and Sandra's eyes were well-adjusted to the dark. She listened for voices or footsteps, and when she heard none, she made her way slowly but steadily along the trail that followed the stream until she could see the lights from the condos on the hill in front of her.

Continuing to the edge of the forest that bordered her parking lot, she paused, still hidden in the trees, expecting to see flashing red and blue lights from a police car that her mom had called to help find her. But the parking lot was quiet. She ran across and punched in the code to the security lock on the door and then climbed the three flights of stairs leading up to her condo. At the top, she slowed her pace as she walked down the hall, trying to calm her breathing. She hesitated in front of her door before opening it, again listening for any unfamiliar voices from those her mother may have summoned. Still, nothing.

She opened the door and stepped inside, shutting the door rapidly behind her. There was a soft glow from the lamp next to her couch where her mother, who had not heard Sandra come in, sat with her head down and a well-wrung washcloth in her hands.

"Mom," Sandra said quietly.

At the sound of her voice, Susan Lewis looked up, her eyes unfocused, as if observing a dream.

"Mom," Sandra said again, which brought Susan back to reality.

"Sandy! You're okay!"

Susan jumped up quickly and came over to Sandra, wrapping her arms around her and wetting Sandra's shirt with her tears. Sandra stood quietly and let her mom hug her tightly, though she kept her own arms by her side.

She understood the desire for physical contact, but when she received it, her sensory system went into overdrive and made it hard for her brain to think about anything else. She welcomed the touch, but when it was given without warning, she could not react reciprocally.

"Sandy, you are freezing cold. Where have you been? I've been worried sick! I just about called the police," Susan said, eyes still red and her face wrinkled with concern. "You have never been out this late by yourself before. Did something happen? Were you in the woods?"

"Yes, Mom," Sandra replied.

"Yes, what? Something happened or you were in the woods?" Susan said, with frustration. "Oh! I wish you could just talk to me!"

Sandra looked at her mom without trying to respond again. Tears began to well in her eyes and her chin quivered slightly. A simple conversation between a mother and a daughter—how basic a need but always out of reach for her. How hard it must be for her mother as well. The years of uncompromising effort for that one thing that most people take so much for granted. Would they ever have even a single opportunity?

"Sandy, I'm so sorry. I love you so much, and as I sat here tonight in a panic was forced to contemplate what I would do, how I could live, without you," Susan said softly. "First your dad and then you? I would not survive that loss."

Susan grabbed Sandra's hand and led her to the couch. She sat her down and went into the bedroom and brought out a soft down throw cover and wrapped it around Sandra snugly. She then went into the kitchen and heated some water for hot chocolate. A few minutes later, she brought out a mug to Sandra and sat down next to her on the couch.

"Just rest, Sandy," Susan said gently. "We'll figure it out tomorrow."

CHAPTER FOUR

"We might as well give up, Quinn," Adam said. "Whoever that was is long gone and we aren't going to find him in the dark. Let's just get out of here."

Quinn turned to face Mark and Adam, a flashlight in one hand and his gun in the other. He raised the gun and pointed it again at the other two. "Who was it?" he seethed. "Which of you tipped them off?"

"Tipped them off?" Adam retorted angrily. "Like any of us had any idea what you had planned for tonight? Like any of us could have even imagined that you were capable of shooting someone who was asleep in a chair in his own house? You told us that you were just going to break in and look around. Just for kicks. How could we have possibly told someone to wait in the woods for us to bury a body and then take a picture of us doing it? Why would we do that, even if we knew? Do you think we're that stupid?"

"Your mouth is going to get you killed, Adam!" Quinn moved closer and rested the point of his handgun against Adam's forehead.

"Stop, Quinn! Geez, what are you doing?" Mark said anxiously. "You're going to kill us now? We are your friends, remember?"

Quinn looked menacingly at Mark while still holding the gun to Adam's head. "Friends?" he laughed maniacally. "You are not my friends. Why would I be friends with punks like you? I never wanted to be friends with you. I just needed some idiots to take the hit for me after I took out the man who messed up my family!"

"What are you talking about?" Adam asked, trying to contain the anger that had filled him to the breaking point, while fearing that any word now could be his last. "You knew that guy? You planned this whole thing? For months?"

"So now you know," Quinn pressed the gun firmly into Adam's skin. "What should I do? I can't really let you live, but I still need someone to take the fall. So, this is my new plan. We are going to walk back, finish burying the body, and then we are all going on a little trip. If any of you try to run, I will shoot you. If you get away, I will go shoot Tanner and then I'll kill your families. Do you have any questions?"

Neither Adam nor Mark spoke.

"Great. It sounds like we have an understanding. Now turn around and start walking down that trail!"

The three of them made their way back to the clearing, finished burying the body, and tried to cover the fresh dirt with leaves. Then, they made their way back to where Tanner had parked his car. He was pacing back and forth in front of it when they emerged from the woods—Mark and Adam first, and Quinn behind.

"Get in the car, Tanner," Quinn said calmly, while the others kept silent.

"Where have you guys been? You were supposed to ... "

"Get in the damn car, Tanner, now!" Quinn yelled.

Tanner turned quickly and fumbled for his keys. He sat behind the wheel and started the engine. Adam and Mark got in back, and Quinn sat in the front passenger side. Tanner looked in the rearview mirror at Adam and Mark who both looked like they had seen a ghost. They avoided his gaze.

"Is someone going to tell me what's going on?" Tanner broke the anxious silence.

Quinn pulled out his gun and pointed it at Tanner's head. "This is what's going on," he started. "You are going to drive, and you are all going to be quiet, and when I tell you to turn right, you turn right. When I tell you to turn left, you turn left. It's very simple, Tanner. You have any more questions?"

"Where are you..." Tanner began but was interrupted by the sound of Quinn cocking his gun. "No more questions," Tanner quickly finished. He pulled his car onto the dirt road and out to the highway.

"Very good, Tanner," Quinn said. "You are smarter than I thought. Now, turn right. We are going to the mountains."

Tanner did as instructed and pulled onto the smooth pavement of the highway. His hands were shaking as he reached down to turn on the radio. Quinn didn't stop him. The sounds of Queen filled the silence from their favorite classic rock station.

"She's a Killer Queen,
Gunpowder, guillotine,
Dynamite with a laser beam,
Guaranteed to blow your mind. Anytime."

"Turn it off, Tanner, geez," Adam said from the back.

Tanner quickly shut off the radio, and they continued down the road in silence.

After about an hour, the Subaru pulled off the highway.

"Park here!" Quinn commanded. "Tanner, you are coming with me. If you other two make any attempt to escape, I'll shoot Tanner. We will be back in two minutes. Tanner, out!"

Tanner looked quickly in the mirror at the other two. His eyes were full of fear. Adam looked back this time and tried his best to convey some confidence and reassurance in his gaze.

Quinn came around the front of the car and pointed his gun again at Tanner who got out quickly after that.

"This way!"

He and Tanner soon disappeared into the dark.

Adam and Mark looked at each other nervously, and Adam whispered, "We can get out of this, Mark! He's not going to kill us, or he would have done it already. There's three of us and one of him. We've been teaming up against bad guys since second grade, right? Think of all the video game villains that we've destroyed. We just have to come at him from different directions, and someone needs to get his gun."

Mark looked skeptical. "The problem is that in video games, you get a bunch of chances to figure out the monster's weaknesses and how to attack them. Here, if we die, we're actually dead!"

Adam rested his head against the back seat and let out a sigh. "I know. But we've got to do something. I hate being the victim! We can't let this guy ruin our lives. Keep your head about you, Mark. If you have a move, take it! I'll be with you, and hopefully Tanner will catch on."

They sat in the dark for just a few more minutes before they heard footsteps, two pair, causing them both to let out a sigh of relief. The idea that Quinn was not going to kill them was something they kept telling themselves to maintain a ray of hope, more so than a firm belief that it was true. They had both seen the look in his eyes when he shot that man. It was animalistic.

He really couldn't be trusted to make rational decisions with their lives.

They were both startled when Adam's door suddenly opened, and Quinn peered in at them. "Still here, eh? You're either really loyal or really stupid. Get out, both of you!"

They got out of the car and stood next to Tanner who was visibly shaken. Adam put his hand on Tanner's back as a gesture of solidarity and to let him know that they were glad he was still with them.

"Keep your hands to yourself, Adam, and where I can see them! If you guys try anything stupid, and I mean anything, I will shoot first and ask questions later. I have nothing to lose. I can dump your bodies anywhere in these mountains, and it'll be days or weeks before you are found. I will be long gone by then. Your prints are all over that crime scene. I can make your deaths look like a murder suicide as well. So don't test me!"

Adam looked at Mark and slowly brought his hand back to his side. Quinn wasn't wrong about finding their bodies. Plus, he was anticipating them to try an escape. They may not get a chance.

"Okay, Tanner, get back in the car and pull it up to where I showed you. And remember, your two friends saved your life by not running. You should do the same for them."

Tanner drove the car slowly toward the edge of the road. He watched Quinn guide him forward until his front tires were just a foot away from a steep embankment that led directly into the dark waters of a lake. The moon reflected off its smooth surface, and Tanner's thoughts interrupted his nightmare briefly to note how beautiful the scene would have been under different circumstances.

Quinn held up his arms signaling Tanner to stop. "Okay, put the car in neutral and the emergency brake on," he instructed.

"And get out. You three are going to go behind and push when I tell you to."

"You're dumping his car?" Adam asked.

"Get back there, now!" Quinn yelled and again cocked his gun.

"Okay, Okay!" Adam conceded. He and the other two went around the car and put their hands on the trunk.

Quinn reached in through the driver's window and disengaged the parking brake. "Push!" he commanded.

The other boys leaned into the back of the car and felt the tires roll beneath it. The front tires left the side of the road edge, and the car careened down the hill and made a splash in the water below. It floated for a minute before the front end dipped below the surface, and like a duck hunting for food, it dove and then was gone. The ripples from the initial impact on the water spread across the lake but within a few seconds had also dissipated, and the surface soon returned to its glass-like complexion.

"Okay. Now, we hike!" Quinn pushed Tanner ahead, and Adam and Mark followed. "No talking. I'll tell you when to stop. Here is a flashlight, Tanner. You lead the way. The trail is right there."

CHAPTER FIVE

Sandra woke early the next morning, before dawn. She surveyed her condo from her spot on the couch, trying to regain her bearings. When she saw her mom sleeping in the adjacent chair, the memories from last night came rushing back, and she realized it hadn't just been a bad dream.

She rose quietly and moved carefully down the hall, into her bedroom, and then to the master bathroom. At the sink, she splashed her face with cold water to arouse her brain so that it could come up with a plan to solve her dilemma. Actually, her brain would be of little help. It had no motive. It would be her soul that would give her the answer. She just needed to be awake enough to hear its voice.

Looking in the mirror, she could see the reflection of both of her parents. Her high cheekbones and thin nose were her mother's. She had light blond hair, also like her mother's before it had turned a snowy white, her mother's most striking feature. Sandra loved that Susan had let it follow nature's course instead of trying to hide her age with artificial color. She saw her father in her fuller lips and emerald-green eyes. Those eyes. She loved his eyes. His eyes always emanated his best qualities—kindness, patience, and love.

The autism experts frequently told her parents that she could not read their facial expressions and to use words to explain how they were feeling. But the "experts" had it wrong. She ignored the mouth and facial muscles and concentrated on the eyes. They told her everything she needed to know, and they never lied. That is why she failed all the psychological tests; pictures of actors mimicking certain emotions could not reproduce the truth, and she could never guess their true feelings. But when it was real, she only needed a glance to understand.

The experts said she avoided eye contact because she wanted to shut out the world and control her inner environment. Also, wrong. She avoided staring into people's eyes to respect their privacy. She didn't think that they would want to reveal so much. The eyes are the window to the soul.

She remembered his eyes, the man with the gun. They were illuminated briefly by her flash, long enough to burn them into her memory. They were dark, cold, and full of hate—and they revealed to her his soul. When she closed her eyes, all she could see were the cold, dark eyes of a murderer. Had he seen her? Through the flash? Would she meet those eyes again? In the courtroom? In the woods? Or would they come for her in her condo? Could he sense her fear? Could he track it? How could she ensure that those eyes remained behind bars forever?

Sandra dressed quickly in her preferred clothing, a sweatshirt and yoga pants, and went back out to her living room. Susan was still asleep in the chair, snoring lightly. Sandra looked at her, and a flood of memories filled her mind.

She had an unusual way with memories. They were never buried deep but, rather, floated in the periphery of her concentration, immediately accessible and never forgotten. Her memories were catalogued visually, like little video vignettes that were instantly triggered by a stimulus in her visual field.

Watching her mother sleep brought back memories of other times when she saw her mother sleeping. Like after her father's funeral. Susan hadn't slept for days. Sandra remembered the dark circles under her eyes and the grief that spoke from them. Finally, after all the well-wishers and family had left, Susan had sat on her couch and shut her eyes. Sandra watched as her breathing slowed and the tension in her muscles eased. She could feel her mother's grief lift momentarily from her soul and watched her dream. At one point, she smiled, and Sandra knew that her mom and her dad were together again.

What was her mom dreaming of now? Sandra wondered. And what could Sandra tell her when she awakened? How was she going to tell her mom about the body in the woods? Of course, she could show her the picture, but then she would be caught in a police investigation, and she wasn't ready for that. Not yet. She had to be able to tell her story first.

...

Sandra was diagnosed with autism at age five but had lost all her language before her third birthday. Before that, she had apparently been developing normally.

Her parents were so excited when they found out that she was coming. They had tried for twenty years to get pregnant and had seen multiple fertility specialists along the way. None of the interventions had been successful, so after a while, they had just given up.

When Susan missed a couple of periods, she assumed it was early menopause. She didn't even think to check a pregnancy test. She went to her doctor's office one day after what she thought was a stomach virus that wouldn't go away. The doctor ran some tests and then told her the news.

"Susan, it looks like it isn't a virus. It seems that you have a parasite."

"A parasite? How did I get that?" Susan answered with surprise.

The doctor handed her the results of her tests. "Now, do I really need to explain that to someone your age, Susan?" he said with a wink.

Susan read the results, jumped up, gave the doctor a big hug, and ran out of the examination room without saying another word. She drove downtown and interrupted Tony during a board meeting. The two of them drove straight to the furniture store and bought the crib that Susan had been eyeing for years.

The pregnancy was surprisingly uncomplicated although Susan was anxious throughout, afraid that this last chance would end too soon. But at full-term, Sandra was born and, by all accounts, was a normal, healthy baby girl.

Susan had quit her job as a real estate agent and was excited to dedicate herself to being a full-time mom. And she loved it. Even the sleepless nights and diaper changes, the doctor's visits, and the play dates. Everything felt like a gift.

She read to her every night, classics like Dickens and Steinbeck. She played Mozart and Chopin on their stereo system. She studied child development and celebrated each milestone. And Sandra was following the script until...

Until she stopped. Susan couldn't figure it out. Had something happened? Had she fallen? Was she sick? She hadn't had a fever. Maybe it was just a phase. Maybe Susan was over-analyzing it. But Sandra used to want to sit in Susan's lap and look at picture books and would listen when Susan identified the names of each thing. She would even try to say it back. She made eye contact and interacted with them. When did that stop? It seemed sudden, but maybe it had been changing subtly, and Susan hadn't noticed. Now she was fussy, irritable, and preferred being by herself. She wasn't talking either. Hardly ever.

Susan took her to the doctor who shrugged it off.

"You are worried over nothing, Susan," he said. "Haven't you heard of the terrible twos?"

"Yeah, and I expected that she would become defiant and demanding. Not aloof and unattached."

"Well, everybody's different," the doctor said, his only advice.

Susan left, convincing herself to not worry so much. The doctor must know; he had seen thousands of children.

As the months went by, Sandra got worse and stopped using words completely. She also started little rituals around the house—gathering certain toys in groups, turning lights off and on repetitively, walking in patterns on the floor. And the tantrums! The tantrums lasted for hours, and there never seemed to be an obvious trigger.

Susan eventually stopped listening to the pediatrician dismiss her concerns. She knew her daughter, and something was wrong. Tony had a client who was a developmental specialist and arranged for a consultation. After an afternoon of testing and observation, they received the bad news. *Autism, regressive type. Prognosis: guarded.*

The specialist told them that autism was historically rare, but they had started seeing more cases recently. They were not sure why. There wasn't much known about the cause; it was probably genetic. And there were no known effective treatments. She would likely be institutionalized as an adult.

Susan and Tony left the specialist's office in shock. *Autism? Really? Sandra? Institutionalized? Never!*

Susan started researching the next day. Newspapers, research journals, books. She read everything about autism that she could get her hands on. If anyone had a suggestion, she tried it. Diets, supplements, therapies. They tried it all. They learned about a research program at UCLA trying a behavioral intervention called Applied Behavioral Analysis or ABA. Sandra qualified as a subject, so they all moved to California for five years. Sandra made marginal improvement while many of her peers were progressing steadily.

"She doesn't seem to be responsive to anything we try," the therapists complained. "Maybe you should just take her home and try public school."

Public special education was a waste for Sandra—babysitting, more or less. They didn't really try to teach her; they just kept her occupied. So, Susan pulled her out and taught her at home. She had no formal training, but just treated her at age level and hoped that something would sink in.

Susan didn't know it, but this saved Sandra. It was sinking in. All of it. Her mind was like a sponge that had been left out in the arid desert air. It was shriveling and thirsting for stimulation and knowledge. Her mother provided the rain that restored her, nourished her, made her receptive and pliable.

If only she could speak.

...

Susan started rousing from sleep as Sandra sat and watched her. When Susan opened her eyes, Sandra said, "Hi, Mom."

Susan sat up abruptly and rubbed the sleep from her face. "Sandra, how long have you been awake? Is it morning?"

"Almost."

"You're dressed. Did you eat?"

"Not yet."

"I'll fix you something," Susan said and started to rise from her chair.

"No, Mom. Go home."

"Home? I don't want to go home. What about last night? I need to figure out what happened."

"Later," Sandra said.

"When later?" Susan protested.

"Tonight. Come back."

"Okay … if you are sure." Susan knew what Sandra was asking for although she hesitated to leave. Sandra needed some space. And quiet. No distractions. That is how she solved problems.

"I'm sure."

"Promise me that you don't go back into the woods today. Not alone. Okay?"

"I promise, Mom."

"Okay, tonight then. I'll bring dinner."

CHAPTER SIX

Quinn followed the other three into the woods onto the hiking trail, and they were all quickly surrounded and obscured by the dense pines. The trail was relatively flat for about a mile but then began rising steeply and became more technical and rockier. The moon was bright, and when it wasn't obscured by the trees, they could see without the flashlight.

After a couple of hours of hiking, Mark said, "Can we rest for a minute? My feet are killing me."

"Go ahead," Quinn said. "But stay in the open, where I can see you."

"Can I ask where we are going?" Adam said.

"Canada," Quinn replied.

"Canada? Really?" Adam scoffed, and then caught himself and corrected his tone. "Canada. I hear it's nice this time of year."

Quinn cocked his pistol in reply.

Adam raised his arms, "Sorry. I'm sorry."

After a few more minutes, Quinn commanded them back onto their feet and back on the trail. "Get used to hiking, boys, we've got a long way to go still."

The trail continued higher until they were just above tree line, at which point they followed it over a ridge and began descending. As they re-entered the trees, Mark nudged Adam and opened his eyes widely, conveying his readiness to make a move to try to escape. Adam shook his head slightly and signaled with his hand to say "not yet." Mark let out an impatient grunt, wondering how many opportunities they might have. Adam did not acknowledge him and kept hiking forward.

Mark figured that the next time they stopped, he would grab Quinn when he didn't expect it and try to get the gun. Hopefully, Adam and Tanner would see what he was doing and jump to help him. If not, he realized, they could all be killed. But what did they have to lose? He didn't believe that Quinn was really going to let them live.

They walked the rest of the night without a break. Mark was so tired that he didn't know if he could carry out his plan when they finally stopped by a stream for a drink.

"Drink up, boys. This is our last stop before we get there. We crossed the border about a mile ago," Quinn said.

"So, now what?" Mark asked.

"Don't worry about it, Mark," Quinn said. "I know what we're doing. You don't have to."

You don't know what I'm doing, you bastard! Mark thought. He inched closer to Quinn so that when Quinn bent down to get a drink, Mark would be ready to pounce.

But that moment never came. Quinn never took his eyes off them and didn't drink anything himself. When the others had finished, he pointed the gun at Mark and said, "Back off, big man. You get any closer and you'll get a bullet between your eyes."

Mark joined the others, and they carried on down the trail. *How did he know?* thought Mark. *And how does he not need water?*

The last few miles felt like a hundred. They were tired, hungry, and discouraged as they trudged along the trail at a shuffling pace. The trail flattened as they passed a few campsites complete with backpacking tents and Coleman stoves but no signs of life. Mark heard Quinn's gun cock again from immediately behind his head in warning. Within a mile of the camps, they arrived at a trailhead with its parking lot occupied by a few empty cars. The dark sky was now a deep shade of blue signaling the coming dawn.

"Keep going," Quinn said, "to the road."

They walked past the vehicles and onto the highway. As soon as their feet hit the pavement, they were blinded by a bright white light. An amplified voice from the same direction commanded them to halt and put their hands in the air.

The boys did as they were told and within seconds found themselves face down on the cold asphalt, arms forced behind their backs, and steel cutting into their wrists.

"Now, don't move until I tell you. You three are in a whole mess of trouble," the voice said.

Three? They all moved their heads from side to side, making eye contact, the same question evident on their shocked expressions. Mark, Adam, and Tanner were there. *Where was Quinn?*

CHAPTER SEVEN

Sandra closed the door behind her mother and took a minute to focus before she made her next move. After the pause, she walked across her living room and into the second bedroom of her condo. She turned on the light and looked around, sighing deeply before crossing over the threshold. The walls were covered in sound-proof insulating cushions, and the floor was wall-to-wall exercise mats. A kickboxing bag hung from the ceiling in the center of the room and there were exercise balls of assorted sizes lined against one wall. The opposite wall was full of bookshelves stacked with CDs and DVDs. There was a large TV sitting on the center shelf and a nice stereo system adjacent to it with surround sound speakers embedded in the ceiling.

This was Sandra's safe room. This is where she came when she needed to escape from her life. This is where she came to drown out the negative voice inside her head. This is where she could release her pent-up anxiety without anyone else hearing or knowing.

The room was identical to the one that her father built for her in their own house, her mom's house. It was well-used in her younger days, especially the rough years as a teenager when her hormones had surged and brought with them new emotions and desires that left her even more confused and anxious. During those panicked moments, she could feel the negative energy rise within her like boiling water in a teapot that would soon breach the pressure point and demand a release valve.

But now the targets of her energy were the punching bag and the exercise balls. She could hit them or kick them as hard as she wanted without causing any damage. She used drumsticks on the balls which gave the additional effect of noise to empty out the thoughts in her mind that told her she was worthless, damaged, or stupid. She could yell and scream until her voice was hoarse without alerting the neighbors who had called the police more than once before her dad had created the safe room.

Sandra had learned over the years to dampen her emotions before they reached the point of violence and now rarely had a full meltdown, but she still appreciated her safe room where she could turn up her music, practice her kickboxing, and release the energy that made it impossible for her to focus.

She went in and closed the door. She selected a CD from her collection, Beethoven's *Ode to Joy*. It was one of her favorites when she was sad or frustrated. She loved the story of the great composer, completely deaf, directing this great symphony with eyes closed, continuing to wave his arms after the orchestra had finished and the audience erupted in applause. It reminded her that one could still be great, even when given challenges that could be used as an excuse. No one certainly would have criticized Beethoven had he retired after his loss of hearing. But he had more music inside of him that could not be silenced, and he didn't need his ears to hear it. *Joy*. Joy is an expression from within. When she needed that reminder, Beethoven was her go-to.

She turned the music up loud and laid on the floor, her face looking up at the punching bag as it swung like a pendulum just above her. Watching the bag swing was hypnotic and worked just as well for her anxiety as riding high on a swing at the park, one of her favorite activities when she was younger. The rhythmic motion coupled with the music allowed her brain to clear itself and gave her space to focus on her task at hand.

Her mind went back to the events of the previous night. *Three young men, probably teenagers. A body. One had a gun. The others seemed scared. They weren't like him.* Her soul told her that.

She looked at the picture on her phone. The man with the gun stared right at her. He was taller, athletically built, had blond, curly hair. But his eyes were the feature she could never forget. Could she recognize them if she saw him again? She knew without a doubt that she could. Eyes are like fingerprints. To Sandra, no two pair were alike.

She was in danger. She knew it. Men like that do not give up or run away. They try to silence their witnesses. Before she could tell anyone about him, she needed to be sure that he would not be able to know her, where she lived, what her patterns were. He could not be able to follow her into the woods.

Sandra hit the bag again, restarting its momentum, and again suppressing the background noise inside her head for another pause. *I need to tell the police, but how? I can't even manage a conversation with my own mother,* she thought as her mind scanned its video files for possible solutions. *Would they even believe me, that I wasn't involved? That I actually can't speak up and tell them the whole story? Or would they think I was faking it? After all, I don't look disabled. And what if they do believe me? If then, I would need to testify in court. In front of many people. In front of him.*

. . .

Sandra had been in therapy of one sort or another since she was five years old. They had tried everything to teach her how to communicate. Sign language didn't work for her. She couldn't make her hands do what her mouth wouldn't. It's not that her mouth could not create words; she just couldn't get them out of her brain.

She tried using picture exchange systems of various types, but they were too simplistic, and she eventually learned how to communicate the same things with her limited verbal vocabulary. Plus, pictures didn't help her express anything beyond her basic needs. They didn't have a picture for murder.

She had tried to learn how to type. She enjoyed watching the letters come up on the screen, but she made so many mistakes that no one even knew that she was actually attempting to communicate. To her therapists, it just seemed like random letters, and they became impatient and did not let her practice.

Her parents had bought her a laptop to watch movies on when they went on road trips. She had never used it for anything else. Typing was something she did during therapy, not at home on her own. She hadn't ever done it before without help or someone watching her and telling her what she was supposed to try to reproduce. No one had ever just given her a blank screen and told her to type what she was thinking.

...

Suddenly, Sandra reached up and stopped the spinning bag with both hands. *I will try typing.* When the thought filled her mind, she could feel her soul stirring, like Beethoven's audience. He couldn't hear them, but he must have felt them, the vibrations in the floor as they stood on their feet. Maybe they stomped their feet while they clapped so he would know that he had gotten it right. Sandra knew, too. She didn't know how it would work, but she knew that this was the way.

CHAPTER EIGHT

Quinn hid in the shadows of the woods and watched his three companions get arrested under the bright spotlights of the police. He had led the boys to the trailhead parking lot and then slipped behind a car when they started onto the asphalt. Quinn knew what was about to happen. It was all going according to plan—at least since they had left Slater's cabin.

He backtracked up the trail for a few hundred yards and then picked his way through the trees, parallel to the road until he emerged after about a mile near a scenic pull-off where a black BMW sedan was parked, waiting for him.

Quinn got into the car quickly and said, "Let's go! The Canadian police might be looking for me. The others will have told them by now."

"Calm down," the driver said. "If the police are looking for you, you can't act like you are running." He pulled casually away from the turn-off and back onto the highway heading south, toward the US border.

Gary Madison was in his early fifties and had dark curly hair tipped with gray at the edges. He had a muscular build under the black turtleneck sweater that he was wearing. His face was calm, but his eyes reflected the intensity of someone who had spent a lifetime on the wrong side of the law.

"Okay, Jack, but pick it up a little or I'm going to be late for practice," Quinn said impatiently.

"Don't call me by my real name! Ever! Not even when we are alone, you got it?" Gary snapped back. His real name was Jack Harris, but for the last year and a half, he was pretending to be Gary Madison, Quinn Madison's widowed father. "Why were you late?"

"Complications," Quinn said quietly.

Gary looked over at him. Quinn looked a little nervous. "Complications?"

"Somebody saw us. At Slater's," Quinn said, as he kept his eyes focused on the passing scenery.

Gary didn't say anything at first, but Quinn could see in the window reflection that his grip on the wheel had tightened.

"Somebody saw you," Gary repeated, softly but intensely.

Quinn nodded. There was an awkward silence before Gary hit the steering wheel loudly with his hands causing Quinn to jump and look over at his escort.

"How in the hell did somebody see you?" Gary yelled. "No one goes to visit out there at night. Ever! We have been watching for weeks. Were you followed?"

"I did everything you told me!" Quinn yelled back. "We took Tanner's piece-of-junk car, drove around for a half-hour, and I was watching the whole time. Nobody followed us!"

"Okay, calm down," Gary said, regaining his own composure. "How do you know that somebody saw you?"

"There was someone in the woods when we were burying the body. I couldn't see who it was, but I heard them, and ... "

"And what? It was probably just a deer."

"And they took a picture of us at the scene," Quinn said irritably. "Somebody set me up, Jack! When I find out who it is, they are dead. I promise you that!"

"Someone took a picture of you? Impossible," Gary responded, more to himself than to Quinn. "How could anyone have known when to be there? Only you and I knew when we were going to do it."

"That's what I'm saying, asshole!" Quinn said, his eyes cold and boring into the side of Gary's face.

Gary looked straight ahead as he tried to sort out the problem in his mind. He had just become a target, not just of Quinn, but of Quinn's real father, Frank Donovan, who didn't accept excuses and delivered swift retribution whenever he perceived disloyalty.

Neither said anything for a while as they continued south on the highway.

"It wasn't me, Quinn," Gary said, breaking the silence. "Maybe we are both being set up. Your dad's organization is full of people who are more than willing to stab an ally in the back if it clears a path for them to move up the ladder. Obviously, there are others that know why we are here. Your dad can't do everything by himself from prison. There are people writing checks. And I report to Wesley O'Brien. He knows everything ... except which day. Maybe they planted someone out there and waited."

Quinn considered what Gary was saying. He didn't know most of his dad's employees. He had met Wesley, an intense Irish fellow in his early thirties who had risen through the ranks quickly and was now the acting head of the organization while his dad was locked up.

Quinn didn't trust Wesley. He had first met him at their house in Connecticut at a work party. Wesley seemed a little too impressed with their house and their life in the suburbs. He was constantly looking around and commenting on all their stuff, speculating on how much this had cost, or that. He even seemed attracted to Frank's wife, Quinn's mom, although she was at least ten years older than him.

Quinn had used Wesley to get information about his dad's business. Up until then, Frank was unwilling to talk about work when he was home. Quinn had grown up thinking that Frank was a hedge fund manager like half of the other kids' dads in his neighborhood. But as he got older and spent time at friends' houses, he realized that Frank didn't dress like those dads and didn't speak their same language around the house.

Quinn eventually asked his dad exactly what he did at work. His dad studied Quinn, then thirteen-years old, and said "imports/exports." Quinn didn't really understand much about international trade, and as his dad didn't seem to be in the mood to elaborate, he dropped the conversation.

It was three years later, at the work party, that Quinn cornered Wesley and pumped him for information. And Wesley seemed a little too eager to give him answers.

"Ahh, little man. Interested in the family business, now, are you?" Wesley had said in his lilting Irish accent. "Well, now. Where should I start?"

"My dad told me that he works in imports and exports," Quinn offered.

Wesley snorted and choked a little on the wine he was drinking. "Did he now? That's a good one! Your dad does work in imports and exports. Do ya know what commodity he trades?"

"I have no idea."

"Humans, lad. Your dad imports and exports human beings."

Wesley went on to explain how they ran multiple companies that recruited agricultural workers from poor countries, made grand promises of American riches that could transform their dire situations at home, enticed them into unfavorable and illegal contracts, and then sold them off as cheap labor to large landowners to work their farms. In addition to recruitment services, these companies also managed the workers for the farmers and treated them extremely poorly, providing only the bare essentials of food and shelter while forcing them to work thirteen-to-fourteen-hour days of backbreaking labor to pay back the debt of their exorbitant recruiting fees and travel expenses that brought them to America. If the workers complained, they would just ship them home, along with their unmanageable debt and a reputation as a failure. When given a choice, most of the workers took the abuse.

Quinn carefully considered what Wesley had told him over several days before approaching his dad. He liked being rich. He liked the power that wealth provided, even in a high school full of rich kids. He had always been a bit of a bully, he admitted to himself, but now he knew that he came by it honestly. His dad ran a human trafficking ring. How else was Quinn supposed to turn out?

When he finally got up enough nerve, he approached his dad. It was after a football game where he had replaced the starting senior quarterback and, as a sophomore, had led the team on a winning touchdown drive. His dad, a former college defensive end, was in a great mood as they drove home from the game.

"It's about damn time that your brainless coach put you in," Frank said. "That sorry excuse of a quarterback wasn't ever going to take your team anywhere but to the bottom of the standings. I told your coach on the way to the locker room at half time that if he wanted to win, he better put you in. He looked a little scared." Frank laughed out loud. "I guess I have that effect on people. Anyway, I was right, wasn't I?"

"Yes, sir!" Quinn said enthusiastically.

"Let's go celebrate! I think you are old enough for your first drink."

Quinn smiled. He and his football buddies had been stealing liquor from their parents for years.

Frank pulled into a bar and whispered something to the bouncer at the door who smiled and waved Quinn in. They walked through the crowded main area into a private room in the back. Soon, a scantily clad waitress brought a plate full of appetizers and a bottle of scotch.

Quinn and Frank indulged heartily and when Frank was pleasantly intoxicated, Quinn found his moment.

"I know what you do, Dad," he said, a bit hesitantly.

Frank put down his glass and stared intensely at his son. The smile was gone.

"What do you mean, 'What I do'?"

"At your work."

"Oh yeah? And what is it that you think I do?" Frank's dark eyes continued to bore a hole into Quinn's face.

"Wesley told me everything. The farm workers, the contracts, the debt, the abuse."

Frank didn't say anything for several minutes but continued to stare at his son, searching his eyes for evidence of anger or disappointment. That's not what he found. Instead, he saw something distinct, though unexpected. *Pride.* He knew that look. It was pride.

"Okay. So now you know. What are you planning on doing about it?"

"Dad. I want in. The family business. I'm ready."

CHAPTER NINE

Chuck Peters was a large man, intimidating by most standards. He had close-cropped silver hair, a style he had never given up after his days in the Marine corps. He put on his uniform and looked at himself in the mirror. He had always respected what the uniform was supposed to represent. *Duty. Honor.* He had not always lived up to those standards, and it still hurt when he saw himself dressed in the mirror. But that was for another day. Today, he was going to represent those ideals to his best ability. He had had this same conversation with himself every day for the last twenty years.

His father, an army man himself, had instilled in Chuck from as early as he could remember that a real man was a protector, someone who others looked to in a crisis, someone who others could always rely on, who would always be there, and would always do the right thing. That is what led Chuck into the military and then into law enforcement.

He started his police career in Chicago—big city crime. And there he soon learned that the black and white lines that had defined his moral thinking were crossed way too easily. Actually, he had first learned that lesson in the military, in Vietnam, where he, and most other soldiers, had done things that they were not proud of. That is why he joined the police force when he got out.

He wanted to atone. Unfortunately, he made mistakes there, too. And those mistakes had cost him dearly.

He knew that he needed to get out, at least, away from Chicago. He would start over, in a small town, in the west. A new life, but still a cop. He found a job in Thompson Falls, Montana and after a few years, had transferred to Whitefish, quickly moving his way up the ranks in the department from patrol officer to sergeant. When Chief of Police Dan Stevens decided to retire, Chuck was appointed to the job.

Now he was in charge. He would set up his department to do things the right way, so that none of the officers who worked under him would ever feel pressure to make compromises. This would be his chance for redemption. To regain what he had given away.

Chuck loved it here in Whitefish. Most folks were law-abiding. Sure, there were problems but usually minor things—petty crimes, burglaries. Violent crime was almost unheard of. He did get the occasional threat of violence. Almost everybody around here owned a gun or two, sometimes more. Guns had always been a big part of the Montana culture, but they were used for hunting and target shooting—not like in Chicago, where guns were a symbol of power on the street, and the only hunting was for members of rival gangs. In Chicago, it was always hunting season.

Chuck felt comfortable here. He had been here now for going on twenty years. The people in Whitefish knew him, and he knew them. Of course, he couldn't know everyone personally, but he knew those that he had to keep his eye on. He rarely had any trouble with those people, either. He had a way of talking to folks that was disarming, like he had their best interest in mind. His size probably helped some, too, he figured.

That morning, September 17, 2010, seemed like any other. He woke up at 6 am, got dressed, turned on the coffee maker, and threw some bread in the toaster. Little did he know that his day was about to be spent investigating a murder.

. . .

Chuck pulled into the lot at the police station and parked his patrol car in the spot marked "Chief of Police." He opened the door and pulled his big frame to a standing position. He had recently started feeling the decades in his joints. As he approached the glass front door, he saw one of the sergeants, Sean Davidson, a linebacker-sized man in his mid-twenties, running down the hall toward him. Chuck stepped back slightly so he would not get hit by Sean bursting through the door.

"Whoa there, hoss, where's the fire?" Chuck said.

Sean bent slightly as he caught his breath. "I saw you pull in ... I just hung up the phone. Someone's been killed out at Dane Mather's place!"

"What?" Chuck said with a look of shocked disbelief. "At Dane's place? Are you sure?"

"Yeah! Gordon Richards went by this morning. They were supposed to go fishing. He said the door was open, and there is blood everywhere."

"Damn ... Damn!" Chuck stood quietly on the sidewalk for a moment trying to collect his thoughts. It's not that he didn't know what to do. He had been involved in murder investigations before, while working the streets of Chicago. But this one was different. He was the only one that knew that Dane Mather was not actually Dane Mather.

Almost two years ago, Dane had moved to town by himself. But he didn't come entirely by himself—he came with a file. It was in a dark blue envelope with the seal of the Federal Bureau of Investigation stamped on the front along with the words *Classified: For Chief of Police only.* It was delivered to him personally by an FBI agent dressed in a dark suit.

Chuck had opened the envelope and read over the file. Dane's real name was James Slater. He was being relocated here as part of the witness protection program. He had provided key testimony in a federal money laundering case that put his former bosses in prison.

Now, he was dead. At least, Chuck presumed the blood belonged to Dane ... er James. One thing he did know was that the Feds were going to be all over this like flies on stink. His department's handling of the crime scene was going to be scrutinized like he had never dealt with before. It was up to him to be sure that they didn't screw anything up.

"Who is there?" Chuck asked Sean calmly.

"Gordon. And Jason Kraft is on his way."

"Call Jason and tell him to keep Gordon outside and not to go in himself. It's very important. I'll be right there."

"Yes, sir. What do you want me to do?"

"Nothing. Stay here. Don't tell anyone else. This is way bigger than you can even imagine, Sean. We need to buy a little time. I'll explain later."

Chuck went back to his car and sat in the driver's seat. He reached over to the glove compartment and found the card from the FBI agent who had brought James's file. Brent Atkins. He dialed his number as he pulled out of the parking lot and turned left onto the street. The patrol car drove off quickly. No sirens.

CHAPTER TEN

Adam sat in the back of the squad car of the Royal Canadian Mounted Police and looked out the window at the pine trees and the brightening sky. Sitting back was uncomfortable with his hands cuffed behind him.

How did this happen? How did I and my two best friends, who had never been in trouble with the law, suddenly find ourselves under arrest in Canada? International fugitives. And where was Quinn?

Adam seethed as he sat there, awaiting transport to who knows where, while the real criminal was still free. He thought back. *When did I last hear Quinn's voice? It was right before we crossed the parking lot. Quinn was still close by. Maybe they could still find him.*

"Excuse me," Adam spoke to the officer sitting behind the steering wheel working on his laptop, starting to process their files.

The officer looked up slowly and then glared back at him. "Don't talk!" he said curtly. "Just sit there and think about the pain you have just caused your families."

"But ... " Adam protested.

The officer turned around angrily now and pointed a finger at Adam. "I said don't talk. Why are you still talking?"

Adam said quickly, "You missed one of us. There were four, not three."

The officer stared at Adam and didn't say anything for a minute. Then, "Look, son, I'm not sure what you are trying to pull. How do you think we found you? Do you think we just hang out here every morning waiting for Americans to spill across our border? No! We were tipped off that you were coming, that there would be three teenage boys coming off the trail at dawn who were wanted for murder in the States. And so, we came; and sure enough, so did you. Three teenage Americans. Not four. Three. So, if you think it's funny to try to send us on a man hunt for your invisible friend, I'd think again."

"I'm just trying to tell you that you are letting the real murderer get away," Adam said sharply.

"Is that so?" the officer mocked. "You are just trying to be helpful, huh? Well, I suggest that you just worry about yourself, young man. That should give you more than enough to think about."

Adam sat back, tears of frustration burning his eyes. He looked at Mark and Tanner, both of whom wore defeated expressions.

. . .

About a month ago, Adam had started seeing Quinn differently and worried how he was changing them. Ever since that first game of HORSE in Tanner's driveway, their lives had changed. Suddenly, they were cool.

Quinn drove them around town in his Mustang and took them to parties with football players and popular girls. Adam had to admit that it was a bit intoxicating to have a girl say hi to him that would have never given him the time of day just months before. He still didn't understand why, though. Why did Quinn want to hang around with them? They had absolutely nothing to offer him.

As the summer wore on and the school year approached, Quinn started changing. He wasn't as fun and relaxed. He was moody and had a short fuse; and he started becoming more reckless.

One day, as they were filling up his car with gas at the local 7-11, he and Quinn were inside getting Slurpees. As they walked past the rotating rack of CDs, Quinn grabbed one and shoved it under Adam's shirt.

"What are you doing?" Adam asked him, anxiously looking around to see if anyone noticed.

"Just stay calm and act natural," Quinn whispered and grabbed him by the shoulder, pushing him forward to the counter.

"That's a nice car. '68?" the clerk asked, while looking out of the window at Quinn's Mustang.

"'67, actually," Quinn said with a friendly smile. "My dad and I restored it ourselves."

"Ah, I had a '68. I loved that car. Broke my heart when I had to sell it. The Slurpees gonna do it for you?"

"Yes, sir," Quinn said, as he handed over a five-dollar bill.

"All right then. Have a nice day and enjoy those wheels."

"Absolutely," Quinn replied. "You have a nice day as well."

Quinn and Adam walked over to the car and got inside. Mark and Tanner had already bought their stuff and were in the back seat.

"Ahh, man!" Quinn said excitedly. "That was a rush! Tell them, Adam. Tell them what you did!"

"I didn't do anything!" Adam said defensively.

"Ah, c'mon, Adam," Quinn continued. "Don't be modest, now. You guys should have seen him. He lifted a CD right from under that guy's nose. He's a freaking pro!"

Adam took out the CD from under his shirt and held it gingerly between his thumb and index finger, like it was contaminated. He threw it in the back seat where Mark picked it up.

"Neil Diamond's Greatest Hits," Mark read. "You stole Neil Diamond?"

Adam protested, "No, I didn't steal it! Quinn shoved it under my shirt. Give it back. I'm going to go pay ... "

Quinn revved the engine and squealed the tires as he sped away from the parking lot. "I'm sorry, Adam. You were saying?"

Adam turned around and fell silent. Being with Quinn was losing its appeal.

There were other moments. Quinn started stealing every time they were together and wouldn't stop talking about trying something bigger, like breaking into someone's house. Adam tried changing the subject whenever he brought it up, but Quinn was almost obsessed. "I'm not going to take anything. I just want to feel what it's like to be in there, looking at other people's stuff. Just to see how much we could actually get out of it."

Mark and Tanner thought he was just joking and never took it seriously until that night, last night, when Quinn told Tanner to bring his car instead of the Mustang. "We have a little mission to accomplish tonight, boys!"

"A mission?" Adam questioned.

"Yep, Adam. And you're coming, too," Quinn replied as he pulled out a CD from his pack. "Unless of course, you want to explain to the police how this ended up in my car without you paying for it."

Adam looked at the CD and then angrily at Quinn, who just smiled back.

"Okay, but we're just looking, right?"

"Of course, Adam, just looking," Quinn replied.

They all piled into Tanner's car and drove to the edge of town. Quinn directed Tanner down a dirt road and past a cabin on the left. "Keep going and pull up there behind those trees."

Tanner did as directed.

"That's good. Tanner, you stay here and be ready. We'll be back before eight. Mark and Adam, come with me," Quinn said.

"Whose cabin is this?" Mark asked.

"Hell if I know! It's out of the way and nobody's around," Quinn said.

The three of them walked quietly through the woods toward the cabin. As they approached, they could see a soft glow from a lamp inside the main living room.

Adam whispered, "Someone's home. Let's get out of here!"

"No," Quinn interrupted and grabbed Adam's arm roughly. "I've been scouting this place out. That light is always on. But nobody is here, I promise."

They walked up the back porch steps and over the deck, the wood creaking beneath their feet.

"Shhh! Idiots! Be quiet," Quinn mouthed.

"I thought no one was here," Adam said out loud.

Quinn clapped his hand over Adam's mouth. "Adam, shut up or I'll shut you up. We're breaking into someone's house, okay! We don't need to announce it at the door!"

Adam raised his eyebrows in concession, and Quinn released his grip. They tiptoed across the rest of the deck, and Quinn slowly opened the screen to the back door and tried the knob. It was unlocked.

He opened the door and waived the others inside. Quinn walked directly through the kitchen with Mark and Adam close behind. Quinn pushed Adam forward as they approached the living room, where they could now see the lamp and entered the room quietly, Adam in the lead.

There was a fire burning in the fireplace but no other signs of life. Adam pointed at the fire and turned to leave the room, but Quinn blocked him. This time, instead of a hand over his mouth, Adam saw that Quinn had a gun pointed at his head.

Adam stopped in his tracks, his mouth dropping in surprise. Mark was wide-eyed and also looked shocked. Quinn pushed Adam in the chest directing him back into the room.

Quinn waved the gun toward the fireplace, signaling Adam to move in that direction. Adam did as instructed, and as he approached the mantle, he could see that there was someone asleep in the chair—an older man, maybe late 50s. He had a pile of papers in his lap and was snoring lightly.

Adam again tried to back away when Quinn approached the sleeping man. He raised the gun, cocked it, and aimed at the man's head.

"Die, you bastard!" Quinn said and pulled the trigger.

Adam and Mark both froze. Quinn had just killed a man! The gunshot still rang in their ears. The man never moved, as a red hole appeared in the middle of his forehead and blood stained the cushion behind.

Quinn turned slowly and looked at the other two. He had a weird smile on his face, and his eyes looked ... evil.

"Well, I guess there was someone home after all."

Adam and Mark just stared at Quinn and couldn't say anything.

"You crazy stupid son of a bitch," Adam finally broke the momentary silence.

"Pick him up!" Quinn said.

"What?" Adam asked incredulously.

"I said, pick him up!" Quinn pointed the gun again at Adam, who stared back, still trying to process the whole last few minutes.

Quinn slapped Mark in the face and then shoved him over to the dead man's chair.

"You and Adam, pick him up!" He was yelling now. "We are taking him out to the woods, and you two are going to bury his body. Do you understand?"

Mark looked down at the man, now pale-faced and lifeless, and reached out cautiously, grabbing the man's arms and pulling him forward. Clotted blood and bits of brain still clung to the chair as the dead man's head fell forward against his chest with the motion.

Quinn laughed as Mark turned a ghostly white and nearly passed out. "Easy there, Mark. Adam, grab the feet!"

Adam moved forward slowly and lifted the man's feet from the recliner's extended footrest. Mark got behind and put his arms under the man's shoulders, carefully trying to avoid looking at the missing pieces of skull.

They lifted the man out of the chair and onto the floor.

"Okay, now drag him out! Same way we came," Quinn directed.

They did as they were told and got the body outside and onto the deck.

"Stop, now!" Quinn commanded. He pulled out another gun that was tucked in his pants. He held the murder weapon out to Adam, grip first. Adam now noticed for the first time that Quinn was wearing gloves. "Take it, Adam," he said quietly.

Adam looked down at the gun but didn't move.

Quinn cocked the new gun and lifted it up toward Adam's head. "I said, take it!"

Adam reached out and grabbed the gun, wrapping his fingers around the handle, feeling its weight. He had never held a gun before and wondered what it would feel like when it fired.

"Don't get any ideas. There was only one bullet in that one," Quinn sneered. "Now, throw it in the bush."

Adam knew what was happening. He was being framed for the murder. But what could he do? Quinn had another gun. He threw the gun in the bush and went around the body to help Mark drag him down the steps.

CHAPTER ELEVEN

Chuck pulled his car onto the dirt road that led to Mather's place. As he pulled in front of the cabin, Jason got out of his patrol car. Jason was tall and athletic looking, though it was evident that his best years were behind him, his gut competing with his bullet-proof vest for attention.

"Stay there for a minute, Gordon," he said to the man sitting in his back seat. "I need to talk to the chief alone for a bit, okay?"

"Sure thing. I'm not going anywhere."

Gordon was sitting in the back seat, a nervous man with grey at his temples. He looked visibly shaken and unsettled. He had never seen that much blood before and thinking about his friend made him nauseated.

Jason walked slowly over to Chuck's car, adjusting his belt nervously. He was fairly new to the Whitefish Police Department and wasn't sure how Chuck was going to react to a murder in his town. Whitefish was a peaceful community. Murders didn't happen here! Accidents, sure—but not murders.

"Chief," Jason nodded slightly to Chuck, who had gotten out of his car and was waiting for Jason to join him.

"Morning, Jason. C'mon over and get in. I need to tell you a few things before we get busy here," Chuck spoke in a calm voice, putting Jason at ease.

Jason and Chuck went back to the chief's patrol car and sat in the front seat.

"What'd you see, Jason?" Chuck asked quietly.

Jason looked straight ahead. "Nothing, sir. Sean told me to stay outside. I just got Gordon out of there, and we've been waiting for you."

"That's good, Jason. That's real good. See anything suspicious around the lot?"

"Nothing, Chief. It's just quiet—like a normal morning."

"Well, I'm afraid this morning is gonna be far from normal—not that any murder in Whitefish is normal, but this one's special. Dane was under the protection of the Feds."

"The Feds? ... Dane? What for?"

"Whistleblower case. He told on some bad dudes he used to work for. So, they gave him a new name and sent him out here to Montana to start a new life. But it looks like his old life just caught up to him."

"Hmmm ... guess so, Chief."

"I called the FBI contact for him. He's in Missoula—on his way. We've got to secure the scene without any mistakes. This is gonna be a big deal. It takes some big kahunas to go after someone in witness protection. The killers will have planned it carefully. Might not be much evidence. We can't overlook even minor details."

"Yes, sir."

"All right, I'll check out the house. Give Sean a call and have him come take Gordon in for questioning. I'm sure the Feds will want to talk to him, too, so be sure he stays accessible. Then, you go secure the entrance off the highway and search the woods around the house. I'll meet you around back when you're done."

"On it, sir!" Jason turned and walked back to his car while radioing into dispatch.

Chuck grabbed a camera from his car along with evidence bags and some blue rubber gloves and headed for the cabin. First, he took a good look around the driveway. He had noticed some tire tracks in the dirt before he had turned in and went back to mark the area and take some pictures.

Then he walked the perimeter of the house. He saw the blood leading from the back door with footprints adjacent to and on top of the trail. He followed the blood into the house and into the living room. The recliner looked like it had shifted a little from its original position based on dust marks on the floor. There were papers scattered on the floor, tax forms with Dane Mather's name on the top. The papers were unstained and looked untouched. There was blood and other tissue on the head cushion of the recliner. Chuck saw a hole in the upholstery in the rear of the chair. He followed the presumed path of the bullet until he found it embedded partially in the floorboards a few feet away. *9mm.* Chuck circled the spot on the floor, took a picture, and then removed the bullet and bagged it.

He then looked around the rest of the cabin. No sign of struggle, forced entry, or obvious theft. *Seems like whoever did this wanted Dane, not his stuff*, Chuck thought. Chuck took pictures of some of the footprints along the blood trail. Two sets. Both looked like sneaker tread. One was moving forward, the other backward. *Two suspects dragging the victim. Why remove the body?* Chuck wondered. *That just creates more evidence.*

He went back outside and dusted the door handles for fingerprints. Didn't see any. He walked down the steps of the deck and saw a glint of metal reflect from the bush at the side of the stairs. Chuck examined the bush more closely and discovered a 9 mm handgun. *Incredible*, Chuck thought. *They tossed the murder weapon in the bush at the crime scene? This doesn't fit with a sophisticated crime ring. They would never leave such an obvious trail of evidence. The whole thing isn't making any sense.*

Jason returned from searching the perimeter just as Chuck was bagging the weapon.

"Is that a gun?" he asked with surprise.

"It sure is. Appears to be the murder weapon. These guys were amateurs, Jason. I can't figure," Chuck said. "Did you find anything in the woods?"

"Yeah, the gravesite. It's just through that grove of trees. Fresh dirt. Looks like a shallow grave. Two sets of footprints around the site that lead away to a parking area behind some trees. Third set of prints there and some tire tracks. Seems like it won't be too hard to find these guys."

"Seems like you're right. And that's what bothers me," Chuck said. "I can see why Dane was a target, but his enemies are professionals. They wouldn't have done it like this. Yet, nothing else was disrupted in his house, so a failed burglary is unlikely. Who else knew about Dane, and why would they want him dead?"

"No clue," Jason said. "Gordon said that Dane was quiet and didn't know many people. Gordon took him fishing a lot because he was always alone otherwise. Felt sorry for him."

"Well, stand post until the FBI comes. I'm going to head back to the office and run some forensics," Chuck said, as he headed toward his car. "Don't let anybody go in the house except the FBI. Okay?"

"Yes, sir," Jason confirmed with a lazy salute.

CHAPTER TWELVE

Sandra got up from the floor in her sensory room feeling motivated and confident. She just needed to type out a message. It had been years since she had tried typing and in a totally different context. She had improved in so many other ways since then; maybe this would be easier, too.

She went to the kitchen and found her laptop, buried at the bottom of one of the drawers. She took it over to the kitchen table and plugged it in. A picture came on the screen. It was of her mom and dad building a sandcastle on a beach. She was in the scene, too, but sitting a few paces away and looking at something off-camera.

Sandra remembered that day. She was watching the waves roll in and out, washing the sand clean, and depositing a fresh layer on the beach. As each wave retreated, the sand on the surface tumbled toward the ocean, exposing shells and the occasional crab, which would scurry a few yards and bury itself again before getting washed out to sea.

The ocean had always fascinated her. *They say the moon creates the tides. How incredible*, she thought, *that something so far away could affect the water on earth.* The influence of gravity from competing bodies compelled the ocean to shift and move with cyclical indecision. And that created the beach where her family was relaxing.

Sandra felt the heart of the ocean like she felt the heart of the forest. It was another part of Earth's great whole. She understood the push and pull and the struggle of the creatures that depended on it. Their life, like her life, was shaped by forces outside of their control; perhaps hers, too, was being directed by a heavenly body far removed.

Sandra redirected her focus from the screen to the keyboard. The letters lined up in a random order in three rows. *Who decided to start with q?* Sandra studied the letters, speaking to them in her mind. *I need you, letters.*

Letters had always played a comforting role for her for as long as she could remember. She remembered her mother teaching her letter sounds when she was a toddler, before her mind became cloudy. The ABC song played like a soundtrack in her head. In fact, Sandra never forgot her ABCs, even when her newly learned words retreated from her mind as she slid further into her disability. It is what confused her doctor at the time.

"She knows her ABCs, Susan. That is advanced! There is nothing wrong with her mind."

Sandra thought about letters all the time. She recited the ABCs forward and backward. She knew what number corresponded to each letter based on its position in the alphabet. She had accumulated boxes full of plastic letters of assorted colors and had memorized each set. She knew when the yellow D was missing from a particular set and couldn't sleep until they had either found it or bought a new set with a yellow D. Her letters protected her from meltdowns. She could spell words in her head using the color combinations from different sets, and if she got it right, her anxiety melted away.

But it was all done inside her mind. No one knew that she could spell or read. When she was asked by her teachers or her therapists to read words on flash cards or arrange the letters on the floor, the letters wouldn't cooperate. They abandoned her during times like that, when an outsider tried to control them.

I need you now, letters. This is for me. No one else is here. Please help me now. I need you.

Sandra ran her fingertips gently over each key, imagining that she was waking them up from a long slumber. *C'mon, H, time to wake up. I need your help. Wake up, N. Now is the time.* She addressed each letter by name and gave it a purpose.

This was not therapy. This was her asking them for permission to use them for a greater good. She knew the power that they held. A power abused by so many. They were taken for granted by most. But not her. She understood. She would be responsible.

Sandra focused again on the screen. There were a few of the standard thumbnails along the left margin. She had watched her mom type documents before and knew that the Microsoft Word icon would open a blank page. She tapped the finger pad to wake up the arrow and then moved it to the right place and tapped again. MS Word options opened, and she selected a blank document. A white page opened on the screen.

At the top left of the page was a blinking straight line, inviting her to begin. She stared at the line, pondered it. Why was it blinking? It seemed impatient, almost mocking. *C'mon, I'm ready,* it said. *Start typing!*

It's not that easy for me, Line. I've never done it before. Not really.

Sandra looked again at the keyboard. All the letters were in their places. She just had to touch them. She knew how to spell. She knew what she wanted to say. *Just touch them with your fingers, Sandra.*

It seemed so simple. But whenever she had tried in the past, the letters would scatter as she approached them with her finger, like a herd of frightened sheep. She couldn't understand how that happened. Her brain. Why would it do that to her? It had taken so much from her already. Why couldn't it let her type? Just that. She could deal with not speaking, but not being able to communicate was just plain torture. Selfish brain. She hated it for that.

Just type your name, her soul spoke. *We will trick your brain. Your name isn't like communication. Start with that.*

The S was right there on the second row, second from the left. *S for second.* Her finger hesitated and then went for it. She looked up at the screen.

FTCCCC.
Stupid, selfish brain. Try again.

DSSD
That was better. At least the S was there.

She was going to try to just get one letter, even if it was wrong. It was like her finger knew how to start but not how to finish and got stuck holding down the key.

SSS.
Okay. Right letter. Three is not bad. I might get it.

D
Solid.

DSSSV
Aargh! Keep focus.

S
Yes! I did it.

Sandra continued in the same way to the other letters in her name and eventually got them all, but the effort was mentally exhausting, and she could feel the negative emotions swirling and bubbling like a volcano about to erupt. She had to take a break. She needed fresh air.

CHAPTER THIRTEEN

The BMW pulled up to a large metal gate supported by twin columns of river rock and topped with an elaborate wood-framed arch. Gary rolled down the driver's side window and punched in a code. The split gate opened slowly, allowing the car to drive through and enter the private estate. As they rounded a bend in the tree-lined driveway, the view opened to a spacious grass-covered yard presided over by a beautiful post-and-beam home whose exterior was constructed from a tasteful balance of rock, timber, and glass. The house drew in its guests with a covered entrance whose roof was supported by full tree-sized logs and adorned with a tongue-and-groove ceiling. There was enough space under its eaves for several cars, protecting them from any sort of harsh Montana weather.

The house was perched on the edge of a sloping hill that overlooked the deep-blue glacial waters of Lake Whitefish. Golden aspen leaves illuminated the scene like sunlight and the shifting reds and oranges of the decorative maples and oaks completed the emerging autumn palette, creating an ambience worthy of the cover of a mountain living magazine.

The black sedan pulled around the side of the house and into one of the bays of the four-car garage. Quinn got out of the passenger side and tried to reenergize his body by doing some squats and lunges on his way into the house. He was going to be late to practice, but he had not eaten all night, and his body was depleted. He grabbed a protein smoothie from the refrigerator and a muffin from the bread box and headed out of the door. On the way, he gathered his football gear and threw it in the back seat of the Mustang. *Calm yourself down, Quinn*, he said to himself. *You have got to act normal today.* Being late for practice was already a bad start. Bringing attention to himself was the last thing he wanted. The Mustang's tires squealed as he pulled away from the gate.

He arrived at the high school several minutes after the team had already started their warm-up routine of stretching and calisthenics. The head coach, Bryce Dalton, a former star at Whitefish High who had played a few years of junior college ball before realizing that coaching was going to be his default path of staying around the game, yelled at him for being late and pointed him to the back of a row. This made Quinn seethe inside. He was a captain and belonged in front, facing his teammates, watching them to ensure full effort. Today was the first time he had ever been late. Why couldn't his coach let it slide this once? Several of his teammates threw some verbal barbs his way as he passed them on his way to the back. Quinn scowled and muttered some colorful words back at them, just quiet enough that the coach couldn't hear.

After warm-ups, the offense and defense divided up for drills. The quarterbacks and receivers got together and began throwing the ball and running routes. Quinn was off. He consistently threw high and was getting frustrated. One of his receivers said something, and this lit the fuse. On the next throw, Quinn pelted him in the back of the head with the ball as soon as he started off the line. His target stopped running, turned slowly, and then sprinted directly at Quinn. A brawl ensued with at least a dozen players picking sides. The coaches tried to intervene, but it took several minutes to separate the players and restore some order. Quinn sustained a bloody nose in the melee, and the coach sent him to the sideline for the trainer to pack it with gauze. The rest of the team started running sprints as punishment.

After a few minutes, Coach Dalton came over to the sideline and lit into Quinn. "What the hell is the matter with you? I saw that whole thing! That last throw was the only time the ball has even come close to a receiver. I know it is a bye week, and we didn't have a game last night, but I still expect you to focus. So, what's your problem? Enlighten me."

Quinn finished wiping the blood from his upper lip and glared into his coach's eyes. Coach Dalton, a little startled by the dark intensity of Quinn's stare, took a step back.

"There is no problem," Quinn said coldly.

Dalton hesitated and then said more calmly, "Then go join your teammates doing sprints. They are all running because of you, Captain!"

Quinn grabbed his helmet, avoiding more eye contact with his coach, and ran back onto the field.

CHAPTER FOURTEEN

Adam sat on the hard bench of the holding cell where they were being detained in Calgary, Canada. He had tried to sleep but could not shut off his mind. Mark was curled up on the bench next to him, breathing slowly and not moving, although Adam could tell he was still awake. Mark hadn't said a word since they were arrested. Adam knew that he was furious that Adam had discouraged them from escaping. Tanner had stretched out on the concrete floor, laying on his back, eyes closed, and snoring. Adam wondered how Tanner could shut it out like that.

Adam stood up and looked out of the small, barred window that was high on the wall of their cell. He couldn't reach it but could see the blue sky. Sunlight beamed through the glass and rested on his face. Would this be how he would experience nature for the rest of his life? Sunlight through a barred window?

Adam knew that he would be the prime suspect. He had held the murder weapon and left it at the scene. There was blood on his shoe. A jury was sure to see it as a clear-cut case and would convict him of murder. Life behind bars for a crime he didn't commit. Tanner and Mark might get punished, but only as accessories to the crime.

How did he get mixed up in this? How did he not see it coming? Getting caught for shoplifting, maybe, but not this. Who could ever have predicted that the star quarterback, the most revered kid at Whitefish High School, was a cold-blooded killer?

Adam could now see how he played them from the beginning. He should have walked away after that first incident at 7-11. That is when he knew that the all-American boy routine was just an act. But he hung around anyway, letting their newfound high school popularity cloud his better judgment and the voice inside of him that was screaming, "Danger!"

But now it was too late. He was caught in the trap. Quinn had led him to the bait, and then forced him to eat it while the metal teeth snapped into his flesh. Then he smiled, turned around, and left, leaving Adam to struggle against the chain until his life eventually slipped away.

Adam thought of his parents, his younger sister. How could he face them? Would they believe that he was innocent? He had been gone a lot this summer, with Quinn. He had been moody, short-tempered. Would that be enough to convince them that he was capable of killing someone?

Mark stirred on the bench and then sat up, looking at Adam through red, tired eyes. "It's not your fault."

Adam looked back at his friend. "You were right, Mark. We should have jumped him when you said so. I was just afraid in the moment and thinking we'd get a better opportunity. I didn't want any of us to get hurt. But look at us now. We are trapped in this cage and Quinn is free. My life is over. You guys have a chance still. I'll vouch for you."

Mark sat straighter. "What are you talking about? You didn't do it! Quinn did it! We are all witnesses! We will just tell them the truth. How can they not believe us?"

Adam sighed. "They won't believe us. He will deny that he was even there. He was careful, Mark. He had gloves on.

He never touched the body. He walked to the side of us so he wouldn't leave any footprints. He made me touch the gun. He made Tanner drive his car. He tipped off the Canadians but erased himself from the scene. Three Americans, remember?"

Mark slumped again and looked down. "I really thought we were his friends."

Adam sat back down on the bench. "He set us up from the beginning, Mark. He targeted us. We were nobodies. We followed along like idiots."

Tanner had stopped snoring and was listening quietly to the conversation. When Mark and Adam fell silent, he said, "We'll be okay, guys."

Adam shifted his gaze to the floor. "Really, Tanner? All is well? Do you have some insight that you are keeping to yourself?"

"I just think it's going to be okay, that's all," Tanner replied.

Adam looked at Tanner in disbelief and started feeling angry. Tanner didn't see any of it, not the blood, the brains, nothing. He didn't have to drag a dead man's body or dig a grave. He just drove his car, at gunpoint. He could prove his innocence. Who was he to tell them it was going to be okay?

Adam looked away, suppressing his anger. *He was just trying to help,* Adam said to himself. *These are your true friends. Don't lose them, too.*

They all sat in silence for several minutes. Adam wanted to stand up and start screaming, "I didn't do it!" but he knew that would just make the guards angry. They couldn't do anything for him. They were just doing their job.

He thought again of Quinn, of his sneer when he forced Adam to hold the gun. The trap line was cinching tighter. The more he struggled, the more painful it became. Adam began panicking and started pacing in the cell. He started feeling the walls closing in, and his vision went dark. Mark caught him just as he started to fall.

"What's wrong, Adam?" Mark asked anxiously, as he looked at his best friend's sweat-covered face. He had never seen Adam like this before. Adam always kept his cool, no matter the situation.

"Mark," Adam whispered, wheezing. "I can't breathe!"

CHAPTER FIFTEEN

Agent Brett Atkins pulled off the highway and removed the yellow tape that blocked his path. He drove onto the dirt road and then stopped again so he could replace the tape. He continued down the road until the cabin came into view and then pulled into the driveway. Chuck's patrol car was still parked in front. He had sent Jason back to the station to see what they had found out from Gordon. Chuck was sitting on the front porch, waiting.

"Chief Peters, nice to see you again," Agent Atkins said, as he offered his hand. Atkins was prototypical FBI—sunglasses, suitcoat, serious, flat expression.

Chuck grabbed his hand with a firm shake. "Yes, though not under these circumstances."

"No, very true. So, tell me what you've got so far."

"Well, Agent. Things aren't really adding up for me," Chuck said.

"Oh yeah? How so?" Atkins replied.

"This crime was not committed by professionals, that's for sure. They shot him in his recliner. He must have been asleep because there was no sign of a struggle. Then they dragged the body out of the house leaving a trail of bloody footprints. And, get this, we found the murder weapon in a bush just off the deck. Then they buried the body in a shallow grave a hundred yards from here with an obvious trail both to and from the gravesite. There are tire tracks and footprints where they parked. Doesn't it all seem too easy?"

"Hmmm, you're right. The guys that Slater put away would not have left a single clue," Atkins acknowledged. "Botched burglary?"

"I thought about that, but none of his stuff looked messed with. He had a nice sound system and a couple of nice flat screens; even his wallet was left untouched with a couple hundred dollars still in it. It's not like they got scared off and fled the scene. They took the time to bury the body."

"Did you find any prints?" Atkins asked.

"Nothing on the door handles," Chuck said. "I haven't dusted the gun. They can do that at the station. We should check the rest of the house more carefully. I haven't had time for that yet."

"Okay. Well, the trail is too obvious, you're right," Atkins said. "There is something going on here hiding underneath the surface. But let's see where it leads."

"Sounds like a plan, Atkins. I'll take the evidence to the station and see if we get any hits in the database. You going to look around?"

"Yeah. For a bit. Go ahead and call the coroner, and let's dig up the body. I'll stay here and wait for him. Let me know if you find anything."

"Will do. I'll come back in an hour or so. I just want to get this stuff logged in."

Chuck got into his car and headed back to the station. Atkins followed the prints and blood trail to the woods where the body was buried. There were two shovels in some tall grass nearby. *Did they come with shovels? Or did they break into his shed?*

At the cabin, he had noticed a tool shed separate from the garage. He went back and looked around. There was a padlock on the door and none of the windows were broken. He could see various garden tools including shovels hanging neatly on a rack when he looked through the dusty windowpane.

So, they planned this ahead of time and brought their own shovels but didn't bother to take them with them. Peters is right. This doesn't make sense, Atkins said to himself. *Slater had lived in Whitefish now for three years. He was a nervous guy and was unsettled about the protection we were offering him. Yet, he never reported anything suspicious to us before now, when he ends up dead by some seemingly bumbling fools who made it easy to find them. What am I missing?*

. . .

Chuck pulled into the station, took the box of evidence out of the backseat, and carried it into his office. After he sat at his desk, he pushed the speaker on his phone.

"Kathy, can you ask Sean to come in here please?"

A few minutes later, Officer Davidson knocked on Chuck's door and poked his head into the room. "You needed me, Chief?"

"Yeah, Sean. I need you to take this evidence to the crime lab in Missoula. I want the professionals to look it over. Don't touch anything. Just leave it in the box, okay?"

"No problem, Chief. Did you find anything?"

"Everything, Sean. Too much, in fact. That's why we need to be careful. I feel like somebody is getting set up here."

Sean left the office with the box, and Chuck leaned back in his chair. Just then, Kathy interrupted his stretch from his phone speaker.

"Chief, you've got a phone call. Says it's an old friend."

CHAPTER SIXTEEN

Sandra closed the laptop, pushed back the kitchen chair, and stood up. She had that all-too-familiar restlessness in her legs, the need to move, to run. *Not now*, she thought, trying to suppress the relentless urge. *I don't have time now. I've got to keep working. I'm making progress. My plan will work if I can just practice some more. It's still illegible to others. I need more time.*

She saw the sun peering in through her kitchen window, beckoning her to come outside. *I can't,* she reasoned. *It's not safe. He might be there, waiting for me to return. To the scene. To see it in daylight. To see if the police know. No. I can't.*

She turned away from the window and walked down the hall to her sensory room. She went in and turned on the light. The kickboxing bag was hanging still. It beckoned to her. *Let me help you. I will be your anxiety. Come and beat me down.*

She walked across the room to her supply box and picked up the gloves. She put them on and cinched up the laces with her teeth. *Okay, bag. Help me.*

She began slowly, warming up her muscles, getting used to the feel of her gloves hitting the swinging bag, finding the rhythm. Between a series of punches, she gave it a kick. That was more satisfying. She started kicking repeatedly, trying to transfer her anxiety to the bag, to visualize it as an evil spirit that departed from her and found a new home where it could be trapped and then destroyed by being hit and kicked until it was too weak to cause any more damage.

But it wasn't working. The anxiety was strong today. It was in the mood for a fight. It would not be fooled by the bag. Not today.

She had to try something different. Maybe she could drown out its voice with sound. She went to the stereo and thumbed through her vinyl record collection. She needed something loud, hard. Classic rock. *AC/DC. Aerosmith.* Her records were organized alphabetically. She kept going until she reached *Metallica.* She grabbed the album, put it on the turntable, and turned up the volume. The guitar riff from *Enter Sandman* filled the room with energy. Sandra grabbed her drumsticks and started beating on one of her exercise balls along with the music.

For a moment, it was working. She was feeling the anxiety start to decrease. But as the music continued, and the lyrics started, her brain began internalizing the words.

Exit light, enter night.
Take my hand
We're off to Never Neverland.

Suddenly, everything around her started getting darker, like the light was being sucked from the room. Or was it from her soul? The drumbeat was pounding in her head, and the room started spinning. She fell to her knees and crawled toward the door. She could see it in front of her, but it appeared to be getting farther and farther away. She started screaming, but the music drowned out her voice. The guitars were yelling at her now, telling her to give in.

Dreams of war, dreams of liars, dreams of dragon's fire

Sandra clapped her hands over her ears but was unsuccessful in suppressing the sound. The music was inside of her now. She had to keep moving. To get out. To just keep crawling.

Now I lay me down to sleep,
Pray the Lord my soul to keep.
If I die before I wake,
Pray the Lord my soul to take.

Just as she was about to succumb to the overwhelming power of her anxiety, her head hit the door. She was momentarily disoriented, forgetting where she was and feeling trapped in an endless abyss.

Get out, Sandra. Go to the woods.

Her soul's voice brought her back to the present, and she reached up and found the door handle. It felt like a secure anchor in the swirling sea. She held on to it for dear life and used it to pull herself to her feet. Then she opened the door, stumbled into the hall, and quickly shut it again behind her.

She slid to the floor, felt its firmness, and let the light from the kitchen window warm her for several minutes. She could still feel the vibrations of the bass coming from her sensory room. She couldn't go back in. Not now. She needed air—and quiet.

She headed for the front door, but as she reached for the handle, she saw her watch. Her tracking device.

Mom can't know I'm there. She will be watching now.

Sandra hesitated but then grabbed at the watch strap and took it off her wrist. She left it on the dining table, grabbed a jacket, and exited her condo.

She hurried down the stairs and out the building's access door, but then paused, flattening herself against the exterior brick wall, and studied the parking lot. Everything seemed normal. She recognized all the cars. Nothing seemed out of place. She hurried across the pavement until she got to the trail leading into the woods.

The dirt felt welcoming. She could feel its familiar hard pack through her shoes and could tell that her heart began to slow. Moving quickly but quietly, she headed toward the stream, followed it to her spot, and then stepped out of the trees and onto the flat rock that overlooked the pool.

She took off her shoes and socks and dipped her feet in the cold stream. Her feet became numb with the cold, painful at first, but then pleasant. She could feel the rush travel up her legs, connect with her spine, and then to her brain where her anxiety began to flow in the opposite direction, and dump into the pool, to be washed away—out of the woods.

She listened for the treetops, whispering to her with their leaves as they were ruffled by a gentle breeze. She heard a woodpecker's rat-a-tat-tat on a nearby tree and a pair of squirrels chasing each other in a vertical game of tag. *The woods were at peace.*

Sandra stayed next to the stream for an hour, soaking in the fresh air and the calm. She was home here. She felt safe here. She didn't need locked doors or security systems. She just needed space and the protection of the trees and the creatures that shared that space who always signaled danger if you could understand their language.

Her soul felt strong now and ready to go back to work. She stood up and started heading back home.

I wonder if they know about the body, yet. How much time do I have to figure out how to communicate what I saw? If it takes me too long, will the evidence be lost?

She got to a fork in the trail.

Turn left, Sandra. Go home and keep working.

But I need to know if they know. I'll be careful. No one will hear me coming. I'll just get close enough to hear if anyone is there.

Sandra turned right, her curiosity besting her caution. She moved slowly, noiselessly, stopping every few steps to listen. It only took her about twenty minutes to get close enough that she should have been able to hear voices if they were there.

All was quiet. She didn't want to go any further. She didn't want to actually see the grave. She sat for a few minutes under the boughs of a large pine tree. Still nothing. No voices. No sounds.

Well, I guess I have some time, she thought.

She stood back up and began hiking back up the trail toward her condo. After a few yards, she stopped in her tracks. There was that sound again. Shovel hitting dirt. And she could now hear several voices—men's voices muffled by the breeze. She could not understand what they were saying, but it didn't sound like they were hurried or trying to be obscure. She paused for only a few minutes and then carried on up the trail, moving carefully and purposefully.

I've got to get busy. They know.

As she disappeared around a bend in the trees, there was a foreign sound from a nearby bush. A subtle sound, barely perceptible amongst the grating noise of the shovel. Sandra didn't hear it. She was now too focused on her next task. But the sound was unmistakable—the mechanical click of a camera's shudder.

CHAPTER SEVENTEEN

Gary dropped Quinn at the house and immediately turned the car around and drove back toward the crime scene. It was risky, but he needed to see if he could find evidence of the picture taker. That picture could put his boss's son in prison, and he would be blamed for it. He knew a back trail that led to Slater's cabin. That is where he had been doing his surveillance of the comings and goings at the place. His car would be well hidden. He just couldn't be seen by the police. They should be preoccupied with the crime scene and wouldn't look too far into the surrounding woods. Not yet.

He pulled his car off the road about a mile away from Slater's and drove behind a patch of trees. From there, he headed straight into the woods, picking his way through the scrub oak until he reached a trail. Now the going was easier. As he approached the scene, he slowed down and listened. He could hear voices but could not make anything out. They were still near the cabin.

Moving further along the trail, he could now see the area where the body was buried. No one was there. He skirted the edge of the woods, choosing his steps very carefully, and went to the spot where Quinn said the flash came from. It was at the end of another trail that headed up into the hills.

The wild grass was broken and matted in a small area just a few steps into the clearing. *This must be it,* Gary thought. He looked around quickly for any other clues but found none. The grass covered the ground like a carpet and would have hidden any footprints.

He retraced the picture taker's likely path up the trail, but here the ground was hard packed with embedded rocks that would also have obscured any prints. He followed the trail for a few hundred yards, scanning the ground and surrounding brush for any clues. Nothing.

Gary swore under his breath and started to head back to his car but stopped suddenly. The voices from the cabin were getting louder. The police were heading this way. He ducked behind a boulder and squatted down low. He could make a run for it if he had to. They would not be prepared for a chase or a manhunt.

He calmed his breathing and stayed in a ready position, but the voices stopped at the clearing. A few minutes later, he heard a shovel digging at the dirt. *Good,* he thought, relieved. *They are digging up the body. That will keep them occupied and will cover up any sounds from me.*

He stood up again and stepped out from his spot. Again, he froze in place. On the trail, just below him, moving slowly, cautiously, like a deer, there was a young woman. Blond hair, petite. She listened to the shovel for a minute and then turned abruptly and started heading his way. Her face was pretty but expressionless.

He ducked into some shadows and waited as she approached. When she got closer, he pulled his phone out from his pocket and snapped a picture. *That must be the picture taker,* he thought. *Incredible timing.*

He watched her disappear around a bend. *I should follow her,* he thought. But maybe that would be a risky move. If she saw him and screamed, the police would be right there. *It's okay,* he figured. *I know another way.*

CHAPTER EIGHTEEN

Chuck stood up from his desk and walked over to his office door, shut it, and twisted the blinds on the windows closed for privacy. Then he went back to his desk and picked up the receiver on his phone. "This is Chief Peters. Can I help you?"

The voice on the other side spoke quietly. "Good morning, Chuck. Or should I say, Chief? How's your day going so far?"

Chuck felt the hair rise on the back of his neck. "What do you want?"

"Ahh, Chuck. Is that any way to greet an old friend?" the voice answered.

"You are not my friend. I told you that I never wanted to hear your voice again," Chuck spoke softly but angrily.

"But I thought that today might be different, you know, given ... what happened," the voice said.

"How did I know you were involved?" Chuck said.

"Felt a little familiar, did it?" the voice replied with a mocking chuckle.

"What do you want?" Chuck repeated.

"Well, Chuck. I need you to do a little something for me, that's all," the voice said.

"I told you that we are through. No more," Chuck said, his hand started to shake with anger—or was it fear? Not fear for his own safety. He deserved what was coming to him. No, it was fear that he might say yes.

"Now, Chuck. Chief Peters. You know that you still owe me. I can ruin you with a single phone call. Your reputation is really all that you have left, isn't it Chuck? Of course, who would care besides you, right? Not your family. They can't really care anymore, can they? Not after ... well, why bring up bad memories?" the voice said.

Chuck was visibly trembling now; his face was pale and sweat beaded on his forehead. "You know that I am going to kill you if I ever see you again, don't you?"

"C'mon Chuck, we were best friends!" the voice said casually. "You couldn't kill me. Then again, with the right motivation, I guess you can kill anybody. Isn't that right, my friend?"

Chuck was silent.

"So, Chuck. What I need is very simple. Someone got in the way last night. A girl. She took a picture. We waited today to see if she'd come back to the scene. Sure enough. They can never stay away, can they? You know, mind their own business? Anyway, we have a picture of her now," the voice said. "We need you to silence her, Chuck. That's all. Should be easy enough for a guy like you, right?"

Chuck hung up the phone forcefully and walked over to the window. He could see the nearby foothills covered in trees. His reflection stared back at him in the glass. Did he recognize that man? He thought he could leave the past behind him when he moved to Montana, to become a person his father would have been proud of, but can people ever really change? Had he gone too far down a path to ever come back?

"No," Chuck said. "No."

CHAPTER NINETEEN

Sandra reentered her condo and saw that everything was in order. She went back to her sensory room and listened outside the door. Nothing. She opened the door and turned on the light. The bag was hanging in its place, but the drumsticks were scattered, and the largest exercise ball had rolled to the far corner of the room. The stereo was silent. The arm of the record player had returned to its resting position, and the turntable was still. She went to the stereo, grabbed the black disc, and broke it in two with her knee. That felt better. She felt better.

She went back out into the kitchen and made some lunch. Chicken strips and fries in the toaster oven. It was her comfort food. She should call her mom, she thought. She was sure to be worried. *But what could I tell her? How could I let her in on what I am feeling?*

Sandra wished more than anything that she didn't have to face this alone. She would love to let her mom be her partner, her advocate. But her mom didn't see what happened. Only Sandra was there. Only she could explain her photo. She had to keep working. She will call her mom for dinner. Now she needed to type.

Sandra sat back down in front of her laptop and opened the screen. Her efforts from the morning were still there, a jumble of letters. She could see her name in there, but it looked like a word search game.

Wait, a word search game! That's it!

Sandra looked again at the scramble of letters. She just needed to highlight the ones that were important. Sandra had done word searches during therapy. She was good at them. Her therapist thought she was just matching letters, but Sandra never looked at the word list. She loved finding the words unprompted.

Now she had to just find the words for someone else—so they could solve the puzzle of her mind.

She looked again at the letters and then down at the keyboard.

How can I highlight a letter? I'm sure there is a way.

She looked at all of the keys. No one had ever bothered teaching her anything about the word processing functions. *Why would they have bothered for a girl they thought couldn't read? I'm going to have to figure it out on my own.*

Sandra remembered using a crayon on a computer art app to scribble colors on the screen. They taught her how to use a mouse to control the crayon. Maybe she could do the same thing on MS Word. She looked up at the toolbar and saw the icon for a pencil.

There it is! A pencil! I just need a mouse, and I can circle the letters on the screen.

She stood up quickly, hurried to the kitchen, and started rummaging through her junk drawer. There, buried near the bottom, was a computer mouse. She grabbed it, went back to the table, and plugged it in. A second later, an arrow popped up on the screen. She moved the mouse with her hand, and the arrow moved with her.

Sandra let out an excited squeal. She was figuring it out! The arrow paused and waited for her command.

She moved it up to the pencil on the toolbar. When she hovered over it, a drop box appeared. *Highlight.*

Highlight? Sandra thought. *Highlight! That's what I want, but how do I do it? It's not like the crayon. I can't draw with it, unless ... if I click on highlight then maybe it lets me draw.*

She clicked the mouse over the word *highlight* and then tried drawing with the arrow over the letters, hoping to see a colored line. Instead, the letters she passed over became shaded.

That's interesting, Sandra thought. *I'll turn off the pencil and see what happens.*

She clicked again. Now the shaded letters turned yellow. Highlighted.

Sandra stood up. She had figured it out! The energy was flowing all through her body, and she needed to move, to release some of it, or she would never be able to focus.

She went back to her sensory room, grabbed the exercise ball, sat on it, and bounced. She bounced for thirty minutes straight, feeling the compression of the ball beneath her weight, then its recoil lifting her body a few inches into the air. Sandra felt the ball gaining and releasing energy and imagined in her mind the same thing happening to her body. She visualized a large energy meter with a needle indicator bouncing between a high reading and a low reading. This was her body. She bounced until the needle stayed almost stationary with each up and down motion. She was ready again for her computer. She went back to the kitchen table.

Now, she didn't have to worry so much about getting each letter right. She could highlight them afterwards. She started typing. The letters began to fill the page. She could see her intended message buried within.

When she finished typing, she grabbed the mouse and started clicking and shading and highlighting. There it was. Her thoughts were now on a page—immortalized outside of her brain for the first time in her life. Her soul had escaped from the tower. Her brain was defeated, but strangely to Sandra, it didn't seem angry. It actually seemed ... proud? Was it possible that she had misjudged it all along? Maybe her brain wasn't her enemy. Maybe it had been a victim, too. Maybe it helped to protect her, not imprison her. Maybe it knew now that she could defend herself, and so, it was releasing her. Maybe.

Sandra picked up the phone and dialed her mother's number.

Susan answered on the first ring. "Sandy, are you okay?"

"Yes," Sandra responded.

"Can I come over now?" Susan asked, pleadingly.

"Yes, Mom. Come," Sandra said.

CHAPTER TWENTY

Chuck picked up his keys and hurried from his office. He didn't want anyone to see him like this, sweaty and shaken. He needed some space to regain his bearings, to restore his image as the unbreakable leader, calm under pressure, always ready to do the right thing, to make the right decision, to protect his community.

Chuck climbed inside his patrol car and drove away. But not back to the scene. He took the turn toward Glacier National Park. That is where he could clear his head. He had spent countless hours there when he first moved to Montana, trying to forget the past and to start anew. The mountain peaks reminded him that he was just a man, insignificant in scope. He had made some mistakes. Bad mistakes. But these mountains didn't care, didn't even notice him. He would change, renew. Just like nature did every spring. His dark winter had to be over.

Chuck drove through the park entrance and found a pull-off that bordered Lake McDonald. He got out of his car and walked to the lake's edge. It was a prototypical Montana early autumn day—deep blue sky, few clouds, a warm sun, though the air had a hint of the briskness that would soon envelop the region. The leaves on the aspens and birches had just started changing to their fall colors of golden-yellow and red which, adding to the various shades of green and brown, painted the mountainside a mosaic of spotted color, reminiscent of an impressionist artist, a Monet masterpiece done without a single stroke of a human hand.

The water on the lake reflected the sky with a darker shade of blue until one got close, when the depths showed green, then black. At the shoreline, the water was nearly transparent. Under its surface, a highway of felled trees and large boulders created a habitat for fish that could be seen cruising the edges, hoping for an easy meal.

The lake had been formed by glaciers that still sat high on their majestic mountainous thrones, gleaming white, surveying the canyons that they had built with the pressure of their slow-moving ice flow. Now, their kingdom created, their power past its prime, they were disappearing, almost imperceptibly, ready to let the new forces of nature chart a modern course.

Chuck studied the water for a moment, watching its surface for disruptions in the smooth pattern. He reached down and picked up a flat rock, just big enough to fit snugly between his palm and index finger. He stood back up, took a couple of quick steps, and slung the rock with a side-armed motion so that it skipped along the surface of the water several times before disappearing. With each skip, concentric rings formed when the rock touched the water and moved on to its next spot, creating a series of ripples that eventually merged and then faded. *Tiny waves,* Chuck thought. *I am a tiny wave ... and someone else is holding a large bucket full of rocks. Do I fight it? Or do I just disappear and merge again into the flat surface of this lake.*

Just then, a trout jumped from the water at exactly the spot where Chuck's rock had first touched. A new set of rings disturbed the smoothness of the surface. Chuck smiled. *That fish doesn't care about rocks. I need to be a fish. Make my own waves.*

Chuck turned abruptly, determinedly, and walked quickly back to his patrol car. He started the engine, glanced back briefly at the lake, and then headed south—back to Whitefish.

CHAPTER TWENTY-ONE

Agent Atkins stood at the edge of the shallow grave and looked down at the body wrapped in a blue tarp. *Why would they have bothered wrapping it?* he wondered. *It's like they were completely prepared to do a terrible job hiding their crime.* He stepped away for a few minutes while the coroner and his workers lifted the body from the ground. He reached for his phone and dialed Chief Peters.

"Peters, the body is out. Are you headed back this way?"

"I'm five minutes away," Chuck replied.

"Good, there is something about this case that rings a bell, but I can't put my finger on it," Atkins said. "Shot in his chair, bloody footprints, a blue tarp. I know none of those are surprising in and of themselves, but this scene seems manufactured to me."

Chuck was quiet for a minute.

"Peters? You still there?"

Chuck cleared his throat. "I'm here. I'll see you in a few." He hung up the phone.

Atkins shrugged off the awkwardness of that exchange and went back over to the gravesite. The coroner had removed the tarp, and James Slater lay exposed, face up, a bullet hole in the center of his forehead. His eyes were closed, and except for the obvious defect, he looked like he was just taking a nap in the woods.

"No other signs of trauma," the coroner said. "No evidence of struggle, like torn clothes or defensive marks. I think he was shot in his sleep."

"That's what it seems like," Atkins agreed. "Alright, you can take the body with you. Let me know if you find anything different on the autopsy."

Atkins walked back to the cabin and went to the living area. The papers were still scattered on the floor. He put on some gloves and picked them up.

Bills, Atkins thought. *It looks like he was just going through his monthly bills and fell asleep in the chair.*

He looked around the dining area and the kitchen. There was a pile of dirty dishes in the sink. A laptop sat closed on the dining table next to a half empty bottle of wine. Atkins stood at the table and looked back toward the living area. He spotted something under the couch that he had missed before. It wasn't visible from any other angle. He walked back over to the couch, bent down, and reached his arm under until he could wrap his fingers around the object. He grabbed it, pulled it out, and studied the label of the orange prescription bottle in his hand.

Ambien. Written for Dane Mather. Filled just three days ago. The bottle was empty.

Atkins held the bottle while he processed the implications. He went back to the dining table and looked more carefully at the papers. Gas company. *Overdue.* Electric. *Overdue.* One from a furniture store, stamped with *Sent to Collections.*

The next one held his attention. He sat down on one of the chairs and read it again. Unlike the other bills, this one was addressed to *James Slater.* The return address was New York City.

It was an invoice from a law firm. The amount on the bottom simply said "*blood*" in an unassuming font. It would have been easy to miss. The only other marks on the page were in red ink. His name was underlined, and there was a circle around his address followed by an exclamation mark.

"They had found him," Atkins said under his breath. "And Slater knew it."

The sound of a car engine interrupted his thoughts. He stepped out of the door onto the deck and waited for Chuck to meet him.

As he approached, Chuck said, "Atkins, I've got some news."

"So do I," Atkins responded, "but you first. Let's go inside."

Chuck followed Atkins in, and they both sat at the dining table.

"I got a phone call," Chuck started. "On my way over. It was from the Royal Canadian Mounted Police. They arrested three teenagers from Whitefish early this morning at a campground near the border. They said that they received a tip at about 2:30 in the morning that the three of them would be crossing over the mountains and would be there, at that campground trailhead at around dawn. They were told that they had committed murder."

"Wait," Atkins interrupted. "Two-thirty? That was before anyone else knew about the crime."

"Precisely. I asked if they ran a track on the phone. It wasn't registered and the call was too short to find location. Like exactly too short. Maybe somebody knew what they were doing after all."

"Wait until you hear what I found," Atkins said and paused. "I'm not even sure if Slater was murdered after all."

Chuck's eyes widened with surprise. "What do you mean? There is a bloody path from his chair to the woods. Was it not Slater in the grave?"

"Oh, it was him."

"Wasn't there a bullet wound?"

"Right in the middle of his forehead," Atkins confirmed.

"So how can you wonder if he had been murdered?" Chuck asked, confused.

"Well, Chief, James Slater may have already been dead."

CHAPTER TWENTY-TWO

Susan knocked on Sandra's door and then checked the door handle. *Good, it was locked*, Susan thought. *She's being careful.* Seconds later, Sandra opened the door. She looked worn out, like she hadn't slept in days, yet she was smiling. And Sandra rarely smiled. Her facial expressions were not generally a good indicator of how she felt, so Susan was cautious to jump to any conclusions about how Sandra was doing.

Sandra stood back so that Susan could enter. When Susan shut the door behind her, Sandra started bouncing on her feet. That was an undeniable signal—Sandra was happy.

"Whoa, you're in a good mood!" Susan said. "That's not what I was expecting."

"Yes."

"Okay, well, that's great! I'm glad you are feeling better. You had me so worried last night," Susan said. "Are you hungry? I brought some lunch."

She was holding several grocery bags and took them to the dining room table when she noticed the laptop. "Is that your computer, honey? I haven't seen you use that for years."

Sandra bounced a few more times and then pulled a second chair closer to the one in front of the laptop. She grabbed Susan's arm and pulled her toward the second chair.

"Okay? We're sitting?" Susan said.

Sandra sat down next to her mom and woke up the computer screen. "Mom, look."

Susan looked at the screen, but then fumbled in her purse for her reading glasses. When she put them on and looked again, she saw a page full of random letters, some of which were highlighted in yellow. She looked up at Sandra, confused. "Okay? Did you type these?"

Sandra nodded.

"That's great, Sandy. I'm glad you're practicing your typing." Susan started to get up to prepare their food, but Sandra grabbed her arm again and held on.

"Mom, read," she said.

Mom, read, Susan thought. How many times had she heard her say those words? From the time she was a little girl, Sandra had asked Susan to read to her. Every night. Susan had started with children's books and read them so many times, she had them memorized. As Sandra got older, Susan got tired of those simple books and started expanding their library to more age-appropriate literature. She expected Sandra to get bored and drift off, but she never did. Sandra always sat quietly and appeared to listen. Susan wasn't sure how much she was absorbing, but the books were way more interesting to Susan, so she kept at it. Over the years, they had read most of the classics, many famous biographies, and some contemporary novels that highlighted current issues. Susan always discussed the relevant topics with her afterwards as if they were members of a very small book club. Of course, Sandra never answered back, but those moments were their only real source of bonding. Sandra's father had their hikes, and he was the one who taught her about music. But reading was Mom's time.

Susan focused again on the laptop.

JUKIOMCXXXDSWEWAXZWWFTGHFDRESSBN
MMBNNUIJTTRRTTYYBZASXBKOJGFDESTYBIM
KNBBBFRTJHGESEVDWUIOKJOPFDDSNHYTGJNG
TGFHYTRCDEREEVGHYJKIOMJUYYHBNGBVJMC
DSEBNMMHNHGUIKMNHTIJOLPOKKKNBAKJIPLIN
BCDFTYUGFDRSWESBYJHKOIJUBVDCXAGBNMKS
WEFREBNTGFHUYDEJKITRBVFXSAXVCGDERXS

"I'm not sure how to read this, Sandy," Susan said. "There aren't words."

"Yellow."

"What? Yellow? You mean—just the yellow letters?" Susan deduced.

"Yes, mom," Sandra responded excitedly.

"Okay, yellow," Susan acknowledged. "Let's see. *IS AW THEM BURY ... Wait. I SAW THEM BURY ...* " Susan stopped reading and looked up at her daughter. Did she just type her a message? Did she just start a conversation? Her first conversation in 27 years?

Sandra looked back into her mother's eyes. She could see the tears welling up from that deep pool of love for her daughter. Sandra knew then that Susan understood. She understood the significance of this moment. This message was from her. She had figured out how to communicate it. Sandra was no longer alone inside her own head. Her mom was now with her, a true ally.

Susan looked back at the laptop and continued working out Sandra's message. *"I SAW THEM BURY ... A BODY ... IN THE WOODS. THREE ... YOUNG ... MEN. I TOOK ... A PICTURE. YOU CAN SEE ... THEIR FACES."*

Susan looked up again. She didn't know how to feel. She felt like crying for joy because for the first time, she had just heard her daughter's real voice. And she felt like crying in horror for what her daughter had just revealed. Sandra witnessed a murder, and she had evidence against the killers. She was in danger, real danger! Visions of police stations and courtrooms and psychologists and forensic experts flashed into her mind. How was she going to protect Sandra now? The flood of emotion overtook her, and she covered her face with both hands—and wept.

CHAPTER TWENTY-THREE

"Already dead? What are you talking about?" Chuck asked Atkins with surprise.

"Look at what I found in the living room. It had rolled under the couch right next to where he was sitting." Atkins held out the prescription bottle, now stored in a Zip-loc. "It's a prescription for Dane Mather, written three days ago, for Ambien, a sleeping pill. There were supposed to be thirty pills in here, and it's empty, plus there is a half-empty bottle of wine on the dining table. And check this out." He showed Chuck the invoice that he had found amongst the other bills.

"It's addressed to James Slater," Chuck said. "Did you circle it in red?"

"Of course not," Atkins responded. "That was how I found it. It seems that the sender wanted to make sure it wasn't overlooked by our victim. Look at the total owed."

"Blood?" Chuck read. "Ah, I see what you're thinking. Slater killed himself with sleeping pills because he knew that he had been found. Well, that explains the lack of evidence of a struggle. Why would they have shot him though? Seems like their job was already done for them."

"Yeah, well the only thing I can think of is that they couldn't tell what had happened. They must have thought he was just sleeping. And maybe he was. Maybe he wasn't dead yet," Atkins said. "I wouldn't have expected so much blood if he had already died, but who knows."

"Probably not," Chuck agreed. "It definitely complicates things though, doesn't it?"

"Did you get the names of the suspects in custody?" Atkins asked, changing the focus.

"Yeah," Chuck said. "I don't recognize any of them. I have someone at the station tracking them down. I'll go pay a visit to their homes as soon as we're done here."

"Go ahead and go," Atkins said. "I'm pretty much done with what I need to do. I'm going to start making some calls to get the extradition process started. I'll stay in a motel in town. Call me after you talk to the families."

"Will do. Maybe the coroner can determine timing of death relative to the gunshot. I'll fill him in."

Chuck walked out of the cabin and went back to his patrol car. He called the coroner first and then called the station. "Jason, it's Peters. Did you find those kids?"

"Hi Chief. None of them showed up on the fingerprint database or in the criminal justice system. Their last names are fairly common but luckily there is only one Bend family in town. I'll contact the high school next."

"Okay. Give me the address for the Bends. I'll head over there," Chuck said.

. . .

Fifteen minutes later, Chuck pulled in front of Adam Bend's house, a modest but clean red brick rambler with a well-kept front yard. He knocked on the front door and waited while he heard footsteps approach.

Martha Bend opened the screen door, surprised to see a uniformed police officer on her front porch. She was dressed in a white robe, and her brunette hair was still wet. "Can I help you, officer?"

"Well, ma'am, I sure hope so," Chuck replied with his trademark disarming smile. "You see, I'm looking for an Adam Bend, and since you are the only Bends in Whitefish, this seemed like a good place to start. Do you know him?"

Martha put her hand over her mouth in worried shock. "Is he alright? Adam is my son. He was staying at a friend's house last night. I haven't heard from him yet this morning, but I really wasn't expecting to until after lunch."

"At a friend's house? Do you know the friend's name?" Chuck took out a notebook from his shirt pocket and clicked his pen.

"Uh, Quinn Madison. They live over on the other side of town. It's just he and his dad, so I let Adam stay there sometimes. I just feel bad for them, you know? No mom and everything?"

"Do you know the father's name?" Chuck asked.

"No sir, I don't. I've never actually met him. Quinn says he works a lot. It must be lonely. I think Adam makes Quinn laugh. Adam is always making people laugh. Quinn is popular in school, you know. He's the quarterback on the football team and everything! But I don't think he had any real friends until he met those three."

"Three? Who are the three?"

"Well, Adam, of course. And then there's Mark Christensen and Tanner Andrews. They have been best buddies since early on in grade school. They're always together. They were all going to Quinn's last night. Officer, did something happen? Is my boy okay?" The panic started rising again in her voice.

"Well, ma'am. It looks like we have some things to talk about, but I can't give you all the details yet," Chuck said as calmly as possible. "I can tell you that your boy is safe and uninjured."

"Where is he?" Martha asked with little resolution of her anxiety.

"He's in custody, ma'am."

"Custody? Adam? What for?" Martha cried out.

"That is the part I can't tell you yet until I get to talk to Adam myself," Chuck responded. "I know that it is hard not knowing, but you are going to have to trust me for a little bit. I need to go now. I will be in touch later today. Give me your phone number, and I'll call you if anything changes."

Martha stared at him suspiciously for an awkward minute before she stood up, grabbed a pen from her purse, and scribbled her number on the back of a receipt. She shoved it toward him impatiently.

"Thank you, ma'am. I'll be in touch," Chuck said and left the house.

CHAPTER TWENTY-FOUR

Susan sat at Sandra's kitchen table, her face still in her hands. Her mind flashed back to the day that they had received Sandra's diagnosis. She and Tony rode home from the developmental specialist's office in silence, with Sandra strapped in her car seat behind them. After getting her dinner and putting her to bed, they stood at the kitchen sink and started going through the motions of washing the dinner dishes.

Susan picked up a plate and started to scrub it. She scrubbed so hard that some of the paint from the ceramic started fading. Tony reached over and grabbed her hand. "It's clean, Susan."

She put the dish onto the rack and placed the dish scrubber down gently on the edge of the sink.

"Tony, what are we going to do?" Susan said, turning to face him with tears spilling down her cheeks. "Autism? Our only daughter has autism? I can't believe it. It can't be real."

Tony put his arms around his wife and just held her. He didn't have any answers. They had waited so long for a baby, and it was such a surprise when they discovered that one was coming that finding out that their precious daughter had a life-long disability was a cruel blow. Their hopes and dreams for her—dreams of school plays and soccer games and proms, of college graduation, a wedding, and grandkids—gone, just like that. Instead, Tony saw special education, psychologists, and sterile institutions. He held Susan tight so that she couldn't see his own tears.

"We will figure it out, Susie," he said after a few minutes. "We'll just have to figure it out. Our daughter will be safe, with us. She's not going anywhere. I don't care how bad it gets. We'll hire a full staff if we have to. She will be as happy as her brain will allow. That I promise."

Susan pulled away from his grip. She nodded, though words escaped her. *Happy as her brain would allow? Just how happy would that be? Would she be able to talk? To feel emotion? Doesn't autism turn its victims into robots? Unthinking robots that move from task to task, controlled by schedule, or numbers, or someone else's experiences? Would their job as parents be minimized to caretakers only? Would Sandra even know that they were different than her doctors or therapists or "full-time staff?"*

"Susie?" Tony interrupted her thoughts.

She looked up at him, his face blurry through her tears.

"I love you," Tony said softly. "We love Sandra. She will feel it. You can't fake love. Love will heal. Us and her."

. . .

Susan removed her hands from her face, wiped away the tears, and regained her bearings. Her incredible adult daughter sat beside her, looking at her eyes, trying to discern the emotions.

"I'm sorry, Sandy," Susan said. "I'm sorry for crying. I don't know how to explain to you how I feel. For my whole life, I dreamt about how I would be a great mother, how I would have these long heart-to-heart conversations with my kids, to give them pearls of wisdom, to help them solve their problems. When you were born, I was so excited, and nervous. Would I be that kind of mother?

"Then autism came into our lives, and those conversations were taken away. I have done my best without them but have never felt like it was enough. And now, here you are. You just taught me something. You never stop teaching me things, do you, Sandy? You just taught me that we can never give up. Never! You never have. Twenty-seven years old and you just typed out a message to me. A real message! Not regurgitated. It's from you. It's a terrible, painful message, but I'll never forget it. And I will never give up on you, Sandra! Not for as long as I live."

Sandra looked away, out of the window, out at the forest. Her woods. Her mom was part of her like they were. She closed her eyes, and she could feel her mom's heartbeat. She knew what her mother was feeling though it was deeper than human language. Their souls could communicate. They had always had that. She could feel her dad, too. When he died, he became a bigger part of her, like her soul absorbed his. She knew her parents would always be there. Forever.

She was doing all that she could to give her mom a few words to acknowledge the moment, but the words were still trapped in her mouth. But today was different. She didn't have to stop with words unspoken. Today she would have a conversation with her mother.

She grabbed the laptop and pulled it closer. She started typing some new lines. Then with the mouse, she selected and highlighted.

K K N M L P O L J N M N B H G T G G H D S
S S A B B N M M K H T Y J K O P I I U V B G F
K L O O T T R R D D E F F V F D E D R G H U Y
G H T G H J I I M N N B G G H J I K K L K K O O B
V V E H G T Y I I O I U U G G T Y K I O J I U S S
A D D D R R E B N M J U Y B G F R I K O F C M K

Susan read the letters as they began to stand out on the page.

MOM THANK YOU FOR EVERYTHING
I LOVE YOU
YOU ARE MY ROCK

Tears again filled her eyes, and now she was the one whose words sat heavy on her tongue. She grabbed Sandra's hand and just held on, feeling the memories surge through her. The challenges. The tantrums. The heartaches with each missed milestone. But also, the celebrations—of the little moments. A new word. Eye contact. A smile. A family picnic. A trip to the beach. Things other parents took for granted. Sandra had brought them together. They relied on each other because there was no one else. *Yes, I am a rock. We are a family of rocks.*

"Sandra, I can hardly believe this is happening right now. All I can think about is your dad. He would be so happy. You are such an amazing source of strength to me. You need to know that you are perfect to me. I am so proud to be your mom."

MOM YOU AND DAD HAVE GIVEN ME YOUR
   LIVES
I AM OKAY
MY LIFE IS OKAY
I HAVE MY CHALLENGES BUT I AM USED TO
   THEM
I ALSO HAVE JOY AND LOVE AND FEEL CONTENT
   MOST DAYS NOW
THANK YOU FOR SHOWING ME THE WAY

"Sandra, you don't know how much those words mean to me. I have worried about that since the day you were born. That is all a parent could ever want for their child. Thank you for giving me peace at last."

I LOVE YOU MOM
MY ENERGY IS SPENT
CAN WE TALK TOMORROW
LETS EAT, OKAY

"Oh, my goodness, of course it's okay. Tomorrow we will make a plan about what you saw. Let's not ruin the rest of today."

CHAPTER TWENTY-FIVE

Chuck sat in his car for a few minutes as he planned his next move. So, according to his mother, Adam was supposed to be at a friend's house last night and not one of the friends that were with him in custody. And this other friend was the star quarterback at the high school.

Chuck remembered reading about him in the newspaper last fall. Whitefish High had finally won the state championship in football last year, and the whole town had celebrated. Chuck had to organize the parade patrol and had to break up a few parties that had become a bit rowdy. But it was still fun to see that things like high school football still mattered here. That's what he liked about it. In Chicago, people had too many other distractions.

He pulled onto the road and headed toward the high school. The football team should still be at practice, and maybe he could chat with Adam's friend Quinn.

As he pulled into the parking lot, he saw the players leaving the field. He quickly parked and got out.

"Excuse me, son," he asked a young man who was putting his shoulder pads and helmet into the trunk of a car. "Can you show me who Quinn Madison is?"

The football player looked around and then pointed at Quinn as he walked towards them from the other side of the parking lot.

"Thank you," Chuck said.

Quinn was what Chuck expected—handsome, strongly built, walked with a swagger of confidence. As he approached, Quinn saw Chuck standing there waiting, involuntarily stopped walking for a moment, and lost his breath. But then his mind took over again and commanded his body to act naturally and keep moving.

Chuck noticed the pause. He watched as Quinn veered away from him and headed toward a red Ford Mustang. As Quinn was unlocking the car door, Chuck approached.

"Are you Quinn Madison?" Chuck asked.

"Yes, sir," Quinn said as he threw his gear into the back seat. He stood up straight and forced a smile. "Can I help you?"

"Well, maybe," Chuck said, watching for any signs of nerves or unusual behavior. Chuck had interviewed a lot of criminals over his decades in law enforcement and could usually pick out the liars, especially if they were unprepared for his questions. Their gaze would avert, their body would tense, and their voice would quiver, even if slightly. "I need to ask you some questions about what happened last night."

Quinn shifted his weight. "What happened last night?" he asked. "I was just home with my dad."

"Was anyone else with you?"

"Nope, just me and my dad. Why? What happened?" Quinn asked, settling into his role and the lie he had practiced.

"Seems a little hard to believe that the star senior quarterback who drives a vintage red Mustang is home alone with his dad on a Friday night. Don't you have a girlfriend? Didn't you have a game somewhere?"

"It's our bye week. And my girlfriend was busy."

"Is that right?" Chuck responded. "Well, that's too bad. What did you and your dad do last night at home?"

"Nothing," Quinn said. "He watched TV, and I played video games."

"In the same room?" Chuck asked.

"No, I was downstairs, and he was upstairs. Can you tell me why you are asking me these questions, Officer? I'm kind of in a hurry."

"What did you have for dinner?"

"I don't know," Quinn hesitated. "Pizza. We ordered pizza. I've got to go." He moved closer to his car and tried to get in before Chuck grabbed his arm.

"Tell me about Adam Bend."

"What about him?" Quinn said, resisting the urge to shake his arm free.

"Are you friends?"

"No, we aren't friends," Quinn replied tersely. "I hang out with him sometimes because the football team decided last spring that we would each try to find someone in the school who looked like they needed some attention. I saw Adam and his buddies one day playing basketball outside. They all looked like losers, so I stopped and made them my project."

"Has he ever slept over at your house?" Chuck asked.

"Hell no," Quinn exclaimed. "I wouldn't trust that kid in my house! He is a little thief. I've seen him lift things from convenience stores more than once, and he's always talking about breaking into some of these vacation rentals around here and stealing stuff."

"Is that so?" Chuck replied. "When's the last time you saw him?"

"I don't know—a couple of weeks. I'm busy with football now. I don't have time for those kids anymore. I'll say hi to them in the hall in front of some girls, and that'll make them feel special. That's all I got."

"Yes, I can see that," Chuck said. *Typical high school jock,* he thought. *Thinks the world revolves around him, and everyone else is just blessed to know him.* "Okay, young man, thanks for your cooperation. Let's win another championship this year, okay?"

"Yes sir, that's the plan!" Quinn got into his car, revved the engine, and drove away.

Chuck watched him go and thought, *That boy is lying. What is Quinn Madison, star quarterback, fake friend of high school losers trying to hide?*

CHAPTER TWENTY-SIX

Adam sat in a hospital room in Calgary, handcuffed to the rail on the bed. He couldn't remember how he got here. The last thing he remembered was gasping for air, and Mark yelling at the guards for help. He took a couple of deep breaths, in and out, and felt the air move easily through his lungs. *Better*, he thought with relief. He wasn't sure what had happened—he didn't have asthma, as far as he knew.

The doctor was at the doorway speaking with the guard. "Panic attack," he said. "We see them all the time. It can look pretty scary, but there is nothing actually wrong with him. I'll sign his release papers."

Soon the guard unlocked his handcuff from the rail and closed it around his other wrist. "C'mon, Tom Cruise. You should get an Oscar for that performance."

Adam didn't say anything as he shuffled out with the guard. When they arrived back at the police station, Mark and Tanner were standing at the cell door, waiting nervously. They both sighed in relief when they saw Adam walking toward them.

"Are you okay, Adam?" Mark said, as the guard fumbled for the right key.

Adam just nodded.

"No more antics," the guard said and gave Adam a shove into the cell.

The three boys sat down on the bench together.

"They think I faked it," Adam said.

"That wasn't faking," Mark said. "I've never seen anyone that gray before."

"I honestly don't even remember what happened," Adam replied. "In my mind, I saw Quinn sneering at me, and I just lost it, I guess. I really hate that guy!"

"They gave us a phone call," Tanner said. "We've both talked with our parents. I'm sure you can, too, if you ask them."

Adam groaned. "I am dreading that call. How did your parents react?"

"Freaked out," Mark said.

"Yep," Tanner agreed.

"Well, it'll never get any easier, I suppose. Might as well get it over with," Adam said. "Guard? Sir?" he yelled through the bars. "Can I get my phone call?"

The guard walked down the hall and unlocked the cell door. He led Adam to a separate room that was empty except for a chair, a desk, and a telephone. "You got ten minutes."

Adam dialed his mom's number and sighed deeply, sadly.

"Hello?" His mom answered on the first ring and sounded panicked.

"Mom, it's me."

"Adam? Where are you? I'm worried sick! A police officer came by this morning and said you were in jail. Can you believe that? I almost kicked him out of the house, I was so mad. Where are you, baby? I think you should come home."

"The officer was right, Mom."

"Adam? What are you talking about. Stop messing with me. It's not funny!"

"I'm not messing. I'm in Canada. In jail."

"Canada? How did you get to Canada? I thought you were going to Quinn's!"

"That's what I thought, too, Mom. It's a long story. I don't have time to tell you, plus I probably shouldn't say anything without an attorney. But, Mom, whatever you hear, just know that I didn't do it. I swear it! I've got to go, Mom. I love you. Tell Rebecca that I love her, too. And dad. When does he get home?"

"He's on his way. I called him," she said. "Adam, baby? Whatever it is, I'm here for you. You should have known that before you got yourself in trouble. You could have talked to me!"

Adam heard his mom sobbing on the other end of the line. "It's not like that, Mom. I promise," he said quietly. "I love you. I gotta go."

He hung up the phone, and the guard led him back to the cell. He sat down on the bench and thought of how his mom must be feeling right now. Without warning, tears began to flow. Mark and Tanner sat on either side, and Mark put his arm around his friend.

"Adam, she'll believe us," he said softly. "She knows you."

Adam wiped his nose with his sleeve and nodded. He couldn't say anything because it still felt like his throat was in his mouth. They all sat in silence and let the time slip by.

CHAPTER TWENTY-SEVEN

Agent Atkins sat on the bed in his hotel room and reviewed the case in his mind. Something bothered him, but he couldn't put his finger on it. It's not that Slater might have killed himself before he was shot. That wasn't entirely unusual in the witness protection program. It is a difficult life. You can never entirely leave your past behind; it always seems to find its way back to you eventually. Most people in witness protection must change their location and identity every couple of years so they don't get discovered. Ultimately, though, they get tired of running. Then, they are sitting ducks, waiting for the day when they meet their own past. Some can't handle that slow pressure and end it themselves, like Slater tried. What was unusual about Slater was that he didn't even attempt to run. The date on that invoice was weeks ago. He would have had time. It's like he was resigned to his fate.

The thing that bothered Atkins was the crime scene. He had seen it before. But when? And what did it mean? There wasn't anything particularly unusual about getting shot in a chair and dragged out to be buried in a shallow grave near one's house. But it was unusual for the perpetrators to have a tarp and shovels and then to be so sloppy at the scene. The killers were obviously prepared for what they were going to do; why leave footprints, the murder weapon, and a trail to the body? A messy scene was the work of amateurs who stumbled onto somebody and killed them by accident or in anger after a fight. Slater didn't fight. And the guys who wanted him dead are pros. It wasn't adding up.

Atkins took out his phone and called his division chief, Henry Call. Call had assigned him here after they had taken down a criminal ring of human traffickers a couple of years before. That case had absorbed all of Atkins' time for over five years and had earned him a break, away from New York City and big city crime. A few years in Montana was his reward. Plus, he could keep an eye on Slater, their key witness.

"Director Call, here," Call answered. He was a tall, wiry man with gray hair and lines creasing his face from too many years dealing with the worst that society had to offer.

"Hi, Director. This is Brett Atkins."

"Atkins! How's the fishing? I've been thinking I needed to get out there and have you show me the way around a fly," Call replied cordially.

"It has been a nice break. Thank you, Director," Atkins said. "But it looks like my time on the river is going to be limited for a while. Remember Slater? The witness in the New Horizons case? He was killed last night inside his cabin."

"Is that right? They found him already? That was fast," Call said. "Did he reach out to you first and ask to be moved? That's how it normally goes unless he didn't suspect anything."

"Actually, no. And he knew he had been found. I found evidence that says so. In fact, it looks like he was trying to kill himself at the same time he was shot."

"I assume there were no traces of the killer?" Call said.

"Quite the opposite," Atkins replied. "The scene is covered in evidence. Footprints, murder weapon, and a trail to the body. And, we have three suspects who are linked to the crime currently in custody in Canada. Teenagers, from Whitefish. The Mounties said they received an anonymous call in the middle of the night before any of us knew that the crime had even occurred."

"It sounds like Slater was just unlucky then. Killed by some kids that didn't know what they were doing. Probably trying to burglarize him or something, huh?" Call said.

"Except nothing was stolen and they had their own tarp and shovels," Atkins replied. "Not sure how many teenagers carry around a tarp and shovels in their car. Something is definitely not right about this case. I've seen it before. In Chicago. Almost the exact same crime scene.

Do you remember that the defense in the New Horizons case brought up a trial from many years ago in Chicago? The one where it seemed like a cop was involved and had doctored the scene, but no one ever caught him? The attorneys tried to use it as evidence of a systemic problem within the police force and that you couldn't trust evidence gathered by local officers."

"I vaguely recall that. It's a common defense tactic. Question the motives of the law. Works pretty well on some juries," Call replied.

"Well, I remember it well because I attended that original trial in Chicago, as a new agent who was interested in organized crime. The ironic thing is that the same guys that were involved with New Horizons were linked peripherally to the Chicago crime rings. And they got away with it back then. The jury didn't bite, and three innocent teenagers went to jail, convicted on the strong evidence of a burglary gone bad. Only, many years later they got an anonymous tip that proved the crime scene was tampered with by an investigating officer, and the convicted men were released. That officer was never caught, but it did lead to the discovery of illegal networking between the local police force and the crime rings, both in drugs and human trafficking.

I remember it because the victim was found buried in a tarp in his backyard, but there was no sign of entry into his garage, which means the boys had to have brought the tarp and shovels with them. If they were there to just burglarize the place, why have tarps and shovels? That never made sense to me but was glossed over in the trial."

"That's an interesting connection, Atkins. It sounds like you might be onto something," Call acknowledged.

"Yeah, maybe," Atkins agreed. "Anyway, I need to get the suspects extradited. Can you work on that?"

"No problem," Call said. "We can have them on home soil by tomorrow. I can send you some of the files from that Chicago case, if you feel like it could help, to see if you can figure out the link."

"Yes sir. I'd appreciate that. I'll let you know what I find."

"Yes, keep me informed," Call requested. "I know there are other members of the New Horizons ring out there, biding their time. We cut off the head of the beast, but I'm worried that it's one of those creatures that just grows two more in its place."

"You are probably right. Things have been unusually quiet on the human trafficking front, at least on the agricultural side since Frank Donovan was thrown in prison. I'm sure things are bubbling under the surface."

Atkins hung up the call and started pacing the room, but before long, his phone began to ring. It was Chief Peters.

"Agent, I met with Adam Bend's mother. Seems like a nice woman though she was understandably panicked. She had no inkling that her son could be in trouble. She thought he was staying over at a friend's house. Different friend, not one of the other two that are with him in Canada. I believe her, too. Moms always know, even if they won't admit it to themselves. Anyway, I met the friend. He seemed nervous to see me but then put it aside and told me a story. I don't buy it though. He definitely knows something. I'm going to pay his dad a visit next and check out his alibi."

"That sounds good, Peters. We should get the boys home by tomorrow. I spoke with my boss in Washington."

"Great!" Chuck said. "I'm anxious to talk with them. Somebody is lying. We just need to figure out who."

CHAPTER TWENTY-EIGHT

Quinn drove directly home after his encounter with Chief Peters at the high school. He was looking forward to a good long nap to clear his mind and recover his energy before he figured out the next step. As he pulled into the garage, he saw that Gary's car was gone. *Good,* he thought, *I need time alone. Gary is a distraction, and I'm not sure I trust him. If anyone had the opportunity to set me up, it was him. He did seem pretty nervous on the drive home, though. He thought I was asleep when he was talking to himself. Kept cursing Wesley's name. So maybe he really didn't know.*

He grabbed his gear from the backseat and threw his dirty clothes into the laundry room on his way upstairs. He needed a shower first, then sleep. He walked into his bathroom, turned on the water in the shower to let it warm up, and then looked at himself in the mirror. His eyes were red and puffy, surrounded by dark circles. He looked as tired as he felt. He climbed into the shower and let the warm water soothe his aching body.

When he was done, he grabbed a towel, dried off, threw on some sweatpants, and climbed into bed. He sighed heavily as his head relaxed into the pillow and, within minutes, drifted off to sleep.

Suddenly, he was yanked back into consciousness by the sound of their front doorbell. It rang over and over, as whoever was at the door persisted in trying to get someone's attention.

"Just leave," Quinn said, annoyed by the interruption to his nap. "Nobody's home, geez."

But the bell didn't stop ringing.

Finally, Quinn threw back his comforter angrily, grabbed a shirt, and headed down the stairs.

"This better not be some damned delivery driver," he muttered to himself.

Before he opened the door, he looked through the peephole and saw Chief Peters standing on the porch.

"Aahhh!" Quinn said irritably. "I can't handle this right now."

Talking with the police was the last thing he wanted to do. He was too tired and was afraid he would make a mistake. But he was sure that the officer knew he was home now because he had stopped ringing the doorbell and was waiting patiently on the porch for the door to open.

Chuck had seen someone approach from the other side, though the person's features were distorted by the frosted glass of the windows that bordered the large wooden door. After a longer-than-natural pause, the door opened, and Quinn stood in the doorway.

"Hello again, young man," Chuck said. "I hope I didn't interrupt anything important."

"No, just trying to catch a nap," Quinn said, suppressing a yawn and trying his best to act casual. He knew that he looked like he had been up all night and tried to will himself alert.

"Tired, huh?" Chuck commented. "I guess football practice must take a lot out of you. Good thing you didn't stay up too late last night. Right?"

"Yeah ... it's a physical sport," Quinn said cautiously.

"I'm here to talk to your dad. Is he home?" Chuck continued.

"He's not here," Quinn replied.

"Do you know where he is?"

"Not sure. Probably golfing. He might be gone the rest of the day."

"Well, that's too bad. Where does he golf? Maybe I'll go track him down at the golf course," Chuck pressed.

"I think he said he was going into Kalispel to golf with some buddies. I don't know where," Quinn said.

Just then, a black BMW sedan pulled through the gate and drove up the driveway. The car stopped, waited for the garage door to open, and then pulled inside.

"Is that your dad?" Chuck asked.

"Looks like it," Quinn said flatly.

"Well, that was a quick golf day in Kalispel," Chuck commented with a smile. "Can I come in?"

Quinn stepped aside and let Chuck enter the house. Chuck glanced around the large foyer briefly, but his eyes were quickly drawn to the floor-to-ceiling stone fireplace adorned with the head of a trophy elk. The living area was decorated invitingly with a large leather sectional, the travertine floors covered with several expensive-looking rugs. Opposite the foyer, a wall of windows framed the lake and distant mountain peaks. The scene was so pristine, it could have been a painting.

"Nice place," Chuck commented. "What does your dad do for a living?"

"Hedge funds," Quinn said without elaborating.

Chuck heard a door open and then footsteps in the nearby kitchen.

"Dad?" Quinn spoke loudly. "We have a visitor."

Gary rounded the corner and entered the foyer where Quinn and Chuck were still standing.

"What's the matter with you, son?" he said with a smile. "Invite the officer to come in and sit."

He approached Chuck, shook his hand cordially, and then gestured toward the living room. "Kids these days. They refuse to learn common manners. Come on in, Officer. Have a seat. Make yourself comfortable. Can I get you a drink? You know, water or tea?"

"No thank you. I'm fine," Chuck said, as he made his way to the couch.

Gary waited for Chuck to sit and pointed at Quinn to sit down as well, then he settled into a reading chair that faced the couch. "Now, what can we do for you?"

"I'm sorry to bother you on a Saturday, sir," Chuck started. "I understand you had a golf engagement."

Chuck sized Gary up visually. Not as tall as Quinn, strongly built though, darker complexion. Dressed in a black turtleneck shirt and dark jeans. There was some mud on his black hiking boots. Not exactly golfing clothes.

"Oh," Gary glanced quickly at Quinn. "No, got cancelled. My buddy got sick."

"Sorry to hear that," Chuck said.

"Yeah, nothing serious," Gary said. "We'll get back out there next week. Doesn't seem to matter how much I play, though, I never get any better," he chuckled. "You a golfer, Officer?"

"Me? No. Never had the time or the money. Public service doesn't really pay that well, you know."

"I suppose not," Gary said.

"Anyway, the reason that I am here is to ask you a few questions. We had an unfortunate crime in our community last night, and it looks like some teenagers were involved. I'm going around talking to some of the families to see what I can learn."

"No problem, sir. We're happy to help however we can. Right, son?" Gary said and smiled at Quinn.

"Sure," Quinn said flatly.

"Thank you. I do appreciate that," Chuck said.

"So, what happened?" Gary asked pointedly. "Somebody go paint the football field in Colombia Falls in Whitefish colors? It's about that time of year, right?"

"I'm afraid it's a bit more sinister than that," Chuck said. "There was a break-in, and somebody got hurt. We have a few suspects, and they have a connection to your son. So, I am here to confirm his alibi. I met Quinn already, over at the high school."

Gary looked firmly at Quinn. "Your football buddies doing stupid things again, son? I told you that you were better than that. You can be an athlete without being a dumb-ass jock, you know. We've talked about this."

"No, Dad," Quinn said, feigning defensiveness. "It wasn't anyone from the football team. It was those loser kids I was trying to be nice to. Why do you always assume the worst about my friends?"

"The 'loser kids' he is talking about told their parents that they were all staying here last night with Quinn," Chuck interjected. "Do you know who he is talking about? Doesn't sound like it was the first time they would have been here according to one of their mothers."

"Uh, not sure who they are, no sir," Gary said, acting confused. "Quinn has friends over sometimes, but they are all from the team, and none of them have ever spent the night. He's too old for that."

"Can you confirm what Quinn did last night?" Chuck asked.

"He was here all evening. He said he just wanted to relax and not go out. So, we ordered pizza and just took it easy," Gary said.

"He never left the house?" Chuck asked.

"No, at least, not that I know of. I wasn't in the same room with him the whole night," Gary said and paused, " ... but we could check the security footage. That's easy enough."

"That would be fantastic," Chuck said.

Gary invited Chuck into his nearby office and opened the camera recordings on his desktop. He scrolled backwards until he saw Quinn's Mustang pull into the driveway around 5 pm. At 6, a car with a Domino's sign on its roof pulled in, and then out. He scrolled through the rest of the night, and no further events were detected until this morning at 10 a.m. when the Mustang pulled out again for football practice.

"Well, that looks pretty conclusive," Chuck said. "That is extremely helpful, sir. I appreciate you, and I'll leave you two alone to enjoy the rest of your day."

Chuck led himself to the front door and waved at Quinn on the way out. "Go get some rest there, son. It looks like you could really use it."

Quinn nodded back in return and waited for the front door to close. Then, he stood and headed for the office. Gary was leaning back in the chair, his smile no longer present. "A little warning would have been nice."

"He just got here right before you did. How was I supposed to warn you?" Quinn shot back.

"Good thing we doctored the security footage ahead of time. That should put him off your trail for a little bit," Gary said.

"Yeah, until someone shows up with a picture of me burying the body," Quinn responded. "What am I going to do with that little issue?"

"Well, lucky for you, I'm a lot smarter than you. I found the picture taker. In fact, I have her picture on my phone. We just need to find out who she is and where she lives and then ... "

Quinn looked up. "Then she disappears," he finished the sentence.

Gary stared at Quinn. *He really is like his dad. He can talk about killing someone, a woman even, without batting an eye. If he still suspects me, I will be lucky to make it through the night. I'd at least stand a chance on the run. I need to make myself valuable to him.*

"I'll take care of it," Gary said. "We have connections in the local police department. They owe us a favor. If she comes forward, I'll be the first to know."

Quinn stared back at Gary, trying to decipher whose side he was on. He decided to trust him ... for now.

CHAPTER TWENTY-NINE

Sandra watched as her mom prepared the lunch that she had brought with her. Susan made sandwiches and soup, and they sat down to eat. It already felt like a full day, but it was still just early afternoon. Sandra was exhausted both mentally and physically. She was going to need a nap after lunch. It wasn't unusual for her to take naps. It gave her mind a chance to calm the furious pace that it kept during the awake hours. Most people can recharge during the day by meditating or listening to music or just tuning out for a while. Sandra's brain never turned off while she was awake. Her senses were always on high alert, and the memory library was constantly shuffling in and out of her consciousness.

Sandra knew she needed some downtime today if she wanted to survive tomorrow. When they had finished eating, she helped clear the dishes and then went into her bedroom, shut the door, closed the blinds, and climbed into her bed. She fell asleep almost immediately. As her mind drifted away, she smiled. *Today is a good day.*

Susan washed the few dishes in the sink and sat down on the living room couch. She thought through the events of the last several hours and tears again welled in her eyes. She had just had an actual conversation with her daughter. And what beautiful words she had expressed. Her life as a mother had been hard.

Really hard. But today was a good day. Susan closed her eyes and also drifted to sleep.

. . .

"Susie, wake up. It's time to go," Tony said as he gently shook her leg. "We've got to get there early so we get a good seat."

Susan sat up and rubbed the sleep from her eyes. "Right! I can be ready in a few minutes. I was having the weirdest dream. Sandra was in trouble, and we were looking everywhere for her. I could hear her screaming, but it was muffled, like she was underwater or in a cave or something. You and I were desperate, digging holes in the yard and breaking through walls in the house. We could hear her but couldn't tell where the sound was coming from. Finally, we found a secret door in the wall behind the refrigerator. It led to a tunnel. We grabbed a flashlight and stepped into it.

"The walls were lined with bricks but covered in moss, and the tunnel smelled moldy and dank. Sandra's voice echoed loudly inside, so we pushed ahead. As we walked, the tunnel became progressively smaller, until we had to crawl on our knees to keep moving. Finally, we hit another door. There was a keyhole but no door handle. We could hear Sandra crying on the other side of the door. She knew we were there but couldn't say anything to us, like she was gagged."

"Our Sandra gagged? Can you imagine that?" Tony chuckled. "She hasn't stopped talking from the moment she was born. Granted, it took a year or so for us to understand her, but she always knew what she was saying. Anyway, sorry to interrupt. Keep going."

"We banged on the door and kicked against it with our feet until our knuckles were bleeding, and our legs were cramped in knots. But the door didn't budge. We tried digging at the dirt floor, but the door was framed into a stone wall. After a long time trying, we both laid down on the dirt exhausted. Then you said that you would go back to the house and find some tools. I gave you the flashlight, and you crawled away back down the passage. I sat there alone in the dark and listened to my daughter cry.

"I waited and waited for you to come back, but you never did. Sandra's cries were getting weaker, so I knew I had to do something. I pounded on the door some more to no avail. So, I started feeling around the tunnel wall for a loose brick or some other latch that might open the door. Nothing! I debated crawling out to find you, but I couldn't leave Sandra alone. Just as I was about to fall into complete despair, the door swung open. There was Sandra holding the key in her hand and smiling. 'Hi, Mom,' she said. 'Don't worry, I figured it out.'"

"Hmm, that is an odd dream," Tony said. "But if we don't hurry, we are going to miss our daughter's acceptance speech. Can you believe that she is a Nobel laureate? I'm not surprised that it is in journalism though. She is gifted with words."

Susan and Tony arrived at the convention center and found their seats. The program began, and Sandra was introduced. She rose to the podium and paused before speaking. She gazed at her parents and reached for a chain that was tucked beneath her blouse. As she pulled it out where it was visible, Susan gasped. "It's the key!"

"What?" Tony asked confused. "What key?"

"The key in my dream!"

"What are you talking about? That's impossible," Tony said, rubbing his hands. "This is so weird. My hands are suddenly killing me."

Susan looked down at Tony's hands. They were beaten up and bleeding. Her own hands began throbbing, too. She watched as the skin over each knuckle split into an open red wound.

. . .

"Mom?" Sandra gently touched Susan's shoulder.

Susan opened her eyes and looked around Sandra's condo. She looked down at her hands and rubbed her thumb over each knuckle. No blood. They were achy though. But the pain went away immediately as she looked into Sandra's eyes.

"Hi, my sweet girl. My Nobel Laureate!"

Sandra looked confused but smiled. "Movie?" she offered.

"I'd love to," Susan nodded.

CHAPTER THIRTY

Adam was startled by the sound of the cell door opening. He had been lost in his thoughts—scary thoughts about attorneys, juries and worst of all, prison—and had not heard the guard walking down the hall. How was he going to survive being locked in a cell all day, every day? Maybe he should just end it now and not have to face that future. His mind was taking him down dark passages.

No! I've got to stop thinking this way. The truth will come out. We didn't kill that man. We were forced to bury him at gunpoint. We are innocent! The system works for the innocent, doesn't it?

As soon as he had almost convinced himself that everything would be alright, his mind flooded with news stories of people who were exonerated with DNA evidence but not before spending decades behind bars for crimes they didn't commit. His thoughts once again scurried to shadowy places.

"C'mon boys," the guard said sternly. "You're going back to Montana. We got the phone call."

The three of them looked at each other and stood up together. They walked toward the guard who placed them each in handcuffs and leg shackles and led them down the hall and out a back door to a windowless unmarked van that was waiting with its motor running. A police cruiser was positioned in front of the van—there to escort them on the several-hour drive to the border.

The boys sat on benches in the van, and the guard first secured their leg chains to bolts on the floor in front of them and then removed their handcuffs.

Adam rubbed his wrists. He hated how the cold metal of the handcuffs felt, pressed against his flesh. Could he ever get used to that?

"Maybe we will get to see our parents when we get there," Mark said. "I just want to see their faces."

"Me, too," Tanner agreed.

Adam kept his head down, staring at the chain between his legs. Did he really want his parents to see him chained like a dog? Would that help him feel better? And them? He didn't say anything and just leaned back against the side of the van and closed his eyes.

The drive to the border seemed to last only minutes to Adam. Time no longer felt relevant. The van door opened, and they could see several men wearing blue US Marshall jackets standing several yards away, holding shotguns in front of them like they were there to transport El Chapo, not three motley, scared teenage boys.

The Mounties entered the van, guns drawn, and unlocked the chains from the floor and, again, secured the cold metal handcuffs around their wrists. Then, separate officers grabbed each of the boys by the arm and helped them from the van. The sun was bright, and it took a minute for their vision to adjust. The US Marshalls took over for the Mounties, and the whole process was repeated in reverse until the boys were once again alone, secured to the floor of a windowless van.

US soil. Adam wasn't sure if that was a good or a bad thing. He wanted to believe in the rights afforded to them by the Constitution but couldn't help thinking of the many times that those rights had been ignored.

After another couple of hours, the police van pulled into the station in Kalispel, and they were led inside to another holding cell. They were given something to eat and then were made to change into the jumpsuits provided by the guards.

"You will be assigned public attorneys for your defense unless any of you would like to decline and pay for a private attorney," a guard explained during the orientation process.

The boys looked at each other. None of their families had extra money. A private attorney would bankrupt them.

"I'll take the public lawyer," Mark said.

Adam and Tanner nodded their consent as well.

"Okay, your attorneys will be here on Monday morning and will begin preparing you for court."

"What do we do in the meantime?" Mark asked.

The guard just chuckled. He looked each of them in the eye and then smiled cruelly. "You sit." He then closed the barred door with a sharp clang and left.

CHAPTER THIRTY-ONE

Gary watched as Quinn went up the stairs and waited for him to slam the door to his bedroom. He glanced at his watch. "I've got about two hours," he said to himself. "If I don't find that girl, I will lose Quinn. If I lose Quinn, I might as well make a run for it."

He pulled out his cell phone and opened the picture of the girl in the woods. She was average height, had shoulder-length blond hair, and looked fit. Not uncommon in Whitefish where there were a lot of outdoor types. Nothing about her really stood out to him as particularly distinguishing. But when he watched her walk away from the scene, he noticed something different about her. He couldn't put his finger on it exactly. It was how she moved. It was almost animalistic. She frequently stopped, looked around, cocked her head like a deer listening for danger, and chose her steps very carefully. He wasn't sure if that would help him find her, but it struck him as odd.

She had moved up the mountain, following the stream. He stayed out of sight but every time he took a step, she stopped and looked around. She must have uncanny hearing. So, he stayed where he was and watched her for as long as he could. Maybe she lived in one of the neighborhoods on the mountain on the way to the ski resort. There were some nice homes up there and a few condo complexes that bordered the forest. He didn't remember any trailheads in that direction, so she probably didn't drive to the woods. Plus, she seemed to know the trails, seemed at home in the area. *She must come here a lot. It makes sense that she lives close by.*

Gary got in his car and started driving. *Whitefish isn't a big town. Maybe I'll get lucky and see her around. I'll go around to wherever people congregate—the grocery stores, restaurants, the park. But first, I'm going to drive up the mountain and see those neighborhoods. Maybe she'll be outside. She doesn't seem like the type who stays inside all day.*

Gary took the turn that led up to Whitefish Mountain Resort. It was a beautiful road, lined with pines. At places, you could see the waters of Whitefish Lake below. *This is a nice town,* Gary thought. *Maybe in another life, I could have settled here and been happy.*

. . .

Gary, aka Jack Dresher, had been hiding from the law for as long as he could remember. Growing up with a single mother in the Baltimore projects was not a path to success. His mom was always at work, trying to keep food on their table, so Jack and his siblings were left to manage their own time throughout the day. He would show up to school just enough to keep the system off his back and out of their front room. The last thing his mom needed was something else to worry about, not that there was really anything she could have done about it. She had five mouths to feed. Her children's education was a secondary concern, at best.

Jack, instead, spent a lot of time on the streets, getting in fights, and committing petty crimes. Despite that, he somehow managed to stay out of the juvenile system. He was a master of disguising himself and flying under the radar. When he turned eighteen, he left home and found a group of guys that he had run the streets with. He honed his craft of assuming identities and used that to make a reputation in the local crime scene. And he was never caught. With time, he stole enough money so that he could afford to move to Florida where there were a lot of easy targets for his scams. That is where he met Wesley O'Brien, a hard-nosed Irishman who said he was part of an organization that would pay Jack a lot of money for his skills.

Jack took the bait and had been working with Wesley and Frank Donovan ever since. That was about seven years ago. Wesley was right. They had paid him well. But he had also witnessed the cost of doing business with those two. More than once, he was used to exact revenge on those that were disloyal. He didn't like it, but what choice did he have now? It was either to play his role as an actor or become a real victim.

Wesley came to him just over a year ago.

"Jack," he said, putting his arm around his shoulder. "You've done well for yourself since I found you scamming chump change off of retirees in Florida, haven't you?"

"Yes, Wesley, you've been good to me," Jack replied, knowing this conversation was going to end up with an assignment, probably one he wouldn't like.

"Well, you've earned it, my friend. You've earned it."

"You've got something for me, don't you Wesley?"

"I do, Jack. But not the usual," Wesley said with a smile. "This will require your best work."

"Okay?" Jack said hesitantly.

"You know about Frank, right?"

"Of course."

"Yeah, he got nailed. Do you know how?"

"Not any details," Jack admitted.

"Our former business partner, Slater, chirped," Wesley said matter-of-factly. "It seems that Slater felt under-appreciated. Imagine that! By Frank Donovan?" His sarcasm dripped from that statement. "I guess ol' Slater liked me well enough though. It's why I'm still here with you and not serving time with Frank."

"I'm glad for that Wesley, I am."

"Yeah, well, I'm seeing a little business opportunity here for both of us. You ready to talk business?" Wesley asked, staring hard into Jack's eyes.

"Sure, Wes. I'm ready."

"It turns out that Frank knew that Slater had ratted on him before the cops raided the Manhattan office. He had some time to prepare. Did he come to me, Jack? His long-time friend and business partner? No sir, he didn't." Wesley's voice started trembling as he tried to stay calm. "No, Jack. Turns out he already chose his replacement—his seventeen-year-old son. And get this, Jack, he wants me to train him, to groom him. Can you believe that? Do I seem that stupid? This business is thriving because of me, Jack. Me! Not Frank. He is just the figurehead, the big intimidating guy who makes people weak in their knees. Slater and I were the brains behind it all. We did all the dirty work. Does he really think I'm going to trust all that to a snot-nosed kid?"

Jack shook his head in feigned disgust. Truth is, he didn't really care who ran the business. He was just biding his time, waiting for a door to open where he could get out.

"Yeah, well I'm not doing it Jack. I'm taking over. Which means I have some loose ends to tie up. With your help, I can do it all at once. Are you with me, Jack? I need a right-hand man, you know."

"What's your plan, Wes? I'm with you, of course." Jack said, trying to sound convincing.

"Frank has ordered a hit on Slater. He is in witness protection in Montana. Does the government actually think that works? If we want to find somebody, we find them, Jack. Remember that. Anyway, he wants me to do it, but I gave him a proposal. I said, 'What better way to train up your son? I'll do the killing, but I think he should be there, you know, to witness it.' Frank thought that was a good idea.

"I told him that we should take our time, play with Slater's mind a little. Let Quinn see things develop. I got his blessing on that one, too. But I have a little different plan in mind. Frank can't know about it until it's all done. I need some time to win over his guys. That's where you come in, Jack." Wesley paused, took a drink of champagne, and smiled.

"You are going to be Quinn's fake dad and move to Montana with him. A rich widower and his only son. And dear Quinn is going to pull the trigger, Jack. He is going to get his hands dirty. Defend his family honor, you know? He'll do it if he thinks his dad expects it. We just need to be sure he gets caught. Then, Slater will be gone and both Donovans in prison. Easy, right?"

"Sounds easy, Wes," Jack smiled.

"But wait, there's more," Wesley said, trying to sound like a game show host. "The murder also needs to send a message. Remember that case in Chicago that I told you about? We used some definite signals at the scene that are known by the criminal element that this was a hit. The man had double-crossed us. We need to set this scene up the same way. It will be a signal to those that know that there has been a change in leadership, and we expect loyalty. Okay? I'll tell you those details later. Are you ready to change your life, Jack? My new right-hand man?"

Wesley stood, clapped Jack on the back, and raised his champagne glass.

Jack picked up his and clinked the glass to Wesley's. "Your right-hand man," he said, somewhat lacking enthusiasm but smiling broadly for Wesley to see.

. . .

Gary turned onto a side street and into a condo community. *She didn't seem old enough to afford one of the houses up here. Probably lives in the condos.* He drove around the parking lot, but no one was out, so he sat in his car for a while and watched. There were a few people that came and some that went. None were her. After about an hour, Gary figured he better go check some other places. As he was pulling back onto the main road, a blue Toyota forerunner passed in front of him. He only got a glance, but in the passenger seat, he saw a blond girl that could have been his target. He pulled onto the street and followed. *My problem may soon be solved,* he thought, as he gave his BMW a little gas.

CHAPTER THIRTY-TWO

Sandra followed her mother out of the condo and down to the parking area. Susan's car was parked in a visitor's spot, and they both got in, moving with some urgency. The movie theater was across the town, and they needed to drive fast if they were going to catch the previews.

Sandra hated missing the previews. She saw most of the movies that came to town, but there were some that she particularly looked forward to. The previews gave her a sneak peek and often gave a release date that she registered onto the internal calendar in her brain where she could anticipate them months in advance.

The movie theater was a safe zone for her. The dark provided anonymity, and the surround sound drowned out the otherwise constant hum of all the extraneous sounds from her immediate environment, resulting in a sensory reprieve where she could spend two focused hours pretending that she was someone else.

This was what Sandra enjoyed the most—the storytelling. In the theater, she could imagine being the quick-witted heroine who used her beauty and her brain to fluster the dim villains, or the sad, abused housewife that overcame her circumstances to change the lives of her children, or the popular teenager who found a true friend in the shy nobody that everyone else made fun of. She also loved to be transported to far-off places or back in time and imagine what it would be like to live a different life.

Susan pulled into the theater parking lot with about two minutes to spare. The selection of movies left a bit to be desired. The best movies always came out around the holidays and early in the summer. September was a bit of a down month. *Harry Potter and the Order of the Phoenix* was out, so they decided on that one. Susan had read all the Harry Potter books to Sandra, and they both had enjoyed them. The fight between good and evil— the ageless theme. Telling the story through the eyes of teenage wizards was a twist but entertaining, nonetheless.

As they arrived at the theater and parked their car, Sandra was suddenly overcome with a dark feeling, an unexplainable premonition that caused fear to course through her body. It was there for only a moment, and then it was gone.

It wasn't the first time she had felt this way. She had always been sensitive to such "soul warnings", as she called them, and usually changed her course accordingly. The few times she tried to ignore them, things had turned out badly.

She hesitated, still wearing her seatbelt, and sitting in the front seat of her mother's car. What should she do? The soul warning was unmistakable, but she was really looking forward to relaxing in the theater and enjoying a movie with her mother. Today felt different than the countless other times they had gone. Today, their relationship had changed a level, toward friendship, something more reciprocal.

Stay in the car, Sandra. The message was clear. *Stay in the car.*

Susan walked around to the passenger side and opened the door. "Are you coming, Sweetheart?"

Sandra pushed the feeling away and smiled at her mom. She stepped out of the car and looked around cautiously. Nothing seemed out-of-place, so she shut the door and began walking across the parking lot toward the theater. As she slowed for a car to pass in front of them, the feeling again overwhelmed her. She wanted to run, to get inside the comfort zone of the movie theater, and to disappear inside the dark. But the car that was passing them slowed to a near crawl. The driver's window rolled down, and a man with wavy dark hair and tinted sunglasses stared right at her. She quickly looked away. She didn't trust anyone who wore sunglasses. She couldn't read their eyes.

"Can I help you?" Susan asked the man irritably, as she noticed that Sandra was uncomfortable.

"No, ma'am," the man said. "Just driving through." He rolled up the window and picked up his speed.

Sandra had frozen in place with her hands over her ears. *Evil. That man was evil.* She could feel it. She turned and ran back to Susan's car and tried to open the door. When it wouldn't open, she pounded on the glass until the car alarm went off, sending a blaring siren echoing throughout the lot. Sandra covered her ears, fell onto her knees, and screamed until Susan caught up to her and, fumbling with her keys, finally turned off the alarm.

"Sandra, it's okay now." Susan crouched down and put her arms around her daughter, helping her to her feet. "Let's just go home. You can come and stay at my place tonight. Okay?"

Sandra stopped screaming and nodded slightly, wiping the tears from her face. She got into the car and locked the door. Susan sat behind the wheel, took a deep breath, and started the engine. As they drove away, from across the parking lot another car pulled out of a spot that had been hidden from view by a delivery van. The car followed at a safe distance—the driver with his dark wavy hair and tinted sunglasses in a black BMW sedan.

CHAPTER THIRTY-THREE

Chuck sat in his office with the shades drawn and the door locked. He had instructed Kathy not to let anyone disturb him unless it was an emergency. He needed time to think. He had just returned from the Madison house, and things were all messed up in his mind. It was clear that Quinn and his dad knew more than they were letting on. Mr. Madison was a bit too eager to show him the security footage, and although it was a very professional job, Chuck could tell it had been doctored. Identifying doctored videos was a passion that he had developed during his time in Chicago that he had carried with him and updated as the technology changed. And he recognized Quinn now. At least he recognized some of his features. Gary Madison was not Quinn's father.

He thought he had left Chicago behind him, but sins of the past had their way of crawling back into the present. Chuck had already made his decision. He had been making it a little bit each day since he left Chicago. He would atone for all of it, and it looked like he was finally going to get his chance. But if he wasn't careful, more innocent lives would be ruined, and it would be his fault, again.

. . .

"The new recruits are here, Chief. What do you want me to do with them," Officer Franklin asked. He was an overweight, graying cop who hadn't seen field duty in at least a decade.

Chief Pete Stoyanavich, the chief of police of the south side boroughs of Chicago, looked up from his desk and said in a gruff voice with a thick northern Midwest accent, "Take them there in the conference room, Bob. I'll be there in a minute."

"Sure thing there, Chief, will do."

Chief Stoyanovich, Stovie for short, insisted on personally interviewing all the rookie cops each year before they were assigned their partners and given their beats. He wanted to be sure that their partnerships would be ... compatible. Stovie ruled his precinct, had fought hard to get where he was. He needed to be sure that some idealistic rookie didn't mess everything up. Every year there were a few that he worried about. They would come in fresh from the academy feeling all self-righteous, and it took a few years on the streets for them to understand that real police work was always about compromise. If he got paid a little here and there to keep the bad guys thinking that he was on their side, what harm could that cause? It kept the violence at a predictable level at least. A good cop is an informed cop. Surprises get you killed.

Chief Stovie walked into the room, and all the recent graduates stood, looking confident and sharp in their crisp new uniforms. He walked slowly around the room, sizing each of them up. It was a good group, bigger than last year. There was a total of eighteen new cops, seven were women. He left the women alone. They were always harder to break. The eleven men fit the stereotypes—former jocks, a few small guys with oversized egos, the usual. He had a whole department full of the same characters. As he surveyed the group, one stood out. He was military.

Stovie could see it in how he stood at attention with his eyes straight ahead.

"What's your name, son?"

"Peters, sir," the tall, well-built young man with close-cropped hair said with sharpness in his voice.

"What branch of the military did you serve in?"

"The Marines, sir."

"I figured so. I love the Marines. You always make great cops."

"I hope so, sir. It's certainly my intention." Peters looked at his new chief out of the corner of his eye. *He seems to be a nice enough fellow. Hasn't started yelling yet. That's not what I'm used to.*

"Why'd you get out?" Chief Stovie asked.

"I'm needed here at home, sir. My father is sick, and I have a younger sister. My mom needs help raising her."

"Admirable," Chief said. "A strong sense of responsibility. That's good."

"I promised my dad, sir."

Chief Stovie finished making his rounds. "Okay, now. I'm going to make assignments for each of you, and you will meet your new partners in about an hour. If any of you have special interests, now is a good time to tell me, and I'll see what I can do."

A few of the others spoke up with requests.

"What about you Peters?" Chief asked.

"I will do whatever you order me to do, sir."

"Excellent. I like that attitude. I think I have the perfect spot for you."

Chuck was assigned to the south side district, narcotics beat. It was the most violent part of the city and felt like a war zone with rival gangs constantly in a battle over turf and customers. Chuck had done a tour in Vietnam. It felt familiar.

Chuck's partner was a seasoned officer named Daniels. Daniels had been working this beat for ten years, much longer than most cops survived it, either literally or because they needed a change to hold onto their sanity, or humanity. Chuck wasn't sure that either was intact in Daniels. But he knew the streets, knew the leaders, and they knew him. There was almost a feeling of mutual respect, for just surviving long enough to get to where they were.

Chuck learned quickly under the tutelage of Daniels. He learned what street belonged to which gang, what drugs were being peddled, where the drop spots were, when to know that a fight was about to break out. He didn't question why Daniels didn't arrest everyone they saw flashing gang signs or selling drugs. He learned in Vietnam that you don't sweat out the little guys. They were just victims of the war, too. Your job was to keep it all contained, try to limit loss of life, and see if you could nail a few of the guys at the top. There was never any expectation, in Nam or Chicago, that you were going to win the war.

One day, Daniels told Chuck to stay in the car. He had to meet someone alone, a cardinal no-no in the Chicago police force. But Chuck was used to following orders from his immediate superior. He did as he was told. Nothing happened. A few minutes later, Daniels came back, got in the car, and they drove away. Daniels didn't say anything, and Chuck never asked. After that, the stops became a weekly occurrence. Same result. No questions asked. Finally, one day, Daniels made the stop, but before he got out, he turned to Chuck.

"Peters, I'm taking you with me today. But I need to know that I can trust you. You know as well as I do that we put our lives at risk every day fighting a losing battle. The only reason that I have survived this long is that I stack the odds in my favor.

I'm going to show you today how I do that. Remember, our main job is to save lives. Sometimes what we have to do to accomplish that is not in the manual. Got it?" Daniels stared hard at Chuck to gauge his reaction.

Chuck didn't flinch. "Yes, sir."

"Geez, Peters, it's been 8 months. Stop calling me 'sir'."

"Yes, sir. I will do that, sir." Chuck replied without even a hint of a smile.

Daniels rolled his eyes and got out of the car. Chuck followed. They went down a narrow back alley and knocked on a rusted metal door in one of the buildings that looked to be abandoned. There was a voice from the other side that Chuck couldn't make out. Daniels hit the side frame of the door twice with the butt of his gun, and the door opened. They entered the dark building that had been gutted to the support beams and crossed a large empty room until they came to another door with two armed men standing in front of it. The men motioned to their gun belts, and Daniels nodded at Chuck and removed his belt. Chuck hesitated but did the same. The armed men patted them down and then escorted them through the door into a nicely furnished room. Sitting behind a desk was a large, muscular man who appeared to be slightly older than Chuck. Standing next to him was a shorter red-haired man, covered in tattoos.

The larger man stood and came around his desk while offering the two cops a seat in some leather arm chairs. He was at least six-foot five and was hardened like an athlete or someone who had spent a lot of time in prison. He had dark hair, long at the collar and a distinctive flattened nose.

"Is this your new partner?" the large man asked.

"This is him," Daniels repeated.

The large man reached over and held out his oven-mitt sized hand. "My name is Frank. Frank Donovan. Daniels says we can trust you. Is he right?"

Chuck grabbed Frank's hand and gave a firm squeeze to show that he wasn't intimidated. He didn't reply, though, to the question.

"Well," Frank said. "I'll take that as a yes because you seem like a smart enough fellow. And smart fellows would definitely answer yes to that question. Because, Chuck Peters, I know everything about you. Like, you live at 532 Bakers Street with your mom, Vicky, and your sister, Nora. Your dad, James, is in a hospice center on the upper east side of town. I know why you left the military, and it wasn't because of your sick dad, was it Peters? Your sergeant was killed because of a mistake that you made, and it got to your head. Am I right so far?"

Chuck stared at Frank Donovan, trying not to show his anger. How did he know all of that? He never talked to Daniels or anyone else at work about details of his family and especially about his military record. Chuck could see that Frank was a dangerous man to get on the wrong side of.

"A man of few words, I see," Frank continued. "No matter. I like men of action better anyway. So, let's clarify why you're here. First of all, I'm not into drugs. Too messy. I do, however, own plenty of those who run the trade, so I understand your job. The reason I am meeting you today is as a matter of principle. I like to meet the people who work for me in person. It keeps everybody connected, like a family."

"If you don't sell drugs, what do you want with me?" Chuck asked.

"Ahh, he speaks," Frank smiled, holding out his hands toward Chuck in presentation. "The answer to your very good question is nothing. Yet. But you will know when the time comes. In the meantime, you get paid. Double your salary."

"And if I say no?" Chuck asked, though he already knew the answer.

"Ahh. James and Vicky and Nora might not appreciate it if you did."

Chuck sat silently for several minutes. "Are we done?" he asked finally.

Frank moved his arm toward the door, and Chuck and Daniels got up and walked out.

Chuck didn't say anything when he got back to the patrol car.

Daniels looked at him. "The rules on the streets are different, son. Don't fight it. Just collect your money and do what they ask. I've been paid for nine years and haven't done nothing."

"Just drive the car," Chuck said. He never again called him sir.

CHAPTER THIRTY-FOUR

Quinn woke up from his nap a couple of hours later feeling a bit more rested but still angry that their plan had been disrupted. He didn't think Gary could be trusted. He was the only person who knew all the details and could have been there to take a picture. It seemed a little too easy that he just happened to go back to the scene this morning at the exact moment that the 'real' picture-taker decided to visit.

No, Gary was in on it, Quinn was sure of it. But if confronted now, Gary might just shoot him and disappear with whatever money he was getting paid to double cross Frank. It was a bold move with a high risk of dying if he got caught. He must be getting a lot.

Quinn would pretend to defer to Gary for a while longer but would watch him like a hawk. He really wanted to catch the real culprit, whoever was paying Gary. It had to be Wesley. Wesley had the most to gain by removing both he and his dad from the action.

Quinn really wanted to talk to his dad now, to get some help, but his only access to him was through Wesley. No. He was on his own. His dad couldn't help him. But he was determined to live up to his name and make his dad proud. He remembered how he felt when he first saw his dad in his true element at his office and wanted to show his dad that he could be trusted to protect their interests.

. . .

His first visit to Frank Donovan's office was almost two years ago, the day after Thanksgiving. Quinn didn't have school, and their family never worried about buying things on sale, so while much of America was fighting each other at stores like Costco and Best Buy, Frank was going to work. It was a few weeks after Quinn had told his dad that he wanted to learn the family business. Frank asked him if he wanted to go into the office with him that day.

"Absolutely," Quinn said.

His mom raised her eyebrows at Frank in protest, but Frank waved her off and told Quinn to get into the Mercedes. They spent the drive talking football. If Quinn asked him any questions about the company, Frank interrupted him with, "Not now. Not here." Frank never spoke about work outside of his office.

They arrived in the city and drove through Manhattan to a skyscraper in the financial district. They pulled into a secure garage and parked in a designated spot with a nameplate labeled New Horizons. Two uniformed attendants greeted them and escorted them to a private elevator. Another attendant was waiting for them there.

"Good morning, Mr. Donovan," the attendant said, as they entered the elevator.

"Good morning, Art," Frank replied.

Silence followed until the elevator doors opened again, and they stepped into a luxuriously furnished office with leather couches and dark-glass end tables. They walked down a hall lined with floor-to-ceiling glass walls partitioning several offices filled with desks and computers and people hard at work behind them. Each looked up and waved as Frank walked past. At the end of the hall, there was a solid wooden door labeled Frank Donovan, CEO. Quinn's dad opened the door, and they went inside.

Frank's office was a large, corner space looking out over Manhattan with views of the Hudson River. There were several leather chairs lined up around a small conference table. There was a huge mahogany desk facing the room. The walls were decorated on one side with expensive art. The other wall had a large electronic map of the world with small red lights illuminating several countries in Southeast Asia, India, Mexico, and most of South America.

Frank waved his hand toward one of the chairs to indicate that he wanted Quinn to sit. He then went to his desk and turned on his computer. After a minute or two, he grabbed a remote control and pushed a button. A large monitor descended from the ceiling in front of the map wall. He joined his son at the conference table, pushed another button on the remote, and the screen illuminated with an image of a large dollar sign.

"That's what it's all about right there, son," Frank said. He then flashed through other images on the screen. Their house. The several expensive cars in their garage. Their yacht. Several vacation houses that Quinn had been to and some he had never seen before.

"You like all that stuff, don't you, Quinn?" Frank asked.

"Yes, sir," Quinn replied.

Frank clicked the remote again. A picture of Quinn's mom and sister appeared on the screen.

"This is also what it's about, son. In any business, you don't get on top without stepping on toes. In my business, it's way more than that. I have a lot of enemies, people who would do anything to take me down. Your mom and sister have targets on their heads. So do you, Quinn, like it or not. The women in our lives don't need to know any details about what we do here. Understand? It would just make it more dangerous for them, right? You are a man now. If you truly want in, you need to understand what you are getting into. You could have a nice life, Quinn, an easy life. I've made that possible for you. You could go to college, marry a nice girl, get a safe boring job. Are you willing to give that up for a life where you can make a ton of money but are always under threat? The decision is yours, but once I let you in, there is no turning back. Think carefully."

Quinn looked at his dad, at the posh office, at the respect he commanded from his workers and felt pride swelling in his chest. His dad had done it all by himself. Frank had told Quinn previously about his upbringing. He was raised in a broken home with an abusive alcoholic father who spent his paychecks on booze, frequently leaving them no money for food. His mother was beaten down to just a shell of a woman who spent her days in the bedroom, fearing her husband's nightly rages. As soon as Frank was big enough, he confronted his old man who immediately kicked him out to fend for himself on the streets. Frank survived by staying with friends or finding places to sleep outside but still made it to school most days and never missed football practice.

Football saved him and gave him hope for a brighter future. He was big and had learned toughness the hard way. Several college coaches saw his talent, and the University of Michigan gave him the opportunity to develop it. He made the most of it and was on track for a pro career when a serious knee injury derailed it all.

After that, his life spiraled again. He got hooked on pain-killers, dropped out of school, found trouble with the law, and ended up in prison for a couple of years. There, ironically, his life started to improve once more. All Quinn knew was that Frank met some people in prison, and they started a company when they got out. Obviously, it was a good move.

"Dad. I don't want to spend my life stuck in a job that I hate just so that I can play it safe. I'm still in. I'm sure."

"Being stuck behind a desk is better than being stuck in prison. You understand that could be your destination if things turn south?" Frank asked, testing Quinn's resolve.

"I get it, dad. But they haven't caught you after what, twenty years? You obviously have been careful. Just teach me, and I'll do the same."

"Okay, I really want you to have all this someday, so if you are ready and committed, I'm going to tell you everything. Remember, nothing leaves this room. Don't trust anybody, including—maybe especially—people who work here. There are only a couple of people who know it all. They are the guys that I met in prison, who have been with me from the beginning— Wesley O'Brien and James Slater. I'm going to tell you about James in a bit but suffice it to say for now that he is soon to be a dead man. So that leaves one other guy—Wesley. I trust him. But you shouldn't. You will be in his way to take over the busi-ness if I'm out of the picture. Understand all that?"

"Yes sir!" Quinn said enthusiastically.

"Okay. First, I'm going to give you some history. James Slater was my cellmate in prison. He was a quiet guy, a nervous type, but I could tell that he was smart. He took care of the finances for an organization that was involved in sex trafficking. They got caught, and he was doing his time.

"We had a lot of time to talk as you would expect. He told me that if he could do it all over, he wouldn't deal with the sex trade because it gets a lot of attention from the FBI. He would take advantage of the weak federal regulation over foreign workers in low-paying industries and agriculture.

"He had spent time overseas in places where wages were incredibly low and opportunities scarce. There were large groups of unemployed men with families to support who would do about anything to feed their people. Many of them hung around places where people would come ready to hire day laborers for various tasks, and if they didn't get selected, they would spend the day together watching American TV shows and movies. So, their idea of America was all fast cars and beautiful women. Selling them on the American dream would be a piece of cake.

"All you would have to do is get them to sign a contract for 'relocation expenses' that were too high for them to realistically pay back during the contract term, and then they were stuck working for you at rates well below the US market. As their employer, you offer their services to companies that need workers who are willing to pay average or even just below average wages, and then you pocket the difference as administrative pay.

"It is a system that has been enriching those smart enough or corrupt enough to use it since the beginning of time. Look at slavery in the South. It didn't go away after the Civil War. It was turned into indentured servitude. Look at the Great Depression era. The big farmers in California took the same advantages over the poor folks from the breadbasket states who were displaced by the dust bowl. And all of that was done under the sleepy watch of the US government.

"Truth is, politicians don't care about poor people, especially those who are willing to work, and more especially if they are seen as outsiders. So, although there are laws and regulations in place, they are not tightly enforced. All it takes is a group of people desperate enough to absorb the abuse, and there is money to be made. It might as well be us making the money. That is what James Slater taught me in prison."

Quinn nodded his head. "I get it. I learned about Reconstruction in school, where former slaves worked for their previous owners on the same plantation because they had nowhere else to go. The whites still rigged the system in their favor by jacking prices at stores and joining forces to keep wages low. We also read the Grapes of Wrath. Same thing happened. The rich got richer, and the poor didn't have any choice but to just take it."

"That's right. But in this case, we are actually giving people who are poor anyway at least a chance to improve their situation if they stick it out and don't fight the system. We just front load our profit and then make it unpleasant enough that about half of them quit, which means they don't ever break even. That is extra money in our pockets."

"Well, it's their choice then, right? Why is it illegal?" Quinn asked.

"Because the government doesn't think that the contracts that we are making them sign are fair. And we don't always follow safety or labor laws once they get here. And the percentage that we take from their wages for administrative fees are too high."

"Okay. That makes sense. The contracts tie their hands, the work conditions make them want to quit, and the administrative fees provide the daily cash flow."

"You got it. Plus, when they quit, we get a big bonus because they breached the contract and lost the money they paid us in relocation expenses. It's a large amount that they usually have to borrow from a bank or family, so it takes a lot for them to give it up. That's when we have to ratchet up the pain," Frank said.

"What keeps them from leaving and finding another job in the States?" Quinn asked.

"Good question. First, we keep their passports and ID. So, if they leave, they are illegals, and we threaten to turn them over to the immigration officials. Without a passport, they can't fly home. Plus, we keep their wages in an account in our name, and then pay for the living expenses that we provide to them out of that account. So, they have no cash to survive on if they leave. Their account breaks even after three years. If they make it that far, and some do, they can then make a decent amount of money to send home. We want some of them to succeed, right? Why is that?"

"So that they'll tell their friends?" Quinn asked.

"Exactly. Then those that go home early just seem like they were soft. Everybody thinks they can do it before they start," Frank explained.

"Makes sense to me. Is that it?"

"Not entirely," Frank said. "We have to hide a lot of the money, because if we declare our actual profit to the IRS, alarms will start blaring, and the government will start snooping. So, we create shell companies. Do you know what those are?"

"Not exactly," Quinn admitted.

"They are unrelated businesses where we hide the money from the noses of the tax collectors. Think of it like a shell game. Have you seen that before? The game host puts a peanut under one of three empty shells, moves the shells around rapidly, and the player guesses which shell has the peanut."

"Oh yeah. I've seen that game. Everybody almost always loses," Quinn said.

"That's because it is stacked in the favor of the host. He already has a 67 percent chance to win if he does nothing special, but if he is good, he can bump it up to ninety. Do you know how?"

"How?"

"The art of distraction. He distracts the player and moves the peanut from one shell to the other. The player is convinced that he hasn't lost sight of the original shell, and he is right. He loses though because the peanut was moved. We do the same thing but increase our odds even more by having more than three companies. In fact, we have more than a dozen. We move the money back and forth and eventually deposit it in an offshore account where it is protected. I can draw from that account anytime to buy anything I want. That process is called money laundering, and it is highly illegal because you are stealing from the US government by not paying taxes on it. The government hates that. But if you think about it, most of the major corporations don't pay taxes either. They just buy the politicians. We just do it our own way," Frank said with a smile.

"I like it," Quinn said. "What happens if you get caught?"

"Depends. Ten to twenty most likely with early parole. But they never see your offshore account. I think of the risk as an investment. Plus, I set it up so others are doing the dirty work. They all know that if they double cross me, they will pay dearly. If they stay loyal, they are highly compensated. It always works out."

"They pay dearly how?" Quinn asked.

"Well, that's a conversation for another day," Frank said. "Just focus on the money-making side for now."

. . .

Quinn got up from his bed and went into his bathroom. He took a good look in the mirror. He could see his dad's intensity staring back from his eyes. After the last year of his life, he now understood what it would take to protect his family's interests. The man who was responsible for his dad being in prison was dead. That was step one. Step two was finding out who was framing him.

CHAPTER THIRTY-FIVE

Atkins sat in his hotel room in Kalispel, waiting for the secure file from the New Horizons human trafficking case as well as the older Chicago murder case that his boss, Director Call, had promised to send him. The New Horizons case had lasted a total of eight months in court, and there were volumes of documents to review. Atkins had been responsible ultimately for the arrest of Frank Donovan, the ringleader. It was a huge case and was the culmination of years of effort including infiltrating the business with undercover agents to gather evidence and to learn the details of the system. The turning point was when one of the agents gained the trust of the man who had set up the financial system in the organization. That was James Slater, and he was one of the founding members. He was willing to talk, as long as he was granted immunity from prosecution. In exchange, he said he would give up the leader.

Apparently, Slater and Donovan had had a falling out. Donovan had threatened Slater's life on more than one occasion, whenever any money was unaccounted for, no matter how small the amount. Slater felt like Donovan should have paid him more, since he was the one who showed Donovan how to set up the business. Donovan kept the vast majority of the profit which rubbed Slater the wrong way. When he confronted Donovan,

Donovan cut him out. While doing so, Donovan threatened Slater's life and that of his family.

Slater knew that those threats should not be taken lightly. He had seen what Donovan could do to those who were disloyal, so he kept his mouth shut. But when someone else leaked information about the company that led to some lower-level arrests, Donovan suspected that Slater was behind it. One day, Slater came home to find both his wife and daughter shot in the head. That was when Slater started talking. He had nothing else to lose.

Atkins had spent five years and all his focus and effort to see Donovan behind bars. They couldn't pin the murder of Slater's family on him as there was no evidence linking him to that crime. They did convict him, however, of tax evasion and money laundering, and he got fifteen years with the chance for early parole.

After the trial, Atkins asked Director Call for a change, at least temporarily. He needed some down time and to get out of New York. He requested Montana, partially for the mountains and fresh air, but also to keep an eye on Slater who would be relocated here under witness protection. Atkins knew that it was only a matter of time before Slater would be found by his former associates, and he wanted to be there to see if they could keep Donovan in prison forever by linking him directly to Slater's murder, if they weren't able to move him in time, that is.

When he got the call from Chief Peters this morning, he knew that they had been too late to save Slater. He didn't feel too bad though. Slater was not a good man. Justice almost always has its way of working itself out. However, if he could nail Donovan for the crime, two bad men would be removed from society.

When he went to Slater's cabin this morning, Atkins expected a crime scene like at the murders of Slater's family—a single bullet hole in the head and absolutely no other trace of evidence. But the scene at Slater's murder was far from that. It was sloppy with all kinds of evidence implicating three local teenagers with clean records and no known link to Slater or Donovan.

That is when he remembered the Chicago case from about fifteen years ago, the trial of which Atkins just happened to observe. The similarities of that crime scene with Slater's were too hard for Atkins to ignore. He remembered thinking at the time that the Chicago crime scene felt manufactured. If three teenage boys had just intended to burglarize the house and get out, why would they bring a tarp and their own shovels to bury the body of their victim in his own backyard? Atkins learned that in organized crime circles at the time, the blue tarp meant something. It was a code word for a targeted killing. The defense team of the boys were inexperienced and underpaid court appointees and completely blew it.

That case had been bothering Atkins for fifteen years. And now, he had his own "blue tarp" case to deal with. It is unlikely that the local Montana police knew what it meant. He had to proceed with caution. It is possible that, like in Chicago, crime money had bought some influence even here in Whitefish, and that someone on the local force could have planted evidence again.

As Atkins sat pondering the job ahead of him, his phone rang. It was from Chief Peters.

"Atkins," he answered.

"Atkins, it's Peters. I just wanted to touch base with you. I have been to the house of Adam's friend, the place he was supposed to stay last night. His name is Quinn Madison. He is the star quarterback on the high school team. I met his dad, as well. Quinn denied being with Adam last night. They live in a nice place on the lake, and his dad had security footage of their driveway and gate. Quinn didn't come or go after five o'clock last night until football practice at ten this morning. But, Atkins, something's not right there. I haven't put my finger on it yet, but I can tell you that video has been doctored."

"Yeah? How could you tell?" Atkins asked.

"There were some very subtle shaky parts at a couple of places that happen when you cut a segment out. At my former job, I spent a lot of time studying security footage."

"Is that right? Where was your former job?" Atkins asked, sounding impressed.

"Chicago."

CHAPTER THIRTY-SIX

Susan pulled into her garage and helped Sandra out of the car and into the house. Sandra was still trembling but had stopped screaming and was ready to put the encounter behind her. She didn't know who that man was, but her soul could sense danger as soon as he rolled down the window and stared at her. She was glad to not be alone tonight.

"Do you need some time in your old sensory room, Sandy?"

"No. I think," Sandra said, shaking her head.

Sandra was mostly just exhausted now. So much had happened in the last 24 hours. She had witnessed a terrible crime, figured out how to tell her mom about it, and had lived through two panic attacks. She had nothing left.

"I'll make dinner," Susan said.

"No, mom. Just bed," Sandra responded. She went down the hall and into her old room. It had been a while since she had stayed here, and she sat on the bed and just looked around. The dresser and shelves were lined with familiar items, comfort items—stuffed animals, boxes of alphabet letters, pictures of their family. These were not just trinkets or toys to Sandra. They were guardians, protectors. This was a safe place, where she could rest.

Sandra crawled under the covers of her bed without changing her clothes and felt the warmth envelop her. *Rest, Sandra. Tomorrow will bring more challenges. But for tonight, you can rest.*

. . .

The sun was warm and bright, and Sandra could feel the breeze from the ocean gently caress her hair. As she walked on the wet sand, holding her father's hand, the tide washed over her feet and caused her to squeal. Her dad squatted down, gazed into her face, and smiled.

"Do you like that, sweetheart?" he asked with his calm, gentle voice. "I thought you would."

She squealed again as the cool water once more washed over her feet.

"Do you want to go in deeper? I'll hold you," Tony said.

Sandra reached up and grabbed around his neck with her arms. He slowly waded deeper into the water, bracing their bodies against the mild waves. Sandra squeezed tight whenever a new wave would come but soon relaxed and let the rhythm of the ocean synchronize with the rhythm of her soul. Her senses were alive but calm. The sound of the waves washing the sand, the cries of the seagulls, other children playing on the beach. She absorbed it all and locked it in. She swayed in the water, secure in her father's arms. She could taste the salt in the air. Nature was talking to her, comforting her, becoming part of her.

"I am here, Sandra. Always here. I will not let you go," her dad whispered into her ear. "You are my hero. I am so proud. You have become so strong. They will try, but you will win. Have courage, my baby girl. Listen to the woods, the trees, the stream. You are part of their family, too. The woods will protect you. I am there also."

. . .

It was warm on her face, the rays of morning sun. She opened her eyes and saw the picture of her parents building a sandcastle on the beach. She was looking out toward the ocean. Her dad was looking at the camera, smiling. His eyes were looking at her now, giving her strength.

She could hear her mom in the kitchen and could smell sausage cooking on the stove. She sat for a moment on her bed, taking inventory of her emotions, listening for her brain to start its running commentary. It was quiet. She could feel her soul in a deeper place, also quiet, but it was a different kind of quiet—one she hadn't felt before, outside of the woods. It felt like ... confidence. She was ready to face a new day.

CHAPTER THIRTY-SEVEN

Chuck woke the next morning, grabbed some coffee, and headed into the station. Last evening, he had met the parents of Mark and Tanner, and like Adam's mother, they were all in shock. Each told the same story: their sons were supposed to be spending the night at Quinn Madison's house. Now, it wouldn't be the first time that teenage boys colluded on a story before going out and getting in trouble, but every one of their parents seemed devastated that their boys would lie to them, to say nothing about burglary or murder.

As Chuck entered the station, Karen told him that there was someone waiting to see him.

"Not now, Karen. Have Sean take care of it," he said dismissively. "I've got to focus on the Mather case."

"I think it's related, sir," Karen said.

Chuck stopped and looked through the glass into the waiting area. There, sitting nervously at the edge of a chair, was an elderly woman with bright white hair.

"That woman is here about Mather?" Chuck asked in surprise.

"She said that she has information, sir."

"Okay, then. Let her in. I'll meet her in my office."

Chuck waited by his office door as Karen escorted the elderly woman, who still seemed quite spry, down the hall. She was carrying a laptop under her arm.

"Please come in, ma'am." He pointed to a chair in front of his desk. "Can I get you anything, cup of coffee?"

"I'm fine, thank you." Susan sat in the chair and set the laptop on the desk.

"I am Chief Peters. Can I ask your name, ma'am?" Chuck began.

"Susan Lewis," Susan said.

"Mrs. Lewis, how can I help you?"

"I have some information about the murder that happened Friday night."

"Murder? In Whitefish? There hasn't been a murder in Whitefish for decades," Chuck said, gauging her reaction.

"I am aware of that," Susan said calmly. "But my daughter, Sandra, witnessed someone burying a body in the woods. She assumed that the body belonged to a victim of a crime."

"Your daughter witnessed a crime? I beg your pardon, ma'am, but why isn't she the one here reporting it?" Chuck asked.

"Well, there is a story behind that," Susan replied, "and the reason why I brought this laptop with me."

"I'm all ears, Mrs. Lewis. Let's hear what you have to say," Chuck said, leaning forward with his hands crossed in front of him on the desk.

"Okay. My daughter Sandra is 27 years old and lives by herself in the condo complex on Forest View Street. She has autism, with limited verbal skills, but she is functional enough to care for her basic needs. A couple of years ago, she wanted to try living on her own, so we bought her this condo. I live close by and check on her every day.

Sandra has been doing quite well with this arrangement and really enjoys her independence. Frankly, Chief Peters, I didn't think she would last a month. But she surprised even her mother," Susan paused.

"Go on," Chuck encouraged.

"Sandra calls me every night when she gets back from her evening hike in the woods behind her complex. She loves being outside and loves the trails in those woods. She can stay out there for hours. She has an incredible sense of direction, Chief. She has never been lost in her entire life.

"Anyway, last night, she didn't call. You would have to know Sandra to know why that would alarm me. She is very dependent on schedule. She has every day planned out in advance. If something happens that disrupts her schedule, she becomes very anxious. So, I know that I will get a call every night at sunset to tell me that she is home.

"Last night, no call ... and I started getting worried. I immediately went over to her condo and let myself in. Everything was in order, so I waited. The longer it took, the more worried I became. I was just about to call you guys when she came in the door. She was unhurt, but something was wrong. She gets a wild look in her eyes when she is upset, almost like a caged animal. She had that look. She couldn't tell me what was wrong, Chief Peters, but I know my daughter, and I know that something had frightened her badly. She eventually told me 'Somebody hurt.' That's all she could get out.

"Anyway, I knew that pushing her further would only make things worse. So, I just stayed the night at her place and let her work things out the only way she knows how. The next morning—yesterday—she asked me to leave and give her some space. I did as she asked. I got a call from her in the afternoon. She said she needed my help, so I went right over. That is when she showed me this." Susan opened the laptop and waited for it to load.

"Before I show it to you, Chief Peters, you need to understand something. Sandra has never typed before. At least, she has never typed out a message or communicated with us on this level before today. So, forgive me if I seem a little stunned by it all.

"We have tried everything out there to teach her how to talk or type or communicate by some other means, any means. Despite hundreds of thousands of dollars and the best therapists in the country, yesterday was the first spontaneous communication in her life beyond simple needs. She found a way on her own to tell you what she saw in the woods Friday night." Susan turned the laptop toward the Chief. "Just read the highlighted letters."

Chief Peters put on his reading glasses and pulled the laptop toward him. Susan watched his face as he studied the message in front of him. His eyes widened, and he looked up at her for a moment and then back at the screen. After another minute, Chuck had finished the message and leaned back in his chair. There was a long pause of silence. Susan waited without saying anything.

Finally, Chuck looked again at Susan. "Mrs. Lewis. I'm going to need to meet your daughter."

CHAPTER THIRTY-EIGHT

Sandra anxiously waited for Susan to return from the police station. It was taking longer than expected, and she wasn't sure what that meant. Would the police take her message seriously? Would they investigate her claim? Or would they blow it off as a hoax? After all, no one saw her type that message. That kind of code writing seemed like something straight out of a kid's adventure magazine, not a legitimate police investigation.

It took two hours before Susan returned. Sandra had been pacing in her sensory room ever since her mom had left. When she heard the door open, Sandra went out to meet her.

Susan came in alone, which was a major relief to Sandra because she wasn't feeling ready to meet with a policeman. Not anymore. The courage that she woke up with this morning had faded as soon as her mom had walked out of the door carrying her laptop. She would need some time in the woods to find it again.

Sandra had always been afraid of the police. She supposed that it stemmed from her time in a contained special education classroom in school. The police were called sometimes if any of the kids had a bad enough panic attack to turn violent. Fortunately, she kept her own attacks controlled enough at school that she was never the target of concern. She saw some of the others get forcibly restrained, though, and she could tell when some of the police officers were getting frustrated and maybe squeezing harder than was necessary. She was always worried that someday they would come for her, too.

"Hi, sweetheart," Susan said. "Sit down, let's talk."

Sandra sat on the couch, and Susan sat beside her.

"Do you know how proud I am of you? And amazed at you?" Susan started, as tears welled in her eyes. "I took your message to the police department. I spoke directly to the chief of police. He is a very nice man, Sandy. And guess what? He believes you. He told me that there was a murder on Friday night. They found a body in the woods, just like you said. He is very interested in meeting you, dear. I told him all about you. He understands how difficult this will be, but it's also very important. You might be the only witness. Do you understand what that means? You might be the only person that can help them catch the killers."

Susan paused for a minute and looked at Sandra. Sandra looked back briefly. She heard what her mom was saying and knew it was true, but she wasn't sure how to feel. Her first emotion was fear. What if she couldn't do it? There would be a lot of people staring at her, depending on her to perform. Her brain wasn't going to like that. It might just say no. *Not my girl. She is my girl. You can't have her. I have held her close for 27 years. I will not give her up easily.*

The second emotion was excitement. This was Sandra's chance to come out from the shadows, from the cracks in the wall of society. People like her are ignored for the most part. It is easier for the able minded to not see her than to stop and consider her, to engage with her. Now they had to listen. *To her.* For once, she had all the power. And she liked that.

"Mom, tomorrow?" she said.

"Tomorrow is fine, dear. I will tell Chief Peters. He will understand. I explained already what an intense day yesterday had been for you."

"Mom, hike," Sandra said. She knew that going to the woods would calm her soul. Her soul was cheering for her. It would help her, but it needed to be fed.

"Okay, Sandy, do you want to go behind the house?" Susan asked.

"Yes, please."

Sandra wanted to avoid the scene of the crime now at all costs. She knew she would have to go back there eventually with the police, and the thought of that repelled her. But her woods were large, spanning hundreds of square miles. She would go the opposite direction. No one would even know she was there. She wanted to listen to the stream and hear the wind in the trees. She could not stay shut inside. It was stifling.

"Can I go with you? I'm worried about you being by yourself out there right now. We don't know if it is safe."

Sandra shook her head vigorously. "Safe!"

"But ... " Susan started to protest.

Sandra stamped her foot and again shook her head. "Safe! Alone. Okay?"

Susan started tearing up but swallowed down her fears. She knew that Sandra drew her energy from being alone in the woods. If she didn't get to go, she would never be able to face the things that she would need to do in the coming days.

"Okay, Sandy, but I'm going to watch your every move, and you need to promise me that you will stay away from people and call me if you sense any danger. I know you need it, but every minute that you are out there by yourself today will probably suck a minute of life out of me. Understand?"

"Yes, mom," Sandra said and grabbed her coat. Her parents' house backed to the same forest, just a few blocks down the mountain from her condo. Today she was going to climb. As she walked through the grass in their backyard and then felt it turn to the crunch of the forest floor, her soul awakened, and her body began to fill again with energy.

She took a trail that led up the mountain, away from the crime scene. The slope became steeper as she went, and Sandra began breathing heavily. The mountain air rushed into her lungs, and it was like filling an empty tank with gas. She climbed higher and higher until she came to an outcropping of rock overlooking the lake and the valley below.

She scrambled to the top and then sat on its edge, closing her eyes, and calming her breathing. She felt the wind on her face and then listened. Far away, she heard the cry of a hawk. She opened her eyes and saw it circling in the air, buoyed by the updrafts. It was searching, scanning, hunting. Then it suddenly tucked its wings and dove straight down. A second later it emerged again with a rabbit kicking and struggling in its sharp talons. After a few more seconds, the rabbit stopped moving, either dead or accepting its fate, Sandra wasn't sure. She followed the hawk until it disappeared into some treetops where she assumed that there was a nest full of hungry gaping mouths waiting to be fed. She thought again of the rabbit. It, too, had just been out there, eating, surviving. The next minute, it was gone.

Was she the rabbit or the hawk? At that moment, she wasn't sure. Was the rabbit sad after the fear had passed? Or did it understand that this was its destiny? A link in the chain of life.

Sandra saw that nature's chain was clean, polished, strong—unless man intervened. Man with bolt cutters cankered with greed, envy, and pride. Man's own chain was weak, broken and rusty. Where she fit among those links was entirely unpredictable to her. But as she surveyed her woods from this perch up above, she knew that no matter what happened between her and man, she would come back here. Always. To join the beautiful chain, the strong chain. Like the rabbit, after the fear was gone, she would stop struggling.

CHAPTER THIRTY-NINE

Agent Atkins closed his laptop as he stood to answer a knock on his motel room door. He had ordered take out breakfast about 30 minutes before. As he rounded the bed and took a few steps toward the door, the motel window glass suddenly shattered in a thousand pieces. Atkins dove to the floor and scrambled back around the bed to reach for his gun on the bedside table. Before he got to it though, bullets riddled the air above him and tore into the mattress, sending cloth and pieces of foam flying all around him. He quickly rolled under the bed frame and hoped for a pause in the commotion. After another thirty seconds of constant gunfire, the room fell silent.

Atkins, amazed he was unscathed, listened intensely for the door to bust open and the footsteps of whoever it was that was trying to kill him coming to finish the job. Two more minutes passed and still it was silent. Atkins slowly scooted out from under the bed and secured his weapon. He could see that the wall behind him was plastered with bullet holes. The door was still closed, but the morning light shined through some large gaps in the splintered wood. On the floor by the window, there was a brick, wrapped in yellow paper.

Atkins stood quickly and pressed his back against the wall, his gun at the ready. He moved deliberately, edging along the room until he reached the window, where he slowly moved what was left of the curtains and looked out from the side of the window frame. There were people running through the parking lot, away from the building. They were unarmed and mostly undressed. *Other motel guests,* he assumed. He saw no one else that looked suspicious, or anything but panicked. In the distance, he could hear police sirens.

Atkins bent down and picked up the brick. The paper cover was from a legal pad and taped carefully in place. He removed the tape and unwrapped the brick. On the other side of the paper was a note constructed from block letters cut from magazines.

"Leave it be!"

That was it. A simple message, though very effectively delivered, Atkins acknowledged, as he took another glance around the room. The laptop, still sitting on top of the bed, was completely destroyed. He would not be able to finish reading the files from the New Horizons case for days. It is not an easy process to get a laptop replacement with the necessary built-in security measures being this far away from headquarters. He had just received the files from Director Call this morning, about an hour before the shooting started, and had just settled in with a morning cup of coffee to begin scanning the hundreds of pages of court testimony. He supposed now that he was not the only one who thought that there was something important buried in there.

Atkins folded the paper and tucked it in his front pants pocket. A few minutes later, five or six police officers from the Kalispel force were yelling through the window, guns drawn, and the door burst open.

Atkins slowly put down his weapon and held his hands up high. "I'm FBI! Stand down!"

"Show us your identification, now!" the lead officer yelled, gun pointed at Atkins' chest.

"It's on the bed stand," Atkins replied, trying to stay calm.

The lead officer motioned to a subordinate to get the ID.

"He's right, sir. Agent Brett Atkins, Federal Bureau of Investigation."

The lead officer lowered his weapon, and Atkins let out a big sigh.

"Damn, man! I thought you were going to shoot me," Atkins said.

"Just doing my job, sir. So, what the hell happened here?" the officer replied, his own adrenaline releasing and sweat now breaking out on his face.

Atkins picked up his gun and reengaged the safety. He went over to the officer that was still holding his wallet and ID and held out his arm.

"May I?"

"Oh, sorry. Of course." She handed it back to him, looking a little sheepish.

Atkins sat down in the frame of a chair whose cushion was torn up from bullets.

"Man, I came to Montana to fish."

CHAPTER FORTY

Chuck leaned back in his office chair and considered what he had just heard. The sole witness to the crime, the only person that could confirm his own growing suspicions about Quinn Madison, had no language skills.

Chuck had a nephew with autism—sweet kid but could be really tough to manage sometimes. Chuck used to spell his brother and sister-in-law a couple of times a month when he lived close to them, pre-military days. He would hang out with Josh while his parents went out to dinner or a movie and tried to pretend for a few hours that they had a normal life. Chuck admired them and felt bad for them at the same time. Most people had no clue what it was like to raise a child with special needs. Josh's parents always looked so tired and stressed out, a few hours a month was the least he could do. After a while, he began to really look forward to his "Josh Time."

Josh was only five years old then—a five-year old puzzle with a built-in code that Chuck wanted to crack. He tried all kinds of things with him—playing with toys, stacking blocks, singing silly songs, rolling a ball. None of it seemed to capture Josh's attention. Eventually, Chuck just sat down on the floor and watched Josh do his thing without putting expectations on him. When Chuck was quiet, Josh came close and would even sit on his lap. That felt like an important breakthrough. After that, Chuck realized that Josh didn't want him to be a therapist. He just needed Chuck to be a calming presence. With time and the new strategy, Josh began responding with more eye contact and even affection.

One day, Garrett, Chuck's brother, told him that Josh had started repeating Chuck's name over and over whenever he got anxious. Josh had something called echolalia, a term for repetitive language. He never communicated using words but sustained an ongoing verbal commentary most of his waking hours. The doctors had told Josh's parents that he was just spewing words, that he didn't understand them, so Garrett informed Chuck not to get too excited that Josh said his name. Nonetheless, Chuck's heart formed a soft spot for his nephew that never went away.

Garrett was eight years older than Chuck and had moved his family away from Chicago when Chuck was in Vietnam. When Chuck returned, he immediately started in the police academy and never made it to North Carolina to visit Garrett and to see Josh again. After starting his job, Chuck didn't have any time off and was distracted most always. He was worried about his father whose health was going downhill quickly and by the constant threat to his mom and sister. He called Garrett occasionally and asked to speak with Josh. He could hear him in the background saying the same things he said when he was five, only now in a deeper voice. Chuck would yell into the phone so Josh could hear him on the other end. There would be a short pause in the verbalizations and then they would resume. "That's all you're gonna get," Garrett explained. "You want more? Come and see him."

Garrett came to their dad's funeral, but Josh stayed in North Carolina with Trisha, Garrett's second wife. His first marriage didn't survive the stress. After that, there were a few more calls before ... well, before what happened ... and Garrett hasn't spoken to him since.

Chuck thought about Josh when he listened to Susan describe Sandra and how she figured out how to type her message. He had always suspected there was a lot more going on in Josh's brain than the constant word salad would have suggested. And now, he was going to meet someone like Josh who just proved something like that. He also thought of the phone call from yesterday morning, the voice from the past trying to weasel back into his present. This was the witness that the voice was calling about, demanding that Chuck take care of her, dispose of her, or his reputation, his job, and very likely, his own life would be at risk. Chuck thought again of Josh. "He started saying your name, Chuck." Garrett's voice jumped again into his mind.

Chuck stood from his chair and walked slowly over to the window and gazed out at the pine trees that surrounded the police station. He was being given a second chance. For Josh. For his sister.

He would protect Sandra with his life.

CHAPTER FORTY-ONE

Quinn woke with a startle Sunday morning to the rising sun warming his face, still in the clothes he was wearing from the night before. He quickly scrambled through his bed sheets looking for his gun. It was nowhere to be found! *Gary has been in here,* he thought. *He's probably in the bathroom right now just waiting for me to wake up. Or maybe it's Wesley. Maybe he wanted to do it himself, which is why Gary was so calm last night. He was just waiting for Wesley to come as soon as I went up to bed.*

Quinn stepped off the bed softly, thinking he could sneak out of the room without whoever was in the bathroom knowing. As his foot touched the ground, he felt the cold metal of his handgun brush against his heel. He looked down quickly and there it was, inconspicuously lying on the carpet next to his bed.

Quinn breathed out a deep sigh. *Get it together, idiot! You need to get it together! Today, you need to stop cowering in your room and go on the offensive. Gary said he saw a girl that he thought was the witness. She would be priority number one. Gary would be next, but I need his help to find her.*

Quinn had spent last evening at home, one eye on Gary and another on game film of the Butte Central Catholic football team, the team they were scheduled to play next Friday night.

Watching game film was his normal way of relieving stress, but last night, he couldn't focus. He kept expecting Gary to pull out a gun and end it all right there. Gary, however, seemed calm and undisturbed ever since he had come home from "running errands" yesterday afternoon.

Quinn had turned down an offer from his friends to go out, saying that he didn't feel well and wanted to rest. In retrospect, maybe he should have gone. He needed something to distract him, and watching film wasn't cutting it. So as soon as he could break away without it seeming too suspicious, he left Gary and went up to his room.

After he had locked the bedroom door behind him, Quinn pulled out his gun from where he had it tucked in the back of his pants. He paced around the room a few times and then sat on his bed. Resting with his back against the headboard and facing the bedroom door, he gripped his gun tightly in both hands. *If anyone comes through that door, I'll be ready,* he thought. He tried to keep his eyes open but the all-nighter from the previous night caught up to him, and his lids became very heavy.

. . .

James Slater was there, sleeping in his recliner. *You are why my dad is in prison,* Quinn thought, as he stared at the resting man. *You ruined my family, and you can just sleep there soundly, in your nice little cabin in the woods? I don't think so.*

Quinn felt the grip of his gun getting warm in his hand as he raised it and pointed at Slater's forehead. Suddenly a black hole appeared in the middle of the pasty white skin.

Nothing happened at first. Slater didn't move, and the hole didn't change. After a long minute, Slater's eyes opened and stared accusingly at Quinn. A smirking grin spread across his face as a trickle of blood dripped from the hole and meandered its way below the center of his eyebrows. It dripped from his nose and formed a small pool of blood at the base of his feet.

Quinn lowered the gun slowly. Slater started laughing, softly at first and then louder and louder until the room was echoing. The trickle of blood turned into a steady flow, and the pool on the floor got bigger, spreading to where Quinn was standing. He stepped back quickly, but the blood followed and surrounded him. Quinn tried to jump over it, but as he leapt from the ground, the blood expanded causing Quinn to land in the middle of the slippery, sticky pool. Quinn started running, leaving behind him a trail of bloody prints—his prints this time.

A fountain of blood began spewing from the hole in Slater's forehead, forming a red avalanche that was coming right for Quinn. Quinn ran harder, trying desperately to escape, when his foot caught on something on the ground causing him to fall hard on his face. When he looked back, he saw Adam Bend's outstretched hand gripping his ankle. Adam started laughing, too, as they both became immersed in a thick coagulating mass of blood, mixed with floating pieces of skull and brain tissue.

· · ·

Quinn bent over, picked up the gun, and headed into the bathroom. He splashed his face with cold water and looked in the mirror. *Play it cool, Quinn. Don't show your fear.* He changed his clothes and tucked his gun again into the waist of his pants. Then he opened the bedroom door and went down the stairs.

Gary was sitting at the kitchen table, casually reading the newspaper and drinking a cup of coffee. He looked up when Quinn entered the room.

"You look better," he observed, as he folded the paper in front of him.

"Yeah. I got some sleep," Quinn replied, trying to act nonchalantly. He went to the fridge, grabbed some orange juice, and threw a couple pieces of toast in the toaster. He then grabbed a plate for the toast and sat down across from Gary.

"So," he said, after taking a first bite. "What's the plan?"

"No plan. Not today," Gary replied.

"Really? You got nothing?"

"We don't need to do anything yet. That will only bring attention to ourselves. The cop thinks you were home. The other three are locked up with more than enough evidence against them. Slater is dead. Nothing has changed. We stick to the original plan."

"Yeah ... but aren't you forgetting something? You know, the witness? Does Wesley know about that?"

Gary looked hard at Quinn for a pause. "He knows. And I know."

"And he doesn't think it's a problem?"

Gary's countenance changed a shade darker, but he suppressed it with another sip of coffee. "We have a way to solve that little problem, and it doesn't involve you."

"What do you mean it doesn't involve me? You think I'm just going to let it slide? That picture links me to the crime and blows my alibi."

"I said it will be taken care of!" Gary's voice now stern. "The less you know the better. Remember, if you get caught, then I get caught too. And I'm not about to get caught. You'll just have to trust me."

"Just trust you, huh? Not sure I can do that, *Dad*!" Quinn said with a sarcastic emphasis.

"You don't have a choice!" Gary said, pounding the table with his hand.

"Yeah? We'll see about that." Quinn stood up and flung his plate across the dining room, smashing it against the wall. He grabbed his keys and went into the garage, slamming the door behind him. A minute later, Gary heard the deep roar of the engine of Quinn's Mustang and then the squeal of tires as it raced away from the house.

Gary picked up his coffee cup and took another sip. Then he took his phone out from his pocket and pushed a few buttons.

"Yeah, it's me … Not well … I think we are going to have to push ahead … Okay … I'll let you know." He finished the call and went to the pantry to get the broom.

CHAPTER FORTY-TWO

Atkins finished answering the questions that the Kalispel police officers asked him, at least most of them. Ever since he learned of a police officer planting evidence in that Chicago case, evidence that convicted three innocent young men, Atkins had trust issues with local police. Some could be bought. So, especially in cases dealing with organized crime, he implemented the "need-to-know" principle and tried to keep as much close to his own vest as possible. He told them about Slater being murdered in Whitefish and that he had powerful enemies and that this morning was an attempt by those enemies to intimidate the investigating officer. The other details he kept to himself.

As soon as the police released him from questioning, he got into his car to plan his next move. He needed to call Chief Peters and find out if anything happened in the case overnight. But he hesitated. *Is the Whitefish Chief of Police a good cop or a bad cop?* Atkins was still trying to figure it out. *He used to work in Chicago. That's a point against him. But he left and is in small town Montana. What good would he do the crime bosses here? Point for him. Then again, he happens to be the Chief of Police in the town where Slater was assigned for witness protection. Could that just be a coincidence? Point against. He's been here for over ten years. Point for. He was one of two people who knew where I was staying. Huge point against. So far, he's losing. I'm just going to bring it up and see how he reacts.*

"Peters? Atkins. How are things? Any new information?"

"Good morning, Agent. As a matter of fact, I do have something to tell you about. How is your morning going?"

"Hmm. Interesting question. It was going great until someone tried to kill me in my motel room about an hour ago. I'm a little curious there, Chief. There are only a couple of people who know where I'm staying, and you're one of those. Should I have reason to be concerned about you? We're on the same team, right?"

"Atkins. Hang up." Chuck said, his tone changed, assuming a new urgency. "Hang up and call me on a different line."

"Me? You think my phone is bugged? My phone has FBI security measures built into it. If anything, it's your phone. You hang up!"

"Fine. Let's meet in person. Back at Slater's. Thirty minutes. Okay?"

"You're not going to shoot me when I get there, are you?"

"Atkins, it's not me! Just meet me there. It'll be just you and me. Okay?"

"I'll see you there," Atkins ended the call and looked at his phone. *Impossible*, he thought. *Is someone in the FBI listening to my conversation? Did Donovan or O'Brien have someone at the FBI on their payroll, too?*

Thirty minutes later, Atkins pulled his car into Slater's driveway. Chuck was already waiting. He raised both hands as Atkins got out of his car, just to be sure Atkins knew that he had no bad intentions.

"Let's go inside," Chuck said and led the way up the porch steps. They went in and sat at the dining room table.

"This is a safe place to talk. I've scanned it already for bugs," Chuck began.

"If you say so, Peters. But if you are connected to the murderers, you would lie about that, wouldn't you?" Atkins said with no trace of sarcasm.

"Atkins. I'm going to tell you something right now that you must swear to me that you won't repeat to anyone. At least, not yet. I promise that you'll understand why in a few minutes. I've got to be able to trust you, though. More innocent lives depend on it." Chuck gazed hard at Atkins, his forehead wrinkled with intensity.

"Well, Peters. I'm not sure how to make that promise without knowing what it is," Atkins said flatly.

"Okay, Atkins, I guess I'm going to have to just tell you and hope you are smart enough to follow me along on this one," Chuck said and took a deep breath. "I know the guys that killed Slater. And it wasn't those three teenagers."

"Well, we figured that Donovan was in on it. That's not incredibly shocking. Is that it?"

"No, Atkins. What I said was that I *know* those guys. Donovan, O'Brien, the rest. I know them because I used to work for them." Chuck paused, waiting for the reaction. Atkins just stared at him, not saying anything.

"You heard me, right?" Chuck continued.

"I heard you, Peters. Go on."

"It was when I lived in Chicago. They paid me. I didn't want to, but they held my family for ransom. I didn't feel like I had a choice back then. Well, obviously, it was the wrong choice and when I tried to get out of it, they killed my mother and my younger sister. I left town, and they let me go. I guess they figured I had suffered enough. I have an older brother who has a family. He is their insurance policy that I wouldn't turn them in. I haven't heard anything from them since, until ... "

"Until?" Atkins coaxed.

"Yesterday morning," Chuck confessed. "Yesterday morning, I got a call from O'Brien. You know him, right?"

"We know him," Atkins acknowledged.

"He's got a thick accent. Irish. I'll never forget his voice. He was the one that called me after I held my dying sister for the last time," Chuck said, his voice cracking with emotion. "Anyway, yesterday, he told me that he had another job for me. Then he sent me a picture of my disabled nephew who lives in North Carolina. Atkins! I don't care what happens to me. I really don't. But you have got to protect what is left of my family! You've got to give me that!" Chuck was trembling now.

"We'll take care of it, Peters. What did O'Brien ask you to do?"

"He said there was a witness to the crime. At least someone who witnessed the body being disposed of. He wanted me to get rid of that witness if they showed up. Well, they showed up. This morning. At least, the mother of the witness did."

"The mother?"

"Yes. The witness is an adult but is disabled. Has autism. Same as my nephew, by the way. She has very limited language but typed out a message in kind of a code, and she has a picture on her phone according to her mother. I haven't seen the picture. I did read the message though. It says 'I saw them bury a body in the woods. There were three of them. I saw their faces.'"

"A code? What kind of code?"

"I'd have to show you. It's quite remarkable, actually. She had never communicated on that level before. Atkins, I will go to the grave to defend her from them. Or prison. You have to believe me. I didn't tell anyone where you were staying. Don't trust anyone, Atkins, including those in the FBI. I've learned firsthand how persuasive these guys can be."

Atkins didn't say anything. He stood up and paced around the room for a few minutes. Chuck stayed seated and let him think.

Atkins stopped at the window and gazed out at the surrounding woods. *It's beautiful here,* he thought.

"Okay, Peters. You've got me. I'll let you take the lead with the witness. Let's nail those bastards this time. But after that, no promises. Do you understand? I'll put a detail on your brother's family. Don't call him yet though. We'll tell him after our business is done here. Deal?"

"Deal."

CHAPTER FORTY-THREE

Sandra returned from her hike feeling more energized and ate the food her mom had prepared for her. She really wanted to get back to her apartment and have a warm shower.

"Mom. Home?" Sandra said to Susan who was busy cleaning the kitchen.

"Okay, Sandy," Susan replied. "Can I walk with you? Or we can drive it, if you want."

"Drive."

"Okay, let me get my things. I'll be ready in two minutes, okay?"

"Okay."

Sandra paced around the living room, waiting for her mom, and processing the events of the morning. Now the police knew about her, and she was committed. *I guess there is no more going back*, she thought. *I shouldn't want to go back, should I? Back to the tower of my castle prison? I was safe there. But now?*

"Let's go," Susan interrupted her thoughts.

Sandra followed Susan out of the door, and they drove the three blocks between their homes. Sandra opened the door of her condo, and Susan went inside.

"Can I see the picture on your phone, Sandy?" Susan asked after she had removed her jacket and saw Sandra's phone sitting on the kitchen counter.

Sandra didn't respond at first. She didn't really feel like looking at it herself. The image was already permanently imprinted in her mind, and each time she saw it, more copies would be front and center.

Susan felt Sandra's hesitance and guessed correctly about the cause of it. "You don't have to see it. I just want to let the chief know what's in it. He asked if I could."

Sandra nodded but then went into her bedroom and closed the door. Susan could hear the shower turn on. She picked up the phone and opened the pictures folder. The photo was a little fuzzy, but it showed three figures standing in a small clearing, two of whom were holding shovels and the other held a gun. They were all looking at the camera. The one with the gun was the most in focus. He was scowling. Susan had never seen any of them before, but they all looked young, probably high school age or maybe early twenties. Anyway, she was sure that this would be very helpful to the police investigation. She picked up her own phone from her purse and dialed the number Chief Peters had given her.

"Chief Peters," Chuck answered.

"Chief, this is Susan Lewis. I'm at Sandra's condo with her now, and I saw the picture. It's kind of blurry, but I think it'll still be helpful."

"Great. We can clean it up. I need to see it though. It's better not to send it electronically. I'm going to have to get her phone. What's that going to do to Sandra?"

"Oh, she'll be fine without her phone. The only reason she has it is that I insist that she take it with her on her hikes so she can call me if she gets in trouble. I can get her a new one."

"Mrs. Lewis, I am not trying to push Sandra faster than she is ready for, but this case is moving at light-speed now, and there are some dangerous actors involved. I need to collect that evidence and meet your daughter. Can I come over now?"

"I understand, Chief Peters. I need to prepare her, though. I already told her it would be tomorrow. If she has a panic attack about meeting you today, it will set everything back, maybe permanently. I'll call you back, okay?"

Susan waited for Sandra to get out of the shower and to get dressed. When she came out, they both sat on the couch.

"Sandra, I called Chief Peters when you were in the shower and told him about your picture. He really needs to come and get it today, sweetheart. I know that everything is probably moving faster than you are prepared for, but someone was murdered, Sandy, and your picture might just get the bad guys behind bars before they kill somebody else, we don't know. Can you be strong again today?"

Sandra knew that her mother was right and knew that this was coming as soon as she made contact with the police. She really didn't feel ready, but did she have a choice? She had already made the decision when she typed that message. Actually, it was before that. It was when she stepped out behind a tree, into the clearing, to take the picture. That was the moment that changed her life forever. She couldn't really take that moment back, so it was up to her to make it all worth it.

"Okay, Mom. It's okay."

...

Chuck knocked on Sandra's door softly. Susan had coached him well. He wasn't wearing his uniform, again at Susan's suggestion. Susan opened the door and let him in. She led him into the sensory room where Sandra had been pacing since her mom had called him back and told him that he could come.

"Sandra, this is Chief Peters, the officer that I told you about. He is here to get your phone but also to meet you," Susan said.

Sandra stopped pacing for a brief pause and stole a glance at Chuck. *He's big,* she thought, *but his face is kind.* She started pacing again.

Chuck smiled at Sandra and eased his body down onto the mat with his back leaning against the wall. He didn't say anything for a few minutes and just gave Sandra a chance to get used to him being there. He watched Sandra out of the corner of his eye but was careful not to stare at her.

Sandra felt some of the anxiety leave her body, and her pacing slowed down. Chuck just waited, patient and non-threatening. He could see that Sandra was becoming much calmer and was looking at him whenever he pretended not to notice. She was a pretty girl—blond hair, athletic build, a healthy tan. The yellow blouse she was wearing accentuated the bright blue of her eyes. After a few more minutes, Sandra sat down on an exercise ball and was still.

Chuck spoke, almost in a whisper. "Hi, Sandra. My name is Chief Peters, but I'd like you to call me Chuck. That's because I don't want you to be afraid of me. I want to be your friend."

"Hi," Sandra said. "Hi, Chuck."

Chuck smiled. "Hi, Sandra. Can I tell you something? I have a nephew with autism. He is a lot like you, actually. He's one of my favorite people in the world."

Sandra looked at him but didn't say anything. She could tell he wasn't lying, though. His eyes spoke the truth.

Chuck continued, "Sandra, I saw your message. And I know that you are telling the truth. What you said really happened. We found the person that you saw buried." He paused and didn't say anything else for a couple of minutes.

Sandra liked him. He wasn't talking down to her, didn't make her feel stupid.

Chuck spoke again. "Your mom told me how you figured out a way to type that message for us. I think it was brilliant. I can't even imagine what you have been through since witnessing that crime. But even more, I can't imagine what it's been like for you to not be able to communicate before now. And then to figure it out on your own. You are obviously a strong and intelligent woman."

Sandra smiled. Her soul was buzzing. *He gets it. He knows I'm in here.*

"Sandra, I just have one request right now," Chuck said.

Sandra held his gaze for almost a minute and then again looked away.

"Practice typing. Every day, okay? I need you to practice. If you practice, it will get easier. Eventually, I'm going to need to ask you some questions. There will be no rush to answer, but the better you get at typing, the easier it will be on you, okay? You are very important to this investigation, Sandra. Don't let that scare you. I just think that what you have to say is going to make a big difference. So, practice every day. Will you do that?" Chuck asked encouragingly.

"Okay," Sandra said and smiled again. She could do that. Yes, she wanted to do that. Typing every day would be hard on her. It took so much of her energy. But she wanted to get better, to get faster with fewer mistakes. Maybe if she practiced enough, she could even do away with the highlights.

Chuck got up with a bit of a groan. "That's a long way down for an old man," he said with a wink. "We'll see you soon, Sandra. Maybe I can drop by tomorrow. Would that be okay? Just to say hi?"

"Yes, okay," Sandra said, a little laugh escaping from her mouth. She felt good. She felt great, in fact.

Chuck left the sensory room and headed toward the front door. Susan gave him a thumbs up when he looked behind him before stepping into the hall.

He was the perfect person for this job, Susan thought.

CHAPTER FORTY-FOUR

Wesley closed his phone and sat for a few minutes in the shade of his poolside cabana. Gary had just let him know about what had happened with Quinn that morning. Quinn's attitude was an interference, for sure, but ultimately might work in their favor. It was their plan all along for Quinn to get caught for Slater's murder and to go to prison, out of the way while they finished the take-over of Frank's business. Frank had to be kept in the dark for a few more months. By then, it would be too late.

They had initially planned on waiting until closer to the trial before they uncovered the evidence that would put Quinn at the scene and would clear Gary of any involvement. But now, someone else had evidence. Better evidence. And Quinn knew he was trapped unless that witness was found and disposed of. His little outburst that morning showed that he was feeling the heat. They just needed to be sure that the witness got to the trial and that Frank didn't figure anything out to notify Quinn that he was being set up.

Gary would keep an eye on Quinn. Wesley needed to pay a visit to his boss, that is...former boss. Wesley smiled and raised a glass of wine, toasting himself in the air. "To you, Frank. Thanks for setting this all up for my future.

. . .

"Wesley, it's been a few months since I've seen you," Frank said after he sat in the chair behind the plexiglass wall and picked up the phone. "I was starting to miss you. You know I can still get mail in here, right?"

"Yes, I'm really sorry Frank. We've been opening a new recruitment service in Cambodia. You know how hectic that gets. How have you been, my friend? Are they treating you well?"

"Well, it is a prison, so ... "

"Yeah. Frank, I'm so sorry you're here. Our team of lawyers are working overtime on your appeals. We hope by the end of the year ... Anyway, I have some excellent news to give you."

"Oh yeah? I could use some of that right now. What is it?"

"Slater ... It's done. Friday night. It was a clean kill. And message conveyed. Blue tarp, you know, the works."

"Excellent! That rat had it coming. Who did you pin it on?"

"I don't know. Three local kids. Quinn picked them out. He told them that the guy needed help moving stuff and sent them in. Slater was already dead. Gary shot him while he was asleep in his chair. Quinn took off and never went inside. Gary made the boys bury the body and then drove them to Canada. He ditched them at a local gas station and called the police to go pick up the three killers. Quinn helped get some of the stuff from their houses that we planted at the scene. Plus, there were footprints, and Gary made one of them hold the murder weapon. Gary was wearing a mask the whole time, and Quinn had another alibi. Don't worry, the boys will be convicted. You know how local police don't like to keep cases open. Small towns need to feel safe. Catching the murderers will make everyone feel better."

"The FBI will be involved, Wesley. Slater was in witness protection. They won't be as easily fooled."

"True, but we have that covered. First, remember Chuck Peters, the cop in Chicago who tried to get out of his commitment to us?"

"Sure. We taught him a very hard lesson."

"Well, he moved to Whitefish. He's the chief of police there. I gave him a little phone call—a reminder of whose side he was on. I reminded him that we were forever friends. He'll help with the FBI. Plus, we have some FBI higher ups on our payroll. It'll all work out just fine. I guarantee it."

"Okay, Wesley. I believe you. How did Quinn handle it?"

"Like a true professional. I can see why you believe in him. He should be coming home in a few months, after the dust settles. I know he can't wait to see you."

"Fantastic! Please tell him that I'm proud of him."

"Of course I will, boss," Wesley smiled reassuringly.

They spent the rest of Frank's time talking about business details and ensuring that everyone was getting paid and remaining loyal. Then, Wesley was escorted out and Frank sent back to his cell. "That should buy us a few weeks at least," Wesley said to himself, as he walked away from the prison and climbed into his Audi.

CHAPTER FORTY-FIVE

Sandra stayed in her sensory room after Chuck left. Her mom also went out and shut the door behind her. Sandra's emotions were running on high alert now. *The policeman seemed nice enough, but they always do when they are on your side. What if he sees the picture and gets mad because it's blurry, or what if I can't handle things in court and I have a meltdown on the stand? How could a jury view my testimony as reliable if I come across as crazy or unintelligent?*

It took all that she had inside of her to type that simple message in the quiet of her own apartment. She didn't think that she could do it in the middle of a crowded courtroom with lawyers pelting her with questions and a judge looking down on her. There was no way that her brain could focus in that setting. She told Chief Peters that she would practice, and she would, but could she really expect to become proficient enough in such a short timeframe? It took her twenty-seven years to get to that simple message. How many more years would it take to type under pressure?

The more she thought about it, the worse she felt and the more that she wished she had never taken that picture. The cops found the body without her. She was sure they could solve the crime without her, too. But now she had identified herself, and there was no backing out. A murder case? Why a murder case of all things? But would she have done it for anything less?

Sandra turned on some music and laid down beneath her punching bag. She got it spinning with a slap from her hand and then focused on the ceiling where the chain hooked into a bolt. The rotating red bag caused her peripheral vision to blur and brought the hook and chain into an almost exaggerated clarity. There were nine links of the chain from the ceiling to the bag that all rotated slowly, forming tight circles. Over and over, she slapped the bag to keep it moving and looked at the links. Nine links in a chain. The first link barely moved, the second a little more. By the ninth link, the chain made a basketball-sized arc.

Nine links, each connected to one before and one after, creating a cone of progressively larger arcs. As she watched each link, one at a time, she felt little circles of light descend from the chain, in proportional sizes to the arcs that each link had formed. Her mother, who had given to her everything that she had to give—her sweat, her tears, her love, her knowledge, her patience—she was the closest circle of light. Sandra felt it surround her and then absorb into her body.

Her father was next. He was her rock, her stable force, her teacher, her advocate. The second circle. It also descended over and then disappeared inside of her. She could feel the jolt of its energy.

She thought of her grandparents. Two on each side. Four more circles, a little farther removed. She didn't know them well. They all had died before she could spend any time with them, but she felt them now. They were there, giving her light when times were dark. Four more circles surrounding her, not absorbed but giving her power.

The last three circles, the largest, descended from the chain, hovered for a minute above her and then merged into one. The ring descended further, encircling her like a protective force field, and filled the room with light. She felt its power, a familiar strength. It was the same power that she felt when she walked into the woods.

Sandra was not raised with religion. Tony and Susan had never expressed any interest in church. Going to a church meeting would be the last thing that Sandra could handle. The singing and clapping and Praise-the-Lord's that she had seen in the movies would just create anxiety in her. But Sandra had developed her own kind of spirituality. The woods were her place of refuge, her temple, the river, the trees and the animals, her godhead. They taught her, gave her comfort, cleansed her, protected her, called her to come home. If there was a heaven, she already knew what it would be like for her.

Sandra let the swinging bag come to a rest just inches above her face, filling her visual field with nothing but red leather. Red. The color of anger. Did she feel angry about her situation? She stared at the bag and tried to analyze her own emotions. She felt fearful and anxious, both because she was worried that she was in danger as a witness and because of the overwhelming tasks ahead of her. She felt sad that a person had been killed. She felt proud that she figured out a monumental step forward in her abilities. But anger wasn't part of any of it. She was motivated only by her desire to do the right thing.

She felt strength in her resolve and now knew that she would not have to face it alone. The rings of light were with her, part of her, there to strengthen and protect. She was ready to finish the job she had started when her camera's flash of light exposed a deep darkness that had contaminated her woods.

Sandra pushed away the red of the bag and got to her feet before it could swing back into her. It was time to get to work. After leaving the sensory room, she saw her mom sitting on the couch with her eyes closed. At the sound of Sandra's footsteps, Susan opened her eyes.

"Hi, Sandy, are you okay?"

"Good."

"Do you need anything?"

"Type."

Sandra went over to the kitchen table and opened her laptop. She sat down in front of a blank white document page and looked down at the letters on the keyboard. They were vibrating in place but identifiable. She reached out a finger to type her name. The S started shaking violently but stayed in its position. She felt her finger connect with the key, and a single capital S appeared on the screen. Sandra smiled broadly. Success on her first try. The remaining letters of her name behaved in a similar way, and on the screen, emerged a perfect S-A-N-D-R-A. She closed the laptop and let out a huge sigh. It was time to go to the woods.

CHAPTER FORTY-SIX

Quinn drove through town trying to calm down and plan his next move. Maybe Gary was right, and he just needed to lay low and let the original plan unfold. Everything would have been fine if it wasn't for that picture. Gary said he knew who it was, but could he be trusted? If Gary and Wesley were setting him up to get caught, they would tell him to leave it all up to them, wouldn't they? As of this moment, Quinn didn't think that the police knew he was involved. That cop seemed satisfied with his alibi when he left their house yesterday. *I can't just let it go. There is something that Gary isn't telling me,* Quinn decided.

He drove toward Slater's place and parked his car off another dirt access road close by. He was going to search the woods himself and try to find any clues about the picture taker. He had to find whoever it was and take care of it himself.

Quinn got out of the car and started hiking along a deer trail that led behind Slater's cabin. As he approached, he could see the yellow tape wrapped around the trees and the pile of fresh dirt where they had uncovered the body. No one was there. He moved slowly now, careful not to leave any prints. He worked his way around to where he remembered the flash coming from and scoured the area for clues. There was nothing, except some bent grass.

Quinn started retracing his own steps that night. He remembered running uphill and taking a path that broke to the left. There was another path that went right. Maybe that was the path the picture-taker had chosen. The path to the right led to the stream. He followed it slowly as the sound of the water became louder. The ground was dry on the trail and not amenable to retaining footprints, although the path was clearly used by humans. That was obvious. It was wider and more worn than a typical animal trail. He continued hiking until he could see the stream. It wasn't large but not easy to cross at that spot. It would have been a good place to hide in the dark, though.

Quinn left the path and followed the edge of the water. The stream had cut a serpentine course through the woods with sections of rapids and areas where it coalesced into small pools. It was hard navigating through the tangles of driftwood and new growth along its banks, but Quinn pushed on. At one of the wider turns in the stream, there was a cut-away in the embankment from the many years of heavy spring overflow, and it formed a little cave covered by an overhang of rocks and trees. *That would be the perfect spot to hide*, Quinn thought, as he approached it from below. He entered the hollow and looked around. The ground was a mix of small gravel and soft dirt. Quinn sat on his haunches for a few minutes and just listened. The sound of the water echoed from the wall, drowning out the other sounds of the forest, and creating a peaceful white noise.

He examined the ground carefully. The hollow could fit six people comfortably. He saw no other signs of human activity— no trash, no remains of a campfire, no cigarette butts, none of the other traces that humans typically leave behind. As he moved to the upstream end, however, the ground became firmer, more compacted. *Someone had been here,* Quinn thought. He could see edges of footprints in the sandy ground but not a definable print.

Quinn left the hollow and looked on the uphill side for an alternate way down into it. Sure enough, there he saw some broken tree branches and disrupted earth leading down the embankment. He was picking his way up the side when he saw it—a perfect, intact footprint. It was much smaller than his own, definitely not from a man. *It was unlikely that a kid would be over here by himself. Probably a woman, a smallish woman,* Quinn thought as he snapped a picture of the print. The pattern of the sole was clearly visible. He followed the trail made by the print until he came to the original man-made path that he had started out on. *A woman.* He was looking for a woman. Maybe a teenage girl. Maybe he even knew her. He doubted that someone not from Whitefish would be wandering around on these trails at night and would know the perfect place to hide.

Quinn kept hiking up the path that followed the river. The woods were quiet. Very few people must come here, even on a weekend. The path eventually forked again with one arm of it heading directly to the stream and the other heading further uphill. He chose the fork leading to the stream. As he approached, he saw a series of flat boulders spaced across the water creating a natural bridge. He stepped from rock to rock until he reached the other side. There were now trails leading in both directions adjacent to the stream. He followed the one heading downhill until it ended at a moderately-sized pool of water with a large flat rock hanging over it where you could sit with your feet close enough to soak in the pool. From that vantage point, he could see the rooftops of some nearby condos. He knew where he was now. Those condos were on the way up to the ski resort.

I bet she lives there, Quinn thought. *I'm just going to settle in here for a while and see if I get lucky.*

Quinn found a spot behind a tree where he could see the pool, the rock, and the path as it emerged from the trees. He made himself comfortable and resolved to wait for a few hours if needed. It was nice here, anyway. The quiet could do his mind some good.

CHAPTER FORTY-SEVEN

Agent Atkins left Slater's cabin after meeting with Chief Peters and drove to the nearest rental car agency. He left his FBI-issued car there, along with his cell phone, and rented a Ford Explorer. He then drove to a nearby town, Columbia Falls, and rented a suite in an extended stay hotel, paid for up front with cash. Now he felt more comfortable that his movements would be untraceable, at least remotely, and he would be watching very carefully for anyone who might be following him. He then went back to Whitefish and set up an office in a spare room at the police station furnished with a desktop computer and a landline telephone. His first call was to his supervisor at the FBI.

"This is Director Henry Call. How did you get this phone number?" Call said after an unregistered number appeared on his cell phone display.

"Sir, it's me, Atkins."

"Atkins? What are you doing calling me from an unsecured line?"

"Well, sir, someone tried to kill me in my hotel room this morning. Only the FBI and the Whitefish chief of police knew where I was staying. I have already met with Chief Peters, and he gave me a convincing argument why it wasn't him. So, with all due respect, sir, my confidence in our supposedly secure conversations is not all that high at the moment." Atkins spoke calmly but with the intensity of someone whose life was under threat.

"What? Someone shot at you?" Call asked with surprise.

"Well, I didn't mention that detail specifically, but yes, that is what happened," Atkins replied, his suspicion of his director now several marks higher. "And they left me a little note, wrapped around a brick—old school-like. The note said, 'Leave it be.' It seems that someone isn't too happy about me reopening old wounds."

"I'm sorry, Atkins," Call said, sounding sincere. "There are powerful criminals involved in those cases. They have bought their influence in a wide network. As much as I'd like to tell you otherwise, I can't be sure that that doesn't include this agency. Money has a way of corrupting even good people. You are kicking a hornet's nest, I'm afraid. Are you sure it's worth it? I could get you out of there immediately."

"No, sir. I will see it through. I'm going to need a new laptop, though. My other one is quite incapacitated. A dozen bullet holes will do that."

"Atkins, I will personally see to it that you get a clean machine, even if I have to deliver it myself. I've been in this position for ten years now. Although you can never be 100% certain, there are people here that I would trust with my life, or more importantly, the life of my family. I'll get you a clean machine! You'll have it by tomorrow. Don't use your phone. You'll get a new one of those, too. I'll contact you through the police station, or you can call again from this number, but only this number. Okay?"

"Okay, sir."

"Atkins?"

"Yes, sir?"

"I'm glad it's you."

"Sir?"

"I'm glad you are there working on this case. I think you are onto something. Clearly someone else does, too. Be careful."

"I'll do my best," Atkins said and hung up the phone. He looked around the bare room and decided that he was going to take the rest of the day off. There wasn't much else he could do today without his laptop. He needed to interview the three suspects that were waiting in jail. He would do that tomorrow. They should have their attorneys with them, and that wasn't going to happen on a Sunday anyway. He already knew what they were going to say. They weren't the culprits. He knew that. He just needed to be able to prove it, or it was likely that with all of the evidence against them, they would still end up being convicted.

Atkins stood up, a little stiff from his dive on the motel floor earlier that morning and grabbed his jacket. Down the hall, Chuck was planning his next steps when his thoughts were interrupted by a knock on his door.

"Yeah. Come on in," Chuck spoke loudly.

Atkins opened the door and poked his head in the room. "Chief, I'm taking a drive. I need some time to process the day's events. I'll pick up a burner phone and call you from it so that you'll have a way to get ahold of me until I get my new phone from the FBI."

"Sounds good, Atkins. Be careful out there!" Chuck replied.

Atkins closed the door behind him and left the department. He walked a few blocks away to where he had parked his rental SUV in the parking lot of a Safeway grocery store. He made note of all the cars that passed him and tried to register faces in his memory. He would get suspicious if he started seeing faces or vehicles that he recognized.

Once he got into the Explorer, he drove around some quiet backstreets, making a lot of random turns until he was confident that no one was tailing him. Then he headed for Glacier National Park.

The drive to the park took about 45 minutes from where he was. It was a clear late summer afternoon with a bright blue Montana sky and a warm but pleasant sun. *It's hard to believe that I am investigating a big city crime like murder in a place as beautiful as this*, Atkins thought, as he followed the curves of the mountain highway.

After driving through the entrance of the park, he continued along the scenic drive around Lake McDonald and started on the ascent up the mountain.

"I want to see a glacier," he said to himself. "I want to sense its power, to feel its quiet destructive force, to see how it changed its own landscape."

As he neared one of the trailheads, he slowed his SUV suddenly when he spotted a small herd of big horn sheep congregating at the side of the road. He watched them watch him. There were two rams in the group. They soon lost interest in him and wandered off into the trees, the ewes following behind.

Atkins pulled ahead to the trailhead parking lot and parked his vehicle. At that altitude, the air carried a bit of a chill but also the fragrance of pine trees and wildflowers. The parking area was almost full, though no one was around.

Atkins started hiking on the well-marked trail as it traversed through a high meadow. As soon as he could, he found a smaller branch from the main trail and followed it along. He needed to be away from people today. That branch climbed through the patchy evergreens that were warped and bent by the extreme living conditions that they endured. He continued up a rise and found a vantage point that was partially hidden between two large crops of granite boulders. From here, he could see several glacier fields, their white tongues extending down the face of the rugged peaks.

He leaned his back against the rock where he was sitting, closed his eyes, and rested. *I'll deal with the rest tomorrow. Today, I am going to focus on a brighter future*, he thought as he drifted off to sleep.

CHAPTER FORTY-EIGHT

Sandra grabbed her jacket and her house key and opened her front door.

"Sandra! Be careful!" Susan called after her as Sandra was exiting the door. "I'll be waiting here for you. And watching you on the laptop. Don't go too far!"

Sandra shut the door and headed downstairs. When she got to the parking lot, she hesitated, once again looking for unfamiliar cars. This would be her new routine.

All was well, so she moved across and onto the welcoming trail. Today she wanted to feel the comfort of her favorite spot by the stream. The cool water would feel good on her feet.

She moved along the trail, walking carefully—out of habit, not fear. The woods were quiet. The animals seemed unalarmed, as she heard none of the warning signals that had become familiar over the years.

When she arrived at the stream, she climbed out onto the rock, took off her shoes and socks, and sat down with her feet plunging into the clear water, sending a chill up her spine but waking her soul.

She sat for a few minutes, her face bathed in a ray of sunshine that had found its way through the trees. The warmth of the sun contrasted sharply to the cold of the water circulating gently around her feet. She tried to settle in, to feel the power of nature start to refill her battery with its energy.

But something felt wrong. She couldn't pinpoint it. The woods remained calm, and her favorite spot was undisturbed. She hadn't seen anyone on the trail. Yet, her soul was unsettled.

Something is wrong! She couldn't explain it, but she knew that it was true. She felt like she was being watched. She had never felt that way in the woods before, at least not in a threatening way.

I need to leave, she thought. *I need to go home, now!* She felt the panic starting to build in her from the place deep inside, like the bubbling lava of a volcano before it erupted.

She quickly took her feet out of the water, dried them off with her jacket, put her socks and shoes back on, and jumped to her feet. She scanned the woods around her for any signs of another human but saw none. The sounds of the stream drowned out all the other noise in this spot, so she could only rely on her eyes and her instincts. She hurried back onto the trail and headed for home as fast as she could without running. She wished she were like a deer who could just bound away in seconds until it found a safer place.

The feeling was getting stronger. It was like everything had reversed. Now she couldn't wait to get out of the woods and to be around other people. She was afraid to be alone.

She reached the parking lot and hurried across, this time not waiting to count the cars. When she reached the access door to the building, she quickly punched in her code and hurried inside. She was up the first flight of stairs when she suddenly paused. *The door didn't latch!* She didn't hear it latch!

In a panic, she sprinted up the next two flights and down the hall to her condo. She grabbed her keys from her pocket but fumbled with them for what seemed like forever until she was finally able to get the key into the slot on the doorknob. As the door opened and she quickly stepped inside, her heart felt like it stopped for a full minute.

There was a voice, a man's voice. Where was it coming from? It sounded like it was inside her condo, but how could that be?

She was trapped! Where was her mother? Had they found her here? Should she run back out? No, she couldn't. Someone had followed her. She was sure of that. The woods had told her.

As she stood frozen in place next to her entrance, her hand still on the doorknob, another voice rang out from her sensory room.

"Sandra? Is that you?" It was her mother. A second later, Susan's head poked out of the sensory room's door. "Why are you back so soon?"

Sandra couldn't say anything. Her voice was nowhere to be found. When she was in panic mode, it scurried away underground like a groundhog that saw a hawk diving for it, ready for a quick meal.

"Sandra, Chief Peters stopped by to check on us. Isn't that nice?"

Sandra felt her heart start beating again, and she filled her lungs with air. She was safe.

She wished that she could scream at the policeman to go check the hall, to catch the person who chased her from the woods. But even if she could speak, what would she say? She couldn't provide a description. She never even saw anyone.

"Then how do you know you were being followed?" he would ask. *The trees told me?* He would definitely think she was crazy then. He would probably throw away her note and move on at that point. *Unreliable source.* She would gain a new label, as if *disabled* wasn't enough.

"Hi Sandra," Chuck said calmly. "Are you okay? You look scared. Did something happen?"

Sandra closed her eyes, and covered her ears with her hands, trying to shut out any external input. She slid down to the floor with her back against the door and listened to her heartbeat pounding through her head. She could hear the air circulating through her nose and filling her lungs before she blew it again out of her mouth.

Her soul was guiding her thoughts now. *Calm. Be calm. You are safe. Be calm.*

CHAPTER FORTY-NINE

Quinn was just about ready to give up and go home when he saw her emerge from the trees and out onto the rock that hung over the river. He had spent the last two hours sheltered under the drooping boughs of a large pine tree, the lowest branches of which nearly touched the ground and created a cover that hid him almost completely. The sound of the river had masked her footfall but also helped him stay undetected.

He was sure that it was her as soon as he saw her. He didn't know why, but he could just tell. Quinn could see that she was comfortable being alone in the woods.

Quinn reflexively felt for his gun in its usual resting spot in the back of his pants. *Damn, I left it in the car*, he thought when his hand came up empty. *I still have my knife though. She is small, should be easy to overpower*, he thought, as he watched her sit down on the rock and start untying her shoelaces.

Perfect. She is taking off her shoes. That'll make it even easier. He would give her a chance to settle in and then make his move.

As he squatted in the shadow of the tree, he took a slow, deep breath. He felt nervous, uncertain. Killing Slater was fairly easy in comparison. Slater had it coming. It was Quinn's duty to defend his family, and the means felt justified. This one, though, was different. She was an innocent woman who stumbled into the crosshairs, and it was going to get physical, cold-blooded.

But what choice did he have? She had the power to put him in prison for the rest of his life.

Don't think, just act. He shook his head quickly as if to erase the moral compass from his mind and slid out from the backside of his hiding spot, away from the river, still obscured from her view.

He retreated from the river for several paces until he found a deer trail that looked like it would circle above the stream behind a stand of trees and come out right where she was sitting. The sound of the water would make it easier to move without being noticed. He could grab her from behind and end it before she even knew that he was there.

With each step, his heart pounded harder and echoed in his ears. It was so loud, he worried that she could hear it, too. *Stop being ridiculous. Calm yourself down, Quinn.*

He moved slowly but methodically up the hill and around the trees. From there, he had a clear view of the rock. *Wait! She isn't there.* His mind began to panic. *There is no way that she heard me!* He took several more steps before he saw her with shoes on moving quickly away from the stream.

Quinn had no time to lose. The trail that he was on stayed higher on the hill but ran basically parallel to hers. He started moving more rapidly, trying to avoid setting off an alarm but realized that he needed to make up ground. Her trail was better, she knew where she was heading, and she wasn't wasting any time getting there.

As he wound through the smaller trees that lined the unmarked deer path, she was gaining valuable separation. He needed to get down to her trail, or she would soon be out of reach. He stepped off the path and slid on some loose dirt. He was making too much noise now and was sure that she must have heard him. He scaled some fallen trees and waded through some thigh-length meadow grass until he finally landed on the hard packed soil of the well-defined trail.

She was far ahead now. There was no reason to keep quiet. He just needed speed. He could see flashes of her clothing between the trees well ahead of him. *Damn, she was moving fast.* He sprinted up the uneven ground, jumping over tree roots and embedded rocks.

When he rounded a bend, he came to another fork in the trail. The main branch continued up the mountain, and the smaller headed toward some buildings that he could just see through the trees. He hesitated momentarily, not knowing which way she went. *She would have gone to the buildings,* he decided and took off on the side trail.

Sure enough, about fifty yards ahead of him, he saw her moving, now at a near run. He followed quickly in that direction and could see that he was closing in. But then the trail ended, and she sprinted across a parking lot toward the condo building. He thought that he might still be able to catch her before she got inside if he went at full speed. Jumping out of the woods, he ran across the lot to the building. As he arrived, he could see the entrance door swinging shut and lunged for the handle, grabbing it just before it latched.

She was already up the first flight and moving fast. He followed behind quickly but tried not to make enough noise to alert any neighbors. The building was three stories, and she ran to the top floor. He finished climbing the last flight and looked down the hall just in time to see the door to number 306 slam shut.

Quinn stood there for a minute and caught his breath. He moved down the hall quietly until he was facing her door. He tried the handle, but it was locked. He could hear some voices from the inside and knew that he had missed his chance.

As he backed away, he felt the knife in his pocket. *Later. I know where you live now.*

CHAPTER FIFTY

Chuck heard the door slam from where he was standing in Sandra's sensory room. Susan motioned to him with her hand to stay put while she let Sandra know he was there. He could hear her say something to Sandra, and then her tone changed to a higher pitch and volume. He stepped out of the room to see what was going on. Sandra was sitting on the floor of her entryway with her back against the door, and her mother was kneeling beside her, holding her hand. Sandra's face was pale, her skin sweaty, and her eyes were wide. She looked like she had seen a ghost.

Susan was trying to figure out what was wrong, but Sandra couldn't speak. Chuck walked over to her and squatted down to her eye level.

"What happened, Sandra? I can help you," he said as calmly and evenly as possible.

Sandra shifted her gaze to him, only momentarily, but he could feel her eyes searching his, penetrating deeply. It was unsettling. *Could she see? See what I did?*

He stood up and went to the window, anything to keep her from seeing everything. Maybe she could only see the result of the man he had become, a tortured, self-loathing fake who had put on this uniform as a daily reminder of choices he had made long ago.

He pulled back the curtains and scanned the parking lot. Nothing seemed awry. Looking back at Sandra, he saw her a little differently now. He knew she was smart after he read her message, but he didn't understand before that she was powerful. He needed to protect her ... if she would let him.

Her eyes were closed, and her breathing started to slow. The color of her skin had returned to its healthy tan. He watched her as she worked through the panic, a skill that she had only developed over the last few years. Prior to that, it would have been a full-on physical confrontation with anyone or anything that got in her way. Her parents both had some scars to prove that.

Susan didn't say anything else. She just sat down next to her, held her hand tightly, and tried to stay calm herself.

Chuck watched them both. He could see the pain etched in Susan's face. Deep wrinkles of worry creased her forehead, lines that had been grooved over many years. Chuck couldn't help but think of his brother. He had those lines, or Chuck had to assume that he did. It had been too long. He had not only lost his mother and sister to his bad choices, but his guilt had caused him to lose his brother, too.

No matter, he thought. It soon ends for me. But, not until this girl gets her chance.

Chuck walked back over to Sandra and looked her in the eye, showing her his conviction. "I will protect you, Sandra. Please trust me."

He took his walkie talkie from his belt and called dispatch. "Send a unit to 306 Forest View. I'm setting up 24-hour surveillance here, starting now."

"Yes, Chief," a voice from the other line responded.

"Susan, you have my direct number, right? I'm going to go down and meet the squad car. Lock the door. Call me immediately if there is a problem."

Susan helped Sandra to her feet and took her down the hall to her bedroom. Chuck opened the door and checked the lock as he left. He was going to need to be sure she didn't leave. He knew that that would be the hardest part.

CHAPTER FIFTY-ONE

Monday morning, Adam thought to himself, as a few rays of the sun peered through the barred window high on the concrete wall of the cell where he had spent the last two nights. After being processed, they were each taken down a long hall to an individual cell. Mark and Tanner were somewhere near him but not close enough for them to see or hear each other. The first night, Adam had said Mark's name aloud as he stood near the separating wall of his cell, hoping that he was next door, and they could talk. But a gruff voice responded, "I'm not your buddy. You damn well better not keep me awake tonight, either, or you will find out real quick that that is true."

Adam went back to the lumpy mattress on the cot that was bolted to the floor and sat with his back against the wall. And he waited. This was going to be the worst part of being incarcerated—the waiting. Waiting for something else to happen, the next meal, the prisoner checks, exercise time, the occasional visit. Always waiting for the next thing to break up the debilitating monotony. Adam hated waiting. He had always been impatient and a little hyperactive. Could he ever settle into the mind-numbing routine of prison life?

He had survived the weekend, and now there was some promise that something would happen today—at least a lawyer visit. The guards had already told him that he wouldn't have regular visitor privileges until after the initial hearing, at the earliest. He was dying to hear his parents' voices again. As hard as it was to talk to his mom on Saturday when he was still in Canada, her voice helped ease his racing heart. But now, he had a constant pit in his stomach that made it almost impossible to sit still or get any sleep. He wished he was more like Tanner who seemed to shut down in stressful environments. *Tanner had probably slept through the entire weekend,* he thought.

Three more hours passed. He ate the cold scrambled eggs and limp toast that they gave him for breakfast. Finally, a guard came to his cell door and told him to get up. The guard instructed him to come to the bars, turn around, and put his two hands through the small window between the bars where the guard placed handcuffs on his wrists. He was then led out of his cell and down the hall to an enclosed interrogation room with a mirror on one of the walls. He was sure that people were watching him from behind that mirror. He sat at the table, and again, waited. Thirty minutes passed, and nothing happened. Adam was struggling to resist the urge to get up and pace around the small room. *Would that make me look guilty?* he wondered and tried to think about something else to distract him. Finally, two men entered the room. One came and sat next to Adam, and the other sat opposite the two of them.

The man across from them spoke first. "State your name."

"Adam Bend," Adam said, while trying to maintain eye contact and look calm.

"Adam, I am Detective Brett Atkins of the Federal Bureau of Investigation, the FBI. This is David Charles, your court appointed attorney." Atkins motioned to the man sitting next to Adam.

Adam looked at his new attorney. He was dressed in a checkered shirt and a wrinkled sports coat, his tie was loose, and his hair wasn't combed. *Not exactly ready for prime-time TV,* Adam thought. He tried to push away his first impression. *This man holds my fate in his hands. I hope he is smarter than he looks.*

"Adam, the reason you are here and the reason that I am involved is that you are accused of the murder of a man who was in federal witness protection, and then you crossed over an international border. That makes this a federal case."

"But I didn't ... " Adam began to protest, the nervous energy spilling out of him.

His lawyer immediately reached over and grabbed his arm, interrupting his thought. Mr. Charles shook his head signaling to Adam to be quiet. Adam fell back into the chair and took a few deep breaths with his eyes closed. He then opened his eyes again and focused on the agent.

"Adam, I am going to ask you a series of questions, and you will have an opportunity to answer and tell me what happened. I would advise you to listen to your attorney. He is here to protect your rights. When you were arrested, the officer described your rights to you, is that correct?"

Adam looked at his attorney who gave him a nod.

"Yes, sir."

"Do you have any questions about those rights?"

"No, sir."

"Okay. Then we will proceed."

Adam nodded nervously. *Will they even really listen to me,* he wondered, *or is my fate already sealed?*

"Adam, tell me where you were last Friday. I want to hear what happened the entire day from the time you woke up until the time you were arrested in Canada. Do not lie, and don't leave anything out. Okay?"

Adam was ready. He had been rehearsing it over and over in his head all weekend. He told the detective everything and then looked at his attorney. Adam had expected Mr. Charles to interrupt during his recounting, but he never did. He just gave Adam a reassuring smile after it was done.

The agent then wanted to go back and hear more about how the three of them had started hanging out with Quinn and how well they knew him, how many times they had been to his house, that kind of thing. When Adam had finished, Agent Atkins just said thank you and left the room.

Mr. Charles stayed behind with Adam for a few minutes. "You did good, Adam," he said, as he put his yellow notepad in a tattered briefcase. "I think he believes you."

"Really?", Adam let out a big sigh. "How can you tell?"

"Because it is usually pretty obvious when people are holding back in their story. You told him everything. We can tell you are sincere."

"Am I going to get out then?" Adam sat up straight, hope spreading over his face.

"Well, that's not really up to him. It's going to be my job to convince a jury that you are telling the truth. There is a lot of evidence that puts you at the scene and actively participating in a man's death. Motivation or coercion is harder to defend. But you'll get my best."

Adam looked him over again. The attorney still looked out of place and like he had just rolled out of bed. "Is your best going to be good enough?"

Mr. Charles noticed how Adam was visually sizing him up and smiled. "Would you feel better if I wore a three-piece suit?"

"Yeah, kind of."

"Adam, like a lot of people around here, I moved to Montana to get away from all of that. I spent my career as a high-profile prosecutor in Washington, D.C. I made all the money that I could ever need. I am here because I want to be, not because I have to be. Does that help?"

"It does. A lot. Thank you." Adam said, a little embarrassed for being so quick to judge. *I hope others won't judge me so superficially.*

The moment was interrupted by the officer who told Adam to stand and then led him back to his cell.

CHAPTER FIFTY-TWO

Sandra woke up with the sun on Monday morning, like she did every day. Her mom was still asleep on the couch, and Sandra tried not to wake her. She really wanted to go outside for a quick walk and some fresh air but knew that she couldn't. The police chief had posted an officer outside the apartment at a spot where he could see if anyone entered the building from either side. The officer had also informed all the neighbors of why he was there and requested that they report any suspicious activity.

After her scare yesterday, she had agreed to the conditions, but a new dawn threatened her resolve. Today, she wondered if she had overreacted and let her anxiety get the best of her. But when she really thought about it, she knew that her feelings were real. The danger she felt yesterday came from deep inside, from her soul, and it came with a clear message: *Get out of the woods!*

In contrast, the panic attacks triggered by her brain had no message, no purpose. Rather, they left her mind scrambled and confused. She had learned over the years that when her soul was trying to tell her something, it was best to listen. Plus, she knew her soul was connected to the woods. It would never tell her to leave unless something was wrong.

So, she would do her best today, in her condo, using her sensory room and all the skills of anxiety-reduction that she had developed. She also wanted to do something useful, to keep engaged. Just waiting for something to happen would be a sure-fire way to an anxiety attack.

Sandra grabbed her laptop and went into her sensory room. After sitting down on the floor mat, she opened the computer and waited for it to load. She then clicked on the Word icon and opened a blank document. She was going to practice writing today. She didn't want to type about what happened in the woods but just wanted to write about whatever came into her mind. It probably didn't really matter what that was; just being able to transfer her thoughts to a page was going to be the best use of her time while she was trapped in her cage.

Hii. My nome isn SSandra Lewis

I an a ssmart and inttuitivve girlll who has aaautism

Iii love naturE and I llovv my pparents

My dad was my beSt frieend but he died

I stilll misss him

My mmmom is also my bestt and noww only friend

I don't knowwwhat will happen to meee when she dieSs

That is whyy I live byy myself

I need to bee ppreparedd

For My whole liffe I have tried to llearn how to ccom-
        municate bbut I never found aaa way until noww

Iii just wwant to ssayy Hello world I am hhhere

I have bbeen here thee whole tttime

Sandra took her hands away from the keyboard and read what she had just written. She was getting better. Her message was clear despite the mistakes, and it had only taken her about an hour to get it out. Although it required a lot of energy commanding her hands to react, it was so rewarding to see her thoughts outside of her head, out where anyone could read them. She promised herself that no matter how good she became at writing, and she had every intention of becoming very good, she would never take for granted what it meant to simply be able to communicate with another human being. She wondered how many people there were out there just like her that may never get that opportunity. When this mess with the investigation was over, she was going to find a way to help others find their voice. She had been given a gift, a gift that she was expected to share.

She rested back against the wall and looked around. Her parents had built this room for her to keep her safe. Pads on the floor and the walls, a padded bag, round rubber exercise balls. The world was a dangerous place. She could get hurt out there. Even her woods could be full of danger, as the last few days had reinforced. But it was time for her to engage now, engage with a world that had largely ignored her outside of the systems that were there to try to change her into one of them. Well, she would never be like one of them. She was going to have to find her way by being who she was. And hopefully that would be enough.

Sandra stood up and stepped over to her punching bag. She hit it a few times until it started swinging. Then she gave it a strong kick. It felt really good. She did it again. And again. Soon she was sweating and breathing hard as she continued to punch and kick the bag. Her mind was clear. It was as clear as it had ever been. She also felt something else that she had previously only ever felt in passing moments. *Joy.* She felt joy. Joy despite her challenges of the past and fears of the present. It was joy that came from a confidence that she had taken life's best shot and was still standing. Not just standing, she was ready to fight back.

CHAPTER FIFTY-THREE

Gary stepped out onto the back patio and took the incoming call. Quinn was in the dining room eating a bowl of cereal before school. He seemed a lot more relaxed today. Maybe he was going to chill and let things carry out according to the original plan.

"Good morning, Wesley," Gary found a chair under a pine tree with views of the lake.

"Is it? I'm not so convinced," Wesley replied, sounding irritated.

"What's wrong? Quinn has mellowed out, and I said I'd take care of the witness," Gary responded.

"I think Frank may be onto us. Turns out that I couldn't hide what we were doing from him. Someone leaked it, and now he knows. He is still a powerful guy, Jack, even from prison. So, we can't wait around anymore, or it'll be too late. I think there's only one way to take care of the problem."

"Which problem? The witness or the kid?"

"Yeah, you're right. We have two problems now. Both have to be solved. We can't wait for the trial anymore. Frank will rally his guys, and the kid will get off. Then they'll both come after us. We must seize power now and hope that most of Frank's guys won't want to wait around until he gets out."

"Sounds to me like maybe we didn't think things through as much as we thought we did," Gary reacted, his voice now steely.

"What does that mean?"

"Well, the only thing that hasn't gone according to plan is an eyewitness, and I know who she is. So, adding Quinn to the list had nothing to do with that. That is a result of bad planning, if you ask me. If we didn't have control over all the lines of communication like you said we did, then of course things would go poorly when Frank found out. Right? We shouldn't have gone forward with it."

"Well, I have control over all the active members of Frank's team. But there was someone I forgot about. It must have been him," Wesley admitted. "No one else would risk it."

"And who is that? I'm dying to know who would betray you knowing that he would die because of it." Gary stood up and looked back toward the house as Quinn's Mustang roared down the driveway and out of the gate.

"It has to be the cop."

"The cop? The Chief of Police?" Gary was surprised. "He works for Frank?"

"He used to. That's why I had our FBI contact put Slater in Whitefish in case we needed to remind the cop that we still control his narrative. The cop was there in Chicago. I designed this hit to mirror that one, as a little message that we hadn't forgotten about him."

"But he's not on the payroll now?" Gary asked. "How did you let him go?"

"Let's just say he paid a hard price for the reprieve."

"He paid you back the money? I didn't think Frank allowed for that." Gary started walking down the outside stairs toward the boathouse. It was a bright sunny morning. There were two swans swimming near the shore next to the dock.

"He didn't pay money, you idiot. He paid in lives. His mother and sister."

Gary didn't say anything. He knew that Frank was capable of killing innocent family members just to make a point. He did it to Slater, too. Gary was thankful that he had no one that could be used as leverage. He had no doubt that Wesley would use the same tactic if he needed to.

"There is another complication," Wesley said.

"Great, what else?"

"Our guy at the Bureau called. The agent working Slater's case is asking around for files from the Chicago trial. He was the one who put Frank in prison. They moved him to Montana afterwards to keep an eye on Slater. We sent guys after him yesterday, but they somehow failed to finish the job, and now he knows that the Slater murder wasn't just a burglary gone wrong. And he knows that we are after him. Since yesterday, he dropped off the grid and is watching his own back very closely. It'll be hard to get to him now without someone from the inside. So, we need to add an employee. Do you understand?"

Gary paused, as he considered what Wesley told him. "Let me get this straight. Our list of problems has now grown to four: the girl, the kid, the cop, and the agent. And I was actually feeling better when I woke up this morning."

"Yeah, well I'm so very sorry to upset you, mate. You do know what it takes to stage a coup, though, right? Did you think it would be easy?"

"That's how you sold me on it, Wesley. You brought me on to be the actor, the sad widower single father. I agreed to kill Slater because the guy was a weasel. I didn't sign up for four others," Gary said angrily, his raised voice causing the swans to stare at him and then start to create some distance.

"Well, Jack, my friend. Shit happens, and you are thigh deep. You want to stay upright, or do I need to flip you head down?"

"What does that mean?"

"You know very well what that means. We have a job to do. Can I count on you to do it, or do I need to come out there myself?"

Gary didn't respond. He took the phone away from his ear and just stared at it. He should have known better. There was never going to be a world where Wesley and he were equal partners. No, Wesley would call the shots, and Gary would be the henchman.

"You still there, mate?" Wesley's voice came from the speaker. "Rest assured that if I have to come out there, I'm bringing extra bullets."

Gary remained quiet. He watched the swans as they swam away slowly.

"Don't make me hang up on you," Wesley's voice now yelling from the phone. "Because if I hang up on you, my next move is a private jet to Montana. I could be there in three hours. You ready for this day to be your last?"

Gary still didn't respond. He was a master of disguises. He could transform himself into anybody, go anywhere. He didn't sign up for this. The money wouldn't help him in a prison cell or six feet underground. He looked again at the phone in his hand.

"You've got one minute," Wesley screamed.

Gary grabbed the phone with both hands, twisted the two halves until they broke, and then threw them at the swans. They took off out of the water with a startled honk. He then took a big breath, turned toward the house, and started walking back across the lawn.

CHAPTER FIFTY-FOUR

Chuck moved slowly down the walkway in front of the police station on Monday morning, sipping on coffee, and trying to work the stiffness from his joints. He had spent the night folded into the driver's seat of his car, keeping an eye on the Madison residence to be sure that Quinn or his fake dad didn't try anything stupid. Everything had stayed quiet until this morning when Quinn's Mustang had roared out of the gated driveway. Chuck followed him to the school and watched until Quinn entered the front doors. *I guess he's going to carry out the charade after all*, Chuck thought. *Looks like I've got a few hours.*

Chuck headed for the station, hoping to find the old cot that had been his bed when he had first moved from Chicago. It wasn't comfortable then and would be way less comfortable now, but maybe he could at least catch a few winks to help him through the rest of the day. Overnight surveillance is a younger man's job, but he already had an officer posted at Sandra's house; he couldn't afford to give up anyone else. So, it fell on him.

Chuck entered the station and waved tiredly at Kathy. "Morning."

"Morning, Chief. You look terrible," she replied with a sympathetic grin.

"I think I probably look better than I feel. I'm going to lay down in my office. Call me with anything that sounds important, okay?"

"Will do," Kathy said and refocused on her paperwork.

Chuck found the cot in a storage closet and brushed away the dust. Now was as likely a time as any for a quick nap. Atkins would be tied up in Kalispel interrogating the three boys this morning, and Sandra promised she'd stay inside. He needed to give Susan a call in a while and see how Sandra was handling being cooped up, knowing that would be a major challenge for her.

Chuck set up the cot next to his desk and sat down on it with a groan. The cot reacted in kind with a creak of protest. "Oh c'mon. You're not so old," Chuck said as he kicked up his feet and wadded up his jacket as a pillow. He had first removed his bulky gun belt and laid it on the desk in arm's reach. Sleep came quickly in defiance of all the coffee and sugar that had sustained him through the night.

. . .

"Hey, Chuck. Where you been?" Nora said, as she leaned back in his office chair. "It's been a while since we've talked. I was beginning to think you had forgotten about me."

Nora hadn't changed a bit after two and a half decades. Still young, still pretty, still full of life. Except that she wasn't—full of life, that is. No, she was dead, and it was because of him.

"Ah, you still beating yourself up about that? Cause you know I've forgiven you, right? Mom has, too. It wasn't your fault, Chuck. You had to make a choice eventually, right? They had you trapped. We're glad you got out, Chuck. You've done a lot of good since then."

Chuck just stared at his younger sister. It didn't matter if he spoke or not, she just read his thoughts.

"They're after you again, aren't they? We figured this day would come. So, what you going to do, Chuck? They're bad men. Can you catch them?"

Chuck looked on the desk, where he had put his gun belt while he napped. He had always had a healthy respect for the law. He had spent his life enforcing it. But he also knew about justice, about how justice was not always served. The system was in place for a reason, and he appreciated the courts and those who did their best to get it right, but the facts were facts. Good people sometimes are wrongly convicted, and bad guys sometimes walk free. Not this time. Not this time.

. . .

The phone on his desk startled him awake. He pushed himself upright and grabbed the receiver. "Chief Peters," he said, as he stood up, walked around the desk, and sat in his empty office chair.

"Chief, the FBI is on line one," Kathy announced.

"Okay, I got it," Chuck said, as he pushed the blinking light. "Atkins, its Peters. What you got?"

"This is not Agent Atkins," the voice from the other line said. "I am a colleague. I am calling to let you know that a former boss of yours is on his way to your town and another former boss of yours is sending guys after him. You better load up your guns. There's gonna be a shootout." The line went dead.

Chuck stared at the phone for a few minutes trying to process if he was awake or still dreaming. He stood up and gave the floor a stomp. *Solid.* He quickly grabbed his gun belt and left the office. He walked briskly down the hall to the gun safe and took out two shotguns and some extra ammo, then left the building through a back door. He didn't want Kathy or anyone else to see him with the extra guns. That would only raise questions that he wasn't prepared to answer. Plus, he wasn't completely sure that Frank or Wesley hadn't bought off some of his guys.

Shit! Sandra! He just realized that she might be under surveillance by a dirty cop. *Okay, Chuck, think. Where can you keep them hidden where no one else would come looking? They would come to my place first, and they could figure out where her mother lives. No, it's gotta be somewhere they wouldn't think to look.*

Chuck steered his patrol car out of the parking lot and headed for Sandra's condo. On the way over, he tried to contact Atkins. He called the jail because Atkins still had not received a new cell phone, but just had to leave a message. Atkins had instructed the staff not to interrupt him during his interrogation under any circumstance. Chuck trusted Atkins. He was the only one. After all, they had tried to kill him, too.

Chuck arrived at the condo building, and all was quiet. Sean was sitting in the patrol car in the parking lot, and Jason had spent the night. *That means at least two officers know where Sandra lives. That's too many. I've got to move her.*

He pulled up next to Sean and got out. "Anything going on?" Chuck asked.

"Nothing, sir," Sean replied.

"Alright. Good work," Chuck said. "I'll take over for a bit. You go get some lunch."

"I'm good," Sean said, pointing to a large amount of food trash in his front seat.

"Well, I need someone to go check on the Madisons. Can you do that? Find out what Mr. Madison is up to. You know where they live?"

"Yes, sir. What should I tell him about why I'm checking on him?"

"I don't know. Make something up."

Chuck waited until Sean drove away and then headed up the stairs. He knocked on Sandra's door and announced that it was him. He could hear someone walk toward the door and unlock the bolt. It was Susan.

"Hi, can I come in?"

Susan stepped aside and let Chuck pass by.

"We are running into some complications. We believe that the men behind the killing, not the boys at the scene, but the men who ordered it are on their way to town to clean everything up. They are really bad men, Susan. Sandra is not safe here. We've got to find another place."

Susan's face turned pale, and she sat down on the couch.

"Where's Sandra?" Chuck asked.

"She's in her sensory room. Where are we going to go?"

"I'm still thinking about that. We can't risk getting anyone else involved. These men have a lot of connections. Don't trust anyone."

"What about you then, Chief Peters? How do I know that I can trust you? You know that it's going to be very hard for Sandra to deal with all of this in a new place, right? She hates motels, and if she isn't at least near her woods, she is going to lose it. How about my place?"

Chuck shook his head. "Too obvious. Susan, you are right to be skeptical about me, too, and what I'm going to propose might sound crazy, but I think it's the only place right now where I can protect you."

"And where is that?"

"The cabin where it happened. Just for tonight until I can figure something else out. They wouldn't think to look there."

"No way!" Susan exclaimed. "We are not spending the night in a place where someone was just murdered. Sandra will freak, and I will, too."

"It's okay, Mom," Sandra's voice came from the sensory room door, now ajar.

Susan and Chuck both looked up at the same time and watched Sandra emerge into the hall. She seemed unusually calm. With her laptop in her arms, she came over and sat down by Susan on the couch. She opened the screen and started to type.

THE CCABIN IS IIN THE WWWOODS AND THE WOODSS WWILL KEEEP US SSAFE

Susan read it out loud to Chuck. There were a few moments of silence as they marveled at Sandra's faith in her woods, but also at her improving ability to communicate it.

Chuck sat down in the chair next to the sofa. "You're a brave girl, Sandra. I will be there with my guns to keep you safe, too. I'm not going to entrust anyone else with that job. Okay?"

Susan looked nervously at Chuck and then at Sandra, who was gazing intently into Chuck's eyes. After several minutes, she looked at her mom, smiled, and said "Okay."

CHAPTER FIFTY-FIVE

Agent Atkins finished interrogating all three of the detained suspects. As he had anticipated, they all told the same story and all proclaimed that Quinn was not only there but was the person who had planned the whole thing and pulled the trigger. They were all legitimately scared and confused. Atkins didn't believe that any of them had it in them to kill someone. Adam confessed to not paying for the CD from the 7-11 that Quinn had made him steal. Even that had been tearing him up since it happened. He wasn't a kid that would be interested in armed burglary.

Atkins knew, however, that he was going to have to prove their innocence given the amount of evidence against them and zero evidence placing Quinn at the scene. The only thing that could confirm their story was the picture taken by that girl, and she would need to testify of its authenticity and be able to describe the event that she witnessed. Chief Peters was right to worry about her safety.

As he got to the front office at the jail, a secretary told him that Chief Peters had called with an urgent message. Atkins found a phone in a back office and dialed the number.

"This is Peters."

"Chief, it's Atkins. You called?"

"Atkins, we've got a major situation brewing over here. Are you secure?"

"I'm not sure. I'll call you back on another line. I need about fifteen minutes."

"Okay, Agent. Hurry, please."

Atkins left the jail and walked the few blocks to a restaurant parking lot where he had left his car. He got in and drove around until he felt comfortable that he wasn't being followed and then found a store where he could buy a burner phone. He then called Peters again.

"Peters, it's me. We can use this phone for the next 24 hours or so. So, what's going on?"

"Agent, I know you've done your research on Frank Donovan and his businesses. You know his second in command? The Irishman?"

"Yes, Wesley O'Brien."

"Well, I got a call from someone about two hours ago who said that he was from the FBI but wouldn't identify himself. He knew of my past connections to those two. He made it sound like Frank and Wesley are no longer friends, and that maybe it was Wesley behind all of this. I'm thinking that Wesley was setting up Frank's kid, and now Frank knows about it. The guy said that Wesley's on his way here to 'clean things up' and that Frank's guys are coming after Wesley. They could be getting here anytime. I'm not sure if they know about the witness, but they have their ways of finding that kind of stuff out. She has a big target on her head, Atkins. I'm taking her into hiding. We're getting ready as we speak."

"Where are you going to take her?"

"Nope. I'm not even going to trust you with that information. It's not just about the girl. It's about her mom and those three innocent boys, too."

"You have a lot at stake here, too, Chief. If you don't cooperate with them, they will destroy your career, if you are lucky. More likely, they'll just dispose of you."

"Yep, I'm well aware of that."

"That's a lot of motive to turn her over. How do I know you're really clean? You compromised once, you can do it again."

"I guess we're just gonna have to see who is standing at the end. As soon as I get off this call, I'm going dark. I can't trust that my phone or my car hasn't been bugged. You will hear again from me tomorrow morning if we all make it through the night."

"Well, it sounds like you've made up your mind. I know you know what's at stake. But Peters, if you betray me and live, I will hunt you down until the day I die if I need to, and I will make you pay not only for these lives but the ones in Chicago, including your own family that were murdered because of your choices. Do you hear me?"

"Agent, I can guarantee that there is nothing you could do to me that I have not been thinking about doing myself for twenty years. I hope you have more than a handgun. You're going to need it."

CHAPTER FIFTY-SIX

Quinn sat in his biology class looking out the window. It was as if he was completely alone in the room, as his classmates and teacher had become a blur of background color and noise. *Why am I even here? My life is on the line, and I'm sitting in fourth period?*

His friends could tell that something was wrong. A few of them had cornered him in the hall between periods.

"What's the matter with you, man?" one of them asked. "You've been acting weird all week."

"Leave me alone!" Quinn said angrily and walked away.

I might as well leave. I can't pretend that everything is normal. I'm more likely to raise suspicion by being here than if I called in sick. Quinn gathered his books and put them in his bag. He stood up and started walking to the door.

"I'm sick," he said to the teacher, who seemed offended by the interruption. Quinn kept walking, checked out at the office, and left the building. He made it to his car and just sat in the driver's seat for several minutes, planning his next move. He had two major problems: Gary and the girl. Gary seemed to be the more immediate threat and was more likely to come after him physically. *I'm not sure what Gary and Wesley are up to, but it's becoming clear that getting rid of me is high on their priority list. I've got to strike first. The girl can wait until later.*

Quinn opened the glovebox in his car, checked that his handgun was loaded, and then started the engine. He drove home slowly, noticing every car and every tree, his senses on heightened alert. As he approached the entrance, he saw that the gate had been forced open, and one of the metal doors was hanging awkwardly on its hinges. Quinn slowed his forward momentum to a near crawl while he continued down the paved driveway. When the house came into view, he could see a silver SUV with tinted windows parked in front of the garage, and the front door of the house was open. Quinn stopped the Mustang and watched for a few minutes. He didn't recognize that car and clearly it wasn't an invited guest. *Where is Gary? Is he in there with the driver of the SUV?* Quinn decided it would be better to not be seen, so he backed up his car out of the gate, parking it a few hundred yards away behind some trees in a neighbor's lot, and then headed back to his house on foot with his handgun tucked into his pants.

He found the spot along the yard's border fence where he knew there was a breach and no cameras. That is where he had snuck out the night that he killed Slater. He stayed hidden amongst the trees until he had another view of the front of the house. He could hear some commotion and yelling coming from the inside through the open door. It sounded like someone was trashing the place.

Just then, another car came down the driveway. He could see glimpses of it through the trees and then watched as a police squad car pull up behind the SUV. *The cop? Was he coming back to arrest me?* Quinn could feel his stomach drop.

The police officer who got out of the car was not the older man who had come previously. It was a younger guy, brown hair, looked fit. He announced himself as he approached the open door. When he crossed over the threshold, the cop just stood there for a minute and looked around. Quinn could see him reaching for his gun but before he could get it from his belt, there was a clap and blood exploded from the back of the officer's head as his body crumpled to the ground. Quinn subconsciously closed his eyes and lowered his head. *Damn! What is going on in there? Was that Gary?*

Just then a large man in a white tank top and loaded with a semiautomatic rifle slung over each shoulder filled the doorway. He grabbed the fallen police officer by the feet and dragged him into the house. A few minutes later, the man appeared again, walked out of the door, and started the SUV. After another minute, Quinn saw a familiar face appear in the doorway: short stature, red hair, long sideburns, covered with arm tattoos and holding a handgun. *Wesley O'Brien.* And he looked angry. Really angry. He slammed the door shut and got into the passenger side of the SUV. The car made a few short, violent rear moves, slamming into the squad car, and pushing it out of the way. It then squealed its tires as it jumped forward and down the driveway.

Quinn laid flat in the underbrush as the SUV sped past, holding his breath, and hoping that he couldn't be seen. *Wesley is here? Why? And why did he tear up the house? Where is Gary? Was he in the back of the SUV? No. That wouldn't make sense. Did Gary bail?*

Questions flooded his brain, and his heart was racing a mile a minute, but he didn't move a muscle for about twenty minutes until he was sure that no one was coming back. He then got up cautiously and snuck around the back to the walkout basement door that was usually unlocked. He entered the house quietly. When he came up the stairs, the kitchen and living room were total disasters. All the cupboards were open, and there were broken dishes and glasses everywhere. The couch was turned over, and all the lamps were broken. He went into Gary's room. It looked like a lot of his stuff was missing, and the rest was strewn all over the floor. He ran upstairs and checked the other bedrooms. They had also been ransacked, including his own. Quinn ran back down the stairs and stepped over the blood trail that led to the coat closet. He opened the door to the garage and sure enough, the BMW was missing from its spot.

Gary is gone. That takes care of one of my problems, but now I have a much, much larger one.

Quinn sat on the garage door steps while he sifted through his emotions. *What's my move? Obviously, Wesley is here because he isn't happy about something. Maybe he told Gary to kill me, and he wouldn't do it. So now he's here to do it himself. Maybe I should just take off, too. But they would find me soon enough. My dad told me how good they were at finding people who ditched. No, I'm not going to run. Right now, I have the advantage. I know he's here, and he doesn't know that I know. I'm going to kill that bastard myself.*

CHAPTER FIFTY-SEVEN

Chuck sat at Sandra's table across from Susan. Sandra was sitting on the end, between them, with her laptop opened in front of her. She seemed a little nervous but was holding it all together amazingly well. *Better than me,* Susan thought. After Sandra came out of her sensory room and showed them her message, she led Susan by the hand to the table and pointed at the chair. Chuck followed, and Sandra directed him to the other chair. She was ready for a conversation, to be part of the discussion, to decide her own fate. She started typing, her finger trembling but still able to find the letters.

TYELL USS THE TYRUTH
WHOO AAARE WEE DRFEALING WITHH

She showed the screen to Chuck and waited for a response. This time, she avoided eye contact. She already knew he was trying to help them.

"Okay, Sandra, you deserve to know," Chuck started, glancing at Susan to gauge her reaction. Susan seemed shocked, by all of it—the danger they were in, yes, but even more by watching Sandra take the lead.

"The boys that you saw are not really the ones behind the murder, except for the one holding the gun. He is the son of a crime boss in New York. They have an international human trafficking business disguised as a foreign worker program. They do bad things to innocent people and make a lot of money doing it.

"The guy that was murdered was in witness protection after testifying against his boss, the gunman's dad, who is now in federal prison. Apparently, the son was the trigger in a plot for revenge. The other boys are just pawns and really didn't know what was happening.

"Well, now it seems that there is some more trouble within their organization, like maybe the second-in-command is staging a coup and trying to get rid of the heir to the kingdom, the boss's son. They might be trying to set him up to get caught for the murder or might just plan on killing him, I'm not sure. Either way, none of them planned on you witnessing the crime and documenting who was holding the gun.

"Your evidence might actually work out in the favor of number two guy but definitely not for the son. And we think he knows about you now. So, he will do everything possible to silence you permanently. We just heard that there are others coming to town. They might all have different agendas; we can't be sure. No matter what, you are caught in the middle of this mess, and we need to get you out of here. They might very well already know where you live."

Sandra's facial expression didn't change after hearing all of this. She stared out of the window for a minute and then back to her keyboard.

I CANN HHIDE IINN THE WWOODSS
II WWILL BBE SSSAAFE TTHERE
KKEEPP MMY MMOMM WWITTH YYOU
SSSHE KNOWS HHOEW TTO FFIND MMEE

Susan came and stood behind Sandra as she typed and read the message over her shoulder. Sandra turned the laptop so Chuck could read it.

"No way, Sandra," Susan protested in a high-pitched voice. "You are not going out there, and I'm not leaving you! Not overnight, not in the dark! You could get lost or hurt or they could find you and ... "

Sandra quickly turned the laptop back toward her and started typing aggressively and amazingly without a single mistake.

I NEVER GET LOST IN THE WOODS

Susan read the new message, gasped, and covered her mouth as she turned away from the table and into the living room, trying to suppress her tears.

"She is not wrong, Susan," Chuck said gently. "If she is comfortable out there on her own, it would be the hardest place for them to find her. Sandra, are you sure you could do that? You wouldn't be scared?"

II AMM SCCARED OF HHUMANSS NNOT AANIMALS INN TTHE FFPOREST
I KNOWE AAW GOOD SSPPOT
TRTHEY WWONT FFIND ME

"Susan?" Chuck asked. "We can't wait here much longer. The men I told you about might be on their way as we speak. We can get Sandra going, and I'll take you to a motel. You'll be safe there. Sandra has a tracking watch, right? You can track her every move all night long if you want. It's a good plan. What do you say?"

Susan couldn't say anything. She had sat on the couch, and her face was covered by both hands. Without removing her hands, she nodded her consent.

"Okay, Sandra, let's go! Get your stuff! Do you have a sleeping bag and a backpack? It's going to get cold out there tonight."

Sandra nodded and went quickly into her bedroom. She stuffed some warm clothes, a flashlight, a down sleeping bag, and some water bottles into a backpack and came back out to the kitchen. Susan had recovered enough to make her a bag full of snacks.

"You can't take your phone, Sandra," Chuck said. "They could track that. Let's set up a signal system. At that cabin. Where it happened. Check there in the morning but stay where no one can see you. There is a window in the back where the deck is. If I put a green Sprite can in the window, it means you can come up the deck and into the back door. I'll be waiting for you inside. But if there is a red Coke can in the window, turn around and go back to your spot and check again later. Okay?"

OK GTREENN ISS GOOD
RTEDD IDS BAD

"That's right. Don't worry about your mom. I will be sure she is safe. Okay, let's get you out there. There are still a few hours of daylight left, so just find somewhere else in the forest to stay away from people. Don't go to your spot until after dark and try not to use the flashlight too much. And no fires, okay?"

Sandra put on her backpack and gave her mom a hug, letting Susan hold on for a few seconds longer than usual, and then followed Chuck down the stairs.

"Let me go out first to be sure no one is watching. I'll knock on the outside of the door twice, and then you can come out. Go straight to the trail and don't stop moving until you are deep into the woods. Try to stay off the main trails. Good luck, brave lady, we'll see you tomorrow!"

After a few minutes, Sandra heard the knock and walked outside. The air was crisp and clean and filled her soul with fresh energy. This was the perfect solution for her. She couldn't have made it another hour locked up in her condo. *The woods will keep me safe,* she thought, as she disappeared into the trees.

CHAPTER FIFTY-EIGHT

Wesley removed the silencer from his weapon and holstered it under his jacket. He was still fuming about Gary's disloyalty and his disappearance. He would find him and deal with him appropriately, but there were more urgent issues to solve at the moment. The first was to find Quinn.

"Find the high school," he instructed his companion. "He drives a red Mustang. There can't be too many of those around this shit hole."

The driver checked his GPS and drove the few miles to the school. They circled the parking lot slowly but did not see a Mustang.

"All right, he's not here. Let's keep driving. The town is not big. We should come across his car soon enough. I doubt that Gary would have warned him. It'd be better for Gary if we find Quinn."

Wesley pulled out his cell phone and dialed. "Yes, we're here ... He's gone ... Not yet."

He hung up and dialed again. "Hello there. This is your new boss. I take it that your bank account just got substantially fatter, didn't it? ... Good. Well now it's time to earn that money. I hear there is a witness ... A woman? In her 20s. Blond hair ... What's that? ... Autistic? You've got to be kidding me. She can't speak? Then what are we worried about? ... She can type? And she has a picture. Have you seen it? ... You haven't seen it ... Quinn? Holding a gun ... Where does she live? ... He's there now? ... Okay, I'll be in touch. We aren't through with you ... More money? No, no, no. This job isn't paid on commission. You are on salary!"

Wesley hung up the phone in disgust. "The greed of these people. The new ones never get it, mate. They don't know who is in charge yet. We're going to have to teach this one. But that can also wait. Look up this address. We're going there first."

The SUV turned and headed toward the lake and then again on the road going up to the ski resort. After a couple miles of winding road, they turned onto a residential street and continued until they saw a group of condos up ahead. As they approached, a police car pulled out of the entrance and passed them on the left, going in the opposite direction.

"Was that him?" Wesley asked.

"I couldn't tell," the driver said. "It's been too many years. Should I follow him?"

"No, don't bother. He will be easy to find. He's the chief of police! Let's get the girl. One thing at a time."

They turned into the parking lot and scanned it for another cop car.

"I thought they'd keep her under surveillance. They are making this too easy," Wesley said as he got out of the car. He walked toward the building with his driver a few paces behind. They checked the front doors of the complex, but they were locked. "Let's go around."

They found the back entrance that was also locked but was out of view from the street.

Wesley nodded at his driver, "Open it."

The driver pulled out some tools and picked the lock. They went inside and up the stairs to the third floor.

"306. Right here," Wesley whispered and motioned again to the driver to get the door open, while he twisted the silencer back onto the muzzle of his gun.

They opened the door and quickly went inside, guns drawn. The living room was empty. Wesley opened the door to the sensory room. Also empty. *Kickboxer? I thought this girl was disabled*, Wesley thought. They checked the hall bathroom, then the master bedroom and bathroom. Nobody.

"Shit! We probably just passed them!"

The driver took a picture down from the wall of the bedroom and showed it to Wesley. It was a picture of Sandra and Susan.

"Alright. Looks like we have some leverage if we need it. I'll have our new employee find out where Mommy lives. That's three strikes against us, though—first, Gary, then the cop and now the girl. Time to stop messing around."

CHAPTER FIFTY-NINE

Quinn left the house through the back door just in case anyone was still watching the front. He wasn't sure if Wesley knew what kind of car he drove, but he couldn't take the risk. His was the only red Mustang in town. He was going to need a different vehicle. Renting wasn't an option; he was still too young. Maybe he could trade with one of his football buddies. One of the offensive linemen drove a beat-up Dodge Ram pickup. He could tell him he needed to move some stuff and would let him drive the Mustang instead. What high school guy wouldn't make that trade?

Quinn made the phone call. He was right. The friend even said he could drive it over. School was just getting out, and he could be there in a few minutes. Quinn told him to just meet him on the street by his house. The exchange was soon completed, and Quinn drove away from his neighborhood in disguised wheels.

He wasn't sure what his next move should be. He could never go back to the house—that much was clear. He was now in need of a place to stay. He couldn't stay with friends; they would ask too many questions and restrict his movements with other expectations. A motel would be better, but would they rent to him, a high school student? Maybe if he paid in cash, they would look the other way.

So, his first stop was the bank. He took as much out of the ATM as he could which he figured would at least get him a couple of nights. He next stopped at the grocery store and bought some food and personal supplies; he wanted to spend as little future time in public places as possible, not being sure how many of Wesley's guys would be roaming the streets with an eye out for him. Then he drove to a motel at the edge of town, a privately owned place, a little seedy, where he figured that there would be a higher chance that they would just take his money and not ask any questions.

He pulled around back and walked through a covered patio to enter the front lobby. He laid down two hundred bucks on the desk and asked for a two-night stay with the option to extend, paid up front in cash. The man at the desk looked up from his magazine for less than one minute and quickly sized Quinn up. Without saying anything, he grabbed the cash from the desk, replaced it with a room key, and went back to reading his magazine.

Quinn grabbed the key and found the room. It was on the ground level, facing the back parking lot. *Perfect*, Quinn thought. When he entered the room, an overpowering mixed scent of cigarette smoke and air freshener filled his nostrils causing him to quickly exhale the stale air. The carpet showed every bit of the at least forty years of misuse. The mattress on the queen bed had lost all its spring, and the dial on the thermostat was broken, leaving a short metal stump that you needed a screwdriver to turn. *I can't believe I paid a hundred bucks a night for this dive*, Quinn thought. *But at least it's out of the way. I don't think Wesley will expect me to be staying here. So, I've bought a little time. Now I need a game plan.*

He shut all the curtains and locked the bolt on the door before he sat down on the bed with his back against the padded headboard. *Okay, let's think of my priorities and figure out what I know and what I don't.*

My first priority is to survive. I don't think Wesley is here to take me back home to Connecticut, unless it's in a coffin. I can't just stay locked up here forever. He'll find me eventually, so I have to go on the offensive at some point, the sooner the better.

My second priority is to get rid of the witness. It won't do me any good to escape Wesley just to land in prison for the rest of my life.

What I know is that Wesley is pissed, and that Gary is gone. He is either dead or he bailed. I don't know where Wesley is and how many guys he has with him. I know where the witness lives and what she looks like. I don't know if Wesley knows about her, although I suspect that Gary told him.

So, until I figure out where Wesley is and what he is up to, I am going to have to stay out of sight. But I can't just sit and do nothing. I might as well take care of priority number two tonight.

Quinn stayed in the room and waited for the sun to set. He then put on dark clothes and an extra magazine clip in his jacket pocket. His handgun was his only weapon, but that should be more than enough for the girl. If he met up with Wesley, though, he would be seriously outmatched. He was going to need to be careful at every step of the way.

He looked out from behind the curtains first to be sure that the coast was clear before sliding out the door and quickly into the truck. The engine rumbled to a start, and Quinn headed toward the mountain. Last time he was at the witness' condo, he had approached from the woods, so he only knew the general area where it was located. He turned up the road that went to the ski resort and checked out every street that seemed residential along the way. Finally, he found a group of condos that looked right. He drove past slowly, watching for any cars on the street that seemed out of place. When he didn't see any, he parked a block away and came back on foot, staying as close as possible to the trees that lined the road. At the condo building, he snuck around the back and looked up to the third set of windows where he thought her condo might be. *Lights were on. She must be home.*

He went to the back entrance and checked the lock, but the handle wouldn't move. Quinn didn't have the skills or the tools to pick it, so he slid back into the shadows away from the streetlamp that illuminated the parking area and the back entrance. He would have to wait and hope that someone would come through that door. After about fifteen minutes, a car pulled into the parking lot, and a woman with a bag full of groceries got out and headed for the back entrance. Quinn watched her punch in a code and pull the door open. He moved like a cat behind her and caught the door just before it latched, just as he had done when he had followed the witness the day before. He held the door for a few minutes to give the woman a chance to make it inside her apartment and then entered the building. He climbed the two flights of stairs, then walked slowly down the hall and checked her door. Locked.

How am I going to get in? Should I knock? What if she isn't alone? I wonder if I could climb to the balcony. He remembered seeing a pine tree that was close to her condo. Maybe he could reach it. Quinn figured that was a better option and headed back down the hall to the stairs.

When he got to the top of the staircase, he heard a door open behind him. He hid on the first stair and peered around the corner, back down the hall. The door to the witness' condo was open, and he could hear some voices inside. He couldn't pick out what they were saying exactly, but it sounded like two men. Quinn quickly descended the rest of the stairs and went outside. It seemed that the witness was either not home, already dead, or was being protected. He hid behind a tree and waited to see who it was that came out of the building.

As he crouched down on his knees to get a better look, he felt it—the cold metal of a gun barrel pressed against the back of his head.

CHAPTER SIXTY

Sandra walked through the trees like she had done countless times before, moving like a deer, paying attention to where she put her feet and keeping her eyes and ears alert to her environment. It felt good to be outside, to feel the breeze on her face and the smell of pine trees in her nose. She was looking forward to spending the night out here alone. Her dad used to take her on overnight hikes quite often in these woods when he was alive, so she wasn't afraid of being out here at night. The creatures that come out at night are just doing what the daylight creatures do, finding food and staying safe. The big predators were there—mountain lions, wolves, and bears—but she wasn't afraid of them. She rarely saw one, and they had always left her alone before. Plus, she was just going to hunker down and stay quiet inside the shelter that her dad had found on one of their extended trips. She figured that if she didn't act like prey, the predators wouldn't bother her. Until then, she had a few hours left to try to forget about the complicated human world where the main predator doesn't follow the rules.

Sandra continued to move steadily away from her condo and deeper into the woods. There were fewer trails out here and therefore, less chance of a human encounter. The air was starting to cool off, and the sky was becoming a softer shade of blue. She grabbed another layer from her pack and put it on. The early autumn nights in Montana could dip to close to freezing. It would have been nice to have a fire.

As she approached the spot where she planned to spend the night, she was more careful. She wanted to be sure that some creature or another human hadn't already laid its claim. It was a man-made shelter that abutted an overhanging cliff as its back wall. The shelter was supported by two large fallen trees that angled against the rock. The cliff was too large to climb and thus provided a protected side. Someone had propped up a bunch of smaller trees against the larger trunks and created a tent-shaped structure large enough to hold two people. She and her dad had slept inside on several occasions. It was comfortable and protected from the wind. Plus, if you didn't know it was there, it was easy to walk right past without noticing.

Sandra hid behind some trees within view of the shelter and waited for a while. She could see that it was in a state of disrepair, but the large trees were in the same position and the smaller logs were scattered around. There were no signs of life, so she emerged from behind the trees and set to work repairing her bedroom for the night.

She replaced the logs against the tree, trying to leave as little space between them as possible. She then cut down some fresh pine boughs and covered the support logs, as well as the dirt floor inside to give her a softer place to lay down. When she was done, she sat in the entrance and ate a sandwich that her mom had made for her. She replenished her water supply at a nearby spring and then pulled out her sleeping bag and climbed in just before it got too dark to see without a flashlight.

She was cozy in the bag and felt well-protected from the elements. She would be happy to stay here for longer if she could build a fire and if her mom would let her. Maybe someday she would find a cabin in the woods where she could live out her life, away from other humans, and just write her story. They would find her eventually but would never know that she was considered disabled in their world. She did just fine in the woods. She didn't have to speak words here to communicate with nature.

As the moon rose above the top of the mountain, Sandra fell into a comfortable sleep.

CHAPTER SIXTY-ONE

Chuck and Susan left Sandra's house and headed toward town. Chuck needed to get Susan settled into a motel, but they also needed to avoid being seen in the process. Susan would definitely be used as a bargaining chip if she was taken by the bad guys. He needed to get Susan out of his squad car and into something less noticeable but keep her protected until she was safely locked behind a motel room door.

Chuck had only one person that he felt like he could trust right now, and that was Agent Atkins. Atkins also happened to be driving an unmarked car and was being careful about flying under the radar. The problem would be solved if he and Atkins could make an exchange for Susan without anyone paying attention.

"Susan, can I borrow your phone?" Chuck asked. "I need to make a call, and I'm not sure if my cell phone is being tracked."

After Susan gave him her cell, Chuck dialed the number to the temporary phone that Atkins was using.

"Atkins, I need your help," Chuck started. "I have Sandra's mother with me. Sandra is in a safe place, but I need to hide her mother as well. Those bastards will go after her if they know. I've got to believe that they are following me and will see where I take her. You are off the grid, so I need you to pick her up and find a motel room for her. She has a laptop and can follow Sandra's every move with that. It's the only way I could get her to agree to separate. Take her to the Holiday Inn on the highway. They have nice rooms, and there is a restaurant that will deliver food to her room. She needs to stay out of sight. I've gone over everything with her, and she agrees to it all."

"Okay, Chief, I can do that. Drop her off at Safeway and have her go inside the store bathroom. Tell her to come out in 15 minutes, and I will be waiting for her in the first handicap spot right across from the main entrance. If that one is full, I'll be in the one next to that. I'll put a yellow Manila envelope on my windshield so that she knows it's me."

"Okay, Atkins. We'll be at Safeway in five minutes."

Susan followed Atkins' instruction and found his car. When she climbed in the passenger seat, he greeted her warmly.

"Mrs. Lewis, I'm Agent Atkins from the FBI. Thank you for all that you are doing, and I'm sorry that you are mixed up in all of this. Your daughter is going to play a significant role in catching the people who are involved in this murder. I regret that it puts both you and her in danger. The police chief is making the right moves to protect you, however. I've already called ahead and secured a room for you. I am going to drop you off behind the motel, and you should go in the back entrance. Your key will be under the name of Bonnie Appleton, and it has been paid for. Go to your room and don't leave. Don't use your real name or your own credit card to buy anything, okay? Get room service and pay in cash. Cover your hair with a towel when the delivery guy comes so he doesn't pay attention to you. Your white hair is very striking."

"Agent, I'm doing my best to stay calm, but honestly, I'm panicking about my daughter. Nothing can happen to her! You've got to promise me! I really don't care what happens to me, except for what would happen to Sandra if I'm gone. I must confess that I've put off making arrangements for her future life without me because it's too hard to think about. And frankly, Sandra has shown me in the last few days that I would have had to rethink it all anyway. But I need time, Agent! That is what I'm asking you for—a little more time."

"Yes, ma'am. I understand and will do my best."

Susan made it inside her third-floor motel without incident and locked the bolt behind her. She slid the chain lock in place, as well. They weren't going to need to worry about room service because there was no way that she could eat anything while her daughter who couldn't speak was by herself at night in the woods while some thugs from an organized crime syndicate wanted to kill her to keep her from testifying against their guy. Nope, Susan would not be sleeping or eating until she was back together with Sandra.

She walked over to the windows, pulled the blackout shades and the curtains shut, and then set up the laptop on the table next to the bed. She opened the tracking app, typed in Sandra's watch code, and watched as a local map populated the screen. A small green light showed up on the background of the topographical lines. She zoomed in until only the woods neighboring their house could be seen.

Sandra was still moving away from her condo. Susan estimated that she was a couple of miles in. That made her feel better. *I highly doubt that anyone would even know where to start if they thought she was in the woods. Plus, how many young women would choose to go there alone at night anyway? This was a good move. But*

I'm still worried about the other dangers out there. How well did Tony prepare her? The two of them spent a lot of nights out there. Did he teach her how to survive?

Susan watched the flashing green dot until it stopped moving. The sky had turned to dusk. *Okay, she is settled in,* Susan thought. *I need to try and relax a little bit.* She grabbed the remote control and turned on the TV. There wasn't really anything on that captured her interest, so she settled on Jeopardy reruns and laid her head against the headboard. She set a timer on her phone for every thirty minutes. Every time it went off, she looked at the computer and found the blinking green light.

CHAPTER SIXTY-TWO

Quinn froze in place, the cold metal of the gun pressed firmly against his scalp. He lifted his hands slowly, up and away from his body. He then felt a hand pat him down until it found his gun and removed it from the back of his pants.

"Lay down!" a voice that he didn't recognize said quietly but intensely.

When Quinn hesitated, he felt a knee hit him hard between his shoulder blades and force him to the ground. His arms were bent sharply behind his back, one at a time, and the sharp plastic edges of zip ties snugged around his wrists tight enough to cut into his skin. The pressure from the knee on his back lifted and was replaced by the sharp pain of a fist grabbing a handful of his hair.

"Get up!" the voice said.

Quinn struggled to his feet, trying not to lose a large chunk of hair in the process. The voice stayed behind him, still out of sight. Quinn's hair was released, but the hand found purchase on one of Quinn's arms and gripped it painfully tight.

"Move!" the voice commanded.

Quinn stumbled forward, tripping over his own feet, causing a wrenching pain to shoot from his wrists all the way up to his spine. He let out a whelp of pain followed by an expletive. At that, the hand on his arm came around and covered his mouth, and he once again felt the barrel of the gun, this time against his temple. He could feel the breath of his captor against his ear.

"You make another sound, and I'll end this right now," the voice said.

Quinn nodded understanding, and the hand released from his mouth and went back to his arm. He moved forward, careful to avoid tripping again. The hand on his arm directed him to a van that was parked on the side of the street. Its side door was open, and Quinn was pushed inside. There were no seats behind the driver and front passenger, so Quinn slid up against the driver's side wall. He only saw a glimpse of his captor as the door slammed shut. The man was wearing a ski mask covering his face and couldn't be identified. He climbed in the passenger seat and motioned to the driver, also masked, to leave. As the van pulled away, the captor showed Quinn his gun to remind him of the consequences of bad behavior.

Quinn tried to adjust his arms so that he could improve blood circulation to his hands which were screaming in pain. It didn't work.

"Who are you guys?" Quinn asked.

There was no reply.

"Do you know my dad, Frank Donovan? Cause if you do anything to me, he will find out, and he will see to it that you are both killed ... Slowly!"

The captor let out a derisive laugh but didn't say anything else.

After about twenty minutes of winding turns, the van came to a sudden halt, and the captor got out. Quinn could hear him talking to someone outside but couldn't understand what he was saying. A few minutes later, the van door opened, and the captor stepped inside. He grabbed Quinn again by the hair and pulled him out of the van causing Quinn to scoot as fast as he could on his knees until he could get to his feet outside. He looked around, trying to orient himself to his new surroundings. The place was familiar. It was Slater's cabin.

"What are we doing here?" he asked his captor, who was now standing in front of him. This was met with a fist to the stomach that knocked the wind out of him and doubled him over.

"No questions."

The captor once again grabbed Quinn's arm and led him up the porch and into Slater's cabin. When they got inside, he was led to the back bedroom. The captor opened the closet door and pulled up a hatch door on the floor. There was a narrow staircase that led down into a dank cellar. The captor pushed Quinn ahead and down the stairs. Not having anything to hold onto, Quinn fell down the last several steps and hit his face on the hard dirt. The captor was immediately behind him and pushed him into a distant corner. There, he secured both of Quinn's feet to a chain that was attached to a concrete slab on the ground. The captor pulled out a switchblade and opened it inches away from Quinn's face. There was a moment of hesitation where it seemed that the captor was deciding whether he should slit Quinn's throat right then or wait until later. The knife moved quickly to Quinn's wrists and cut the zip ties that were binding them. Quinn felt the instant relief of blood rushing back into his hands.

"What do you want from me? Money? I can get you money."

The captor punched Quinn hard in the face which caused his head to snap back and hit the concrete foundation of the cabin. Quinn's world began to spin, and the light from the open cellar door faded to black. Quinn was out cold.

CHAPTER SIXTY-THREE

Chuck drove away from the parking lot at Safeway and parked across the street where he could keep an eye on the front door of the store. He wanted to be sure that Susan made it safely into Atkins' car. He pulled out his speed gun and pretended to use it on the oncoming traffic while he waited. It wasn't long before he saw Atkins pull up in a Ford Explorer and park in the handicap stall. He got out and put an envelope under his wiper. A few minutes later, he could see Susan leave the store, walk quickly to the SUV, and get into the passenger side. They pulled away and headed south toward the highway.

Satisfied, Chuck headed back to the station. When he arrived, he signaled to Kathy who was talking on the phone, that he did not want to be disturbed. She acknowledged him with a thumbs up, and he entered his office and locked the door behind him. He went to the window, closed all the blinds, and left the lights off. He sat down at his desk, turned on his computer, and started an internet search for Frank Donovan and all the companies that helped to place foreign workers in America.

Frank was listed as the CEO of New Horizons only, but Chuck knew that the traffickers were all connected and just posing as legitimate businesses. He wanted to see as many pictures of the executives of those other companies as possible. They would likely be the people that had the most at stake in a leadership takeover.

He scanned through the names and faces and tried to commit them to memory in case he happened to see any here in Whitefish. He knew that Frank employed lower-level thugs to do the actual dirty work, but the higher ups often had a morbid curiosity that led many of them to hang around the periphery during the process.

Before long, a couple of hours had passed, and Chuck was getting anxious. What was happening with Quinn? It was now well after the end of school. Is he hanging out at home or out causing trouble? He then remembered about his deputy, the one that he had sent to check out the Madison house around lunch time. He realized that he hadn't heard back from him and had been distracted by getting Susan and Sandra settled.

"Kathy," Chuck buzzed her on his phone. "Have you heard anything from Sean lately?"

"No sir," Kathy's voice replied from the speaker. "I can try to patch through to him."

"Yeah, please do that." Chuck got up, grabbed his coat and his keys. It was unlike Sean to not report back to him after an assignment. In fact, if anything, Sean usually gave him way more information than he wanted to hear.

Chuck left his office and headed down the hall. "Anything?" he asked Kathy as he passed her.

She shook her head. "Do you want me to send another unit to where he last checked in?"

"No, I got it," Chuck said and kept walking out of the door.

. . .

Not long afterwards, he pulled up slowly to the Madison house and saw the broken front gate.

Something went down here, Chuck thought, as he steered his car down the driveway. As he approached the house, he could see Sean's patrol car with a damaged front end parked at an awkward angle, its rear tires smashing some flowers that bordered the concrete drive. The front door of the house was open.

Chuck got out of his car and took out his gun from its holster on his belt. Everything seemed quiet, but he had a bad feeling about his deputy. He shouldn't have sent him here by himself. He hadn't expected anything to happen yet.

Chuck walked carefully to the front door, keeping out of the direct line of fire should anyone be waiting for him in the house. He realized that this could be a trap for him, but he didn't care at this point. He wasn't trying to be reckless with his life but knew that there was a very high likelihood that things were ultimately not going to end well for him anyway.

When he got to the front porch, he saw a pool of blood that looked sticky and mostly dried. He announced his presence and pivoted into the house with his gun held out in front. There was no response.

A trail of blood from the porch led to a coat closet in the hall. Chuck kept his eyes ahead, scanning for any movement until he reached the closet door. When he opened it, he dropped the arm that was holding his gun. Sean's eyes stared back at him, lifeless and unblinking. There was a dark red hole in the middle of his forehead.

"Those bastards," Chuck said, his voice catching in the back of his throat. He checked for a pulse and when he found none, reflexively reached for his radio to call it in. But then he stopped himself. *I need to give myself a little more time,* he thought, as he got back to his feet and started searching the house. The place was trashed, but there were no more bodies, alive or dead.

He headed back to his car and started the engine. Then he reached for his radio. "Kathy, we have an officer down. I'm afraid that he is dead. Activate the team and get them over here. I have a lead on the perpetrator and can't stay. Tell them to do their best work. This is family."

Kathy was silent on the other end of the line for a minute.

"Kathy, did you copy?"

"Copy, sir."

Chuck could hear her crying.

CHAPTER SIXTY-FOUR

Chuck turned right out of the Madison driveway and headed out of town. He needed to get a few things at his place before dark, when he figured most of the fireworks would happen. He planned to leave his squad car in his driveway and use his Ford F-150 for the rest of the night, to deflect any outside attention from himself. He would grab his radio to stay connected to any chatter but hoped to only use it for an emergency. He was going to have to at least communicate with the team at the Madison house, so they wouldn't get too suspicious about his absence.

Chuck lived in a small cabin north of the lake about ten miles. He had ten acres of mostly pine trees and enjoyed the peace and quiet. He also had a root cellar full of guns, just in case. He hadn't ever really expected to use them, but now, his AR-15 would definitely come in handy. A couple of police-issued shotguns might not be enough.

When he drove up to his cabin, everything seemed quiet, same as usual. A few deer grazed near his porch, also reassuring him that no one had come by recently. They looked up when he pulled in and bounded away when he got out of the car. He went inside and changed his clothes but kept his bullet-proof vest on underneath a dark button-down shirt.

His root cellar was behind the house. It looked like a run-down shed, but he had reinforced it on the inside with concrete walls and floor. He unlocked it and climbed down the few steps. His guns were well organized, hanging on the wall or separated carefully on lighted shelves. He grabbed the AR-15 and as much ammunition as he had and holstered a handgun under each shoulder and another around his leg. He grabbed some night vision goggles and a helmet and left the cellar. *That might at least even things up,* he thought.

The sun was sitting lower in the sky. He figured he had about two hours before dark. Susan was safe in her motel room. Sandra was in the woods and should be in her hiding place by now. He needed to figure out where Quinn was. If he could find Quinn, the others would show up, too.

But how am I going to find him? Chuck thought. *He's obviously not going to stick around the house after someone has been there and trashed it. If he hadn't already seen that, he certainly wouldn't go there now with all the cops hanging around. It's now a crime scene. The second murder in three days. How many more?*

Chuck climbed into his truck and drove back to town. Maybe he'd get lucky and stumble upon Quinn or someone else that he recognized. He was sure that Wesley was here and probably was the one who trashed the Madison house looking for Quinn.

As he approached the main drag in town, he heard the squealing of tires just behind him. He looked in his rear-view mirror and saw a red Mustang speeding away from him.

Incredible! Chuck thought as he quickly flipped a U-turn and accelerated after the car. After a few minutes chase, he could see the Mustang stopped at a stoplight a couple of blocks ahead. Chuck pushed on the gas and swerved around some cars ahead of him who honked angrily at him for his reckless driving, but he made it right behind the Mustang before the light turned green.

As the Mustang started to accelerate, Chuck passed it to the left and veered in front, driving it to the side of the road to avoid a collision.

Chuck pulled out his gun and got out of the truck. The driver of the car had rolled down the window and was yelling obscenities at him until he saw the handgun in Chuck's right hand. He then went very quiet. Chuck approached the window, pulled out his badge, and looked inside. It wasn't Quinn. It looked like another high school kid and his girlfriend out for a joyride.

"Who the hell are you?" Chuck asked.

"Uh ... Ryan," the driver responded nervously.

"Where's Quinn?" Chuck asked pointedly.

"He borrowed my truck. He said I could drive his car," the high schooler named Ryan explained.

"Okay," Chuck said. "So, what does your truck look like, and did he tell you where he was going?"

"It's a Dodge Ram, kind of thrashed. Maroon. He said he needed to move some stuff. We were going to trade back tomorrow. Is Quinn in trouble?"

"Yeah, you could probably say that," Chuck said and holstered his gun under his jacket. "All right. I'm going to give you my cell phone number," he said, as he scrawled out his number on a notepad and ripped off the paper. He handed it to Ryan. "It is very important that you call me if you see or hear from Quinn, okay. Don't tell him! Just call me. His life is in danger, okay? It's important. You got it?"

"Uh, okay," Ryan said as he looked at the notepad paper and put it in the pocket of his jeans.

"And drive safer!"

Chuck walked away from the Mustang and got back into his truck. Now, at least, he knew what Quinn was driving. He drove around town looking, unsuccessfully, for a maroon Dodge Ram.

Maybe Quinn left town. The only thing that would keep him here is the fact that Sandra could testify against him. He would want her out of the way before he disappeared for good.

It was dark now and the activity on the streets was starting to thin out. *I'm going to head up to Sandra's and wait to see if anyone shows up,* Chuck thought. *They'll probably wait until the middle of the night to decrease the chance of anyone else seeing them, but I might as well get there early.*

Chuck headed up the mountain and turned down Sandra's street. He drove past her condo building and was turning around when he saw it—a maroon Dodge Ram parked less than a block from her building.

"He's here!" Chuck said to himself, as he parked his truck and got out quietly. He pulled out his gun, put on his goggles, and walked slowly toward the condo complex, staying close to the trees and out of sight. He ducked into the trees before he reached her condo and made his way around the back, trying to move as quietly as possible. When he got to a point where he could see her window and the back entrance, he stopped.

Sandra's light was on. He was sure that he checked that all the lights were off when he and Susan had left. *Who was in there? Had Sandra changed her mind and come back? Or did Quinn break in? Or did Sandra come back, and Quinn found out?*

Okay, Chuck. What's your next move? he thought. *I've got to get in there in case Sandra is in danger!*

He moved again through the trees until he was as close to the back door as possible. There was a streetlamp that lighted the parking lot and the back entrance, and he wanted to stay out of that light for as long as possible. He knew the access code for the door, so he could get in quickly.

Just as he was ready to make his move, the door opened. Two men dressed in black stepped into the light. Chuck recognized one of them.

How did he get in there? Chuck thought, *and why?* Chuck froze in place and waited for them to walk away. They headed toward the street, and Chuck followed at a distance. The men got into a black car and drove away.

Chuck ran back to the building, entered the code, and sprinted up the staircase. Susan had given him her key in case he needed to get into Sandra's condo for any reason. He pulled it out and unlocked the door. Nothing seemed disturbed except that there were two coffee mugs on the table and the chairs were pulled out.

"Sandra?" Chuck said. "It's me, Chief Peters. Are you here? You're safe now."

He looked in the sensory room. Nothing. Her bedroom door was closed. He paused in the hall for a minute. *Am I too late? Am I going to find her like I found my sister—shot in the head while lying in her bed?*

Chuck opened the door slowly. He could see the foot of her bed. Nothing else in the room seemed out of place. He took a deep breath and pushed the door fully open with his gun held out front. The bed was empty, the covers were smooth. He moved quickly into the bathroom and then the closet. Nothing. Chuck exhaled in relief.

But where was Quinn? That had to be his truck out there. No one was inside it when he passed. He checked. *Was Quinn in the woods? Looking for Sandra?* That's the only thing that made sense.

He was going to have to follow him. *Sandra didn't say where she was going. It had better be a good spot.*

Chuck turned off the lights and locked the condo. He went back down the stairs, left the building, and headed toward the trail. As he started into the trees, he stopped.

Why were those men there? he thought again. *It's one of two reasons. One might be to kill Sandra. But the other might be to catch Quinn trying to kill Sandra. Quinn was here, and now he's not. I don't think he's in the woods.*

Chuck sat down on a fallen log and tried to think. *I could go on a goose chase in the woods all night long, or I could be smarter. No, I need to figure out how those men got into Sandra's condo without a forced entry and what they did with Quinn Madison.*

CHAPTER SIXTY-FIVE

Quinn could hear their footsteps above him. Muffled voices spoke in what sounded like a heated discussion as they moved around the cabin. If they moved directly above him, he could pick up parts of what they were saying, but not enough to piece it together. He figured, based on where he was chained, that he must be below the dining area. After a while of listening to the pacing steps above, he could hear the legs of two chairs scraping across the floorboards.

"What did he say?"

"We hold him as ransom until we get what we want."

"Does his dad know?"

"He will soon enough."

"When will the boss get here?"

"In about an hour, he said."

The voices went quiet for a while until Quinn could hear them both stand up and walk away. He heard the door open, and the footsteps disappeared. *They must have gone outside,* he figured. *At least they're not planning on killing me. My dad will pay them.* He rested his head against the wall and rubbed his sore wrists. He may have even dozed off for a few minutes before he heard a door shut upstairs, then, more footsteps and different voices. *That must be the boss,* Quinn thought, listening intently for an Irish accent.

Snippets of new conversation made its way to Quinn's ears, as the men upstairs moved in and out of position.

"... in the cellar ... "

"He knows ... "

"... send a message ... "

"We'll just have to kill him ... "

The last one sent Quinn's head spinning. *We'll just have to kill him? Were they talking about me? Did my dad say no?*

Sweat broke out on Quinn's forehead despite the chill of the unheated crawl space where he was trapped. He pulled hard against the chain. It was solid.

How am I going to get out of here? No one will find me down here if they kill me now and just leave my body here to rot. My mom will never know what happened. She thinks I came here to play football. My dad lied to her and said the coach was his buddy from U of M and was a former quarterback. He would prepare me for college, he told her. Could she really be so clueless about her husband? Or did she just choose to look the other way?

Quinn spent the next several hours expecting to hear the cellar door open and someone to climb down the steps with a gun to put an end to things. Somehow, after hours of panic at every sound, his body shut down, and he fell asleep.

The next thing he knew, he saw cracks of daylight creeping through the floorboards, and all was quiet above him. He tried to straighten his stiff legs, but the shackles kept them from moving. Instead, he climbed to his feet, hitting his head on a joist. His back was crying out to be straightened but there just wasn't room. He slid back down the wall and waited for what was coming next.

About an hour later, he heard the door open, and a single set of footsteps walked above him toward the bedroom where the cellar door was hidden. *Here we go,* Quinn thought, his heart starting to pound once more.

But nothing happened. The footsteps came back in his direction, where he heard a chair pull out just above him, and then it was silent again. *Someone was up there, just waiting. Waiting for what? For whom? Was he just waiting for the go-ahead to come down and shoot me? Should I scream or beg for mercy?*

Quinn decided to just stay quiet and wait. His fate was sealed. These men weren't the type to grant wishes. *What will be, will be.* He resolved to face his killers with confidence and look them in the eye when they pulled the trigger. It was the only power he had left.

CHAPTER SIXTY-SIX

Sandra woke up before dawn, as the anticipation for the day ahead made it hard for her to stay asleep. Plus, she figured that if she left her shelter while it was still dark, it would minimize the chance that someone would see her in it. She packed up her stuff and put everything back in her pack. She left everything else in the shelter intact should she need to use it again that night. Then she started moving slowly away. She had a several-mile hike before she arrived at the cabin, and, as she got closer, she would need to move slowly and carefully to keep herself hidden, so she wanted to give herself plenty of time.

She felt confident and invigorated after a whole night in her woods. The sounds of the forest at night were like music to her ears, and she never once felt scared. Her mind was as clear as it had ever been, and her soul was giving her strength.

As the night sky turned to dawn, she moved off the trail and deeper into the trees. It was much harder going there, and she had to be careful where she stepped or what she held onto so as not to add any noise. She also began moving in an irregular pattern, like a deer, with frequent stops and short segments of forward progress.

The woods were calm, and the activity of the birds and other small four-legged creatures helped relieve any residual anxiety as she got closer to her destination. The animals were always aware when a human was traipsing carelessly through their home.

As she approached the perimeter of where the body had been buried, though, she felt a shift inside of her. She could almost see the daylight turn a shade darker, like she had just put on a pair of sunglasses. She was moving very deliberately now and decided to skirt away from that spot and approach the cabin from a different angle, staying hidden in the trees until she could see the window of the back bedroom. There, on the windowsill, was a can of soda. Sprite.

Sandra let out a big sigh and slid down to the ground for a minute with her back against a large tree, still hidden from view from anyone who might be watching from the cabin. She just needed to recharge her battery there for a minute before she re-entered the human world with its dangers and expectations.

Right as she was about to take a step out from behind the tree and into the open space that led to the deck, she heard the sound of car tires on the dirt driveway in front of the cabin. She froze in place. *Is that the police chief?* She had assumed that he was already inside, waiting for her. *If not, does someone else know about the signal can? Maybe it's my mom.*

She started moving again but stopped when she heard the voices of several men. She didn't recognize any of those voices, and most importantly, the police chief's was not among them. She held her breath and tried to make her body sink into the tree.

The voices got louder and sounded angry as they approached the cabin. They seemed to be lingering outside, though, which was confusing to Sandra. *Were they waiting for me to show up and mad that I was late?* She didn't know if her anxiety would allow her to deal with people who were impatient or angry with her.

No, I'm going back to the shelter. Something's not right. The police chief was always calm around me, and my mom would certainly correct them if they were being loud or scary.

She started moving as slowly and carefully as possible away from the voices, several layers deep, back into the woods.

Then, a startling sound pierced the air like a crack of lightning. It was followed by several more cracks along with the splintering of wood and broken glass. *Gunshots!*

Sandra moved quickly away, weaving deftly through the trees, not stopping to listen for footsteps or more voices. She covered over a hundred yards in very little time at all. *They must have been shooting at me. Or at least they knew about where we were going to meet. I've got to go back to the shelter and stay hidden. But now, how will I know when it is safe to leave? No phone. No meeting place. No plan. At least my mom knows how to track me on her computer. I'll just wait for her to come get me.*

Sandra suddenly stopped. A sickening feeling rose from deep inside. What if her mom had been waiting for her with the policeman inside the cabin? What if those men had captured her ... or killed her? *No, that cannot be what just happened.*

She felt the ground tilt, and she lost her bearings momentarily, falling hard onto her back in a bed of pine needles. She closed her eyes tightly from the impact while she regained the breath that had been knocked out of her lungs. As she reopened her eyes, all that she could see was the piercing white of the sun that had found its way through the thick canopy of the forest and shown directly onto her face. She squinted her eyes, and as she did, the light separated into all the colors of the rainbow. She just stared at the beauty of the scene above her for several minutes and listened for her soul's voice to give her instructions. Nothing. No voice. But her fear was gone. She sat up, waited for her vision to return to normal, and then made a choice. *I'm going back.*

CHAPTER SIXTY-SEVEN

Chuck heard them pull up. He assumed that it was Atkins and Susan, figuring that Susan couldn't wait to see if Sandra was okay after her night alone. But when he heard multiple male voices, he peeked through the blinds and saw them pulling out their weapons.

"Shit," Chuck said, as he reached for his AR-15 that, luckily, he had brought with him from his truck. *What are they doing here? How did they know?*

His first thought was to run to the back bedroom and switch the cans for Sandra, but as he was backing away from the window, a bullet pierced the glass, causing the entire pane to crack like a spider web and then crash to the floor. Chuck hit the ground and slid away from the window to the side wall. Another volley of bullets came through the window, tearing up the blinds and putting holes in the ceiling and the opposing wall.

Chuck waited for a second and then came up firing as he traversed across the open window. Initially he just aimed at their vehicle, a gray van, but then he saw the men scattering from his gunfire. He saw one of them hit the ground with blood coming from his chest as Chuck's bullets found purchase.

"One down," Chuck said, surprising even himself about how calm he was. He knew that he was outnumbered, but he was at least sheltered behind solid walls, and they couldn't see him. He wasn't sure how many there were. He saw at least three, and one was dead.

The gunfire stopped for a minute, and Chuck planned his next move. He figured that the two other men had probably ran behind the van. They might be on their phones right now, calling for back up. He wasn't sure how many others might be available to come to their aid but didn't really want to wait around to find out. *I've got to make my move now,* Chuck thought.

He stayed close to the wall and slid into the kitchen, never taking his eyes off the front door in case they came bursting through it. He was going to try to get out the back door before they saw him. He could then get into the trees, flank behind them, and hopefully pick them off from there. If he got stuck in the house, it would only be a matter of time before he was surrounded, and then it was all over.

As soon as he hit the tile of the kitchen, he sent another round of bullets through the front window as a deterrent and then ran down the hall toward the back. He made a quick detour into the bedroom and knocked the Sprite can off the windowsill. He had left the Coke can on the dining table. Hopefully Sandra would still get the message.

He slid out the back screen door as quietly as possible and headed across the deck. When he hit the stairs, one of the planks creaked loudly as he stepped down on it. Chuck paused momentarily until he heard someone say, "He went out the back. Get around there!"

Chuck sprinted for the closest stand of trees and dove behind one just as a fresh round of bullets shredded the ground near his feet. *So much for surprising them,* he thought, taking a few seconds to catch his breath. He then aimed his rifle in their general direction and shot off another round as he moved a little deeper into the woods. As soon as he was out of their direct line, he skirted around parallel to the cabin and back toward their vehicle. He could hear voices and footsteps trailing him as he moved.

Through a break in the trees, he could see their van with the side door slid open, facing away from the cabin. He couldn't see anyone around it and figured that both men were behind him now. He had a quick decision to make: try to hide behind a tree and see if he can shoot his chasers or try to make it to his truck and get out of there. Either one was risky. The trees were getting smaller and thinner where he was, and he wouldn't be able to hide completely behind them anymore. If his chasers were careful enough, they could shoot him before he could see them. So, he decided to go for his vehicle.

As he broke into the open driveway, he could hear the van's engine running. *The keys are in it*, Chuck thought. *I'm taking their van!* He ran as hard as he could toward the open van door, trying to make himself as small a target as possible.

He heard someone yell from behind him, "There he is!" Chuck dove inside the open door and climbed quickly into the driver's seat. He put it into gear and squealed the tires as he sped away. Bullets riddled the ground behind him as they shot at the tires, but none of them hit, and the van kept moving forward. He turned quickly onto the pavement of the highway, looking in his left side mirror as two guys with guns ran out onto the road from the trees.

He let out a big sigh and then started laughing and banging his hands on the steering wheel. "Take that, you sons of bitches!"

That's when he heard the familiar click of a pistol being cocked behind him. "Hello, Chuck. Fancy meeting you here."

Chuck grabbed onto the steering wheel tightly. He recognized that voice, and the sound of it made him angry. Really angry!

"You? You're behind all of this? Where is she?"

"I'm afraid you'll have to be more specific, Chuck. Do you mean mother or daughter?" the voice said.

"You rotten-to-the-core bastard!" Chuck muttered.

"Well, to answer your question, mother is right here behind you," he stepped down hard on Susan's foot, and she let out a squeal through the gag binding her mouth. "And, according to this laptop here, daughter is very close by. And you are going to help bring her in, Chief. Now turn the van around and go back to the cabin."

"I'm not going to help you! You can just shoot me now," Chuck said, as he pushed on the accelerator.

Atkins just laughed. "I'm not going to shoot you, Chuck. Not yet anyway. But I will start with mommy here if you don't do what I say. Now do it!" he yelled.

Chuck slowed down, made a U-turn, and drove back to Slater's cabin. He pulled up in front and took his hands off the wheel.

"In the air!" Atkins yelled.

Chuck complied and raised his hands slowly. Atkins waved at his two men who had approached the van with guns pointed.

"Search him! And tie him up!" Atkins instructed. "C'mon mommy, we are going inside."

Susan stole a frightened glance at Chuck while he was being thrown against the hood of the van and his guns removed. Their eyes met briefly, and Chuck tried his best to project calm, but their reality was unbelievably bad. Atkins, the one man that he had trusted through all of this, had betrayed him. And now, the two women he had tried so desperately to protect were both in mortal danger. And he, Chuck, had basically given them right to the bad guy.

CHAPTER SIXTY-EIGHT

The shooting hadn't stopped, and Sandra was having second thoughts about her plan now. *What exactly am I going to do when I get there? I don't have a gun. I wouldn't even know how to use one ... But I've got to know. Is my mom there? Is she still alive? Am I all alone now?*

She started moving slowly away from her spot. It wouldn't be smart to just go directly toward the cabin. If they were waiting for her, that is what they would expect. *I need to circle around and see what I can see on the opposite side. The road side.*

She reached out to steady herself against the trunk of a tree and saw the watch around her wrist. *Take it off!* her soul's voice told her. Sandra took off the watch and put it in the fork between two major tree branches. The tree had a unique shape, and she was confident that she could find it again if she determined that she was still safe. But for now, she did not want to be tracked.

After ditching the watch, she moved a hundred more yards back into the forest and found a place to hide her backpack. She wanted to be as light and unencumbered as possible. With nothing else on her except a utility pocketknife, she disappeared further into the woods.

After several more minutes, the sounds of the gunshots ceased, and the woods were eerily quiet. The forest animals knew there was danger near the cabin, too, and they had all disappeared into their safe places. Sandra's instinct was to do the same, to go far away, back to the shelter, or to find a new place altogether ... but she had to know. She couldn't abandon her mother unless she knew. So, she kept moving, creating a wide circle that would eventually lead her back to the cabin.

When Sandra came to the highway, she waited, hidden in a natural ditch that was covered with a dense bush. Several cars passed with minutes in between. There were no sirens or speeding vehicles. She waited for another car to pass and, when it was out of sight, scurried across the road like a squirrel trying to not get hit by an oncoming car. Luckily, no car came, and she disappeared into the trees on the other side.

Here, she continued circling back, being sure that she stayed far enough from the road that she couldn't be seen. She slowed down to a crawl as she got close to the turnoff from the highway to the cabin. Every few carefully chosen steps, she stopped and listened.

The cabin was set back quite a way from the highway, and she was going to need to cross the road again to get close enough to see it. She knew that the closer she was, the more dangerous it would be. She felt like she was still too visible in her solid blue shirt and hiking pants. She needed some camouflage, something that would make her blend into the shadows.

Nearby, she could hear the bubbling of a spring and moved toward it. As she approached, her boot sank into some rich dark mud. *Perfect*, she thought. She grabbed the mud and made random striped patterns on her clothes and face. She took a handful in each hand and streaked it into her hair. *That should help*, she thought and started back toward the road.

She moved beyond the cabin turnoff by about four hundred yards. The cabin was quite isolated without immediate neighbors, so she didn't have to worry about getting caught on someone else's property. After repeating the road-crossing procedure, she made it safely again to the other side, the same side as the cabin.

She moved one step at a time, inching closer to the cabin with eyes and ears in constant surveillance. If she got caught here, it would be harder for her to disappear. She was now essentially fenced in by the highway and the dirt road that led to and then past the cabin. She wasn't sure where that road ended up but presumed it was at someone else's house. *Could the owners of that place have heard the gunshots and called the police? Was there an army of help on its way?* If help was coming, she would have expected it by now. Yet, it was still quiet in the woods.

Sandra continued her slow progress until she could see parts of the front porch of the cabin through the trees. There was a truck and a van parked out front. No one was outside.

She inched ever closer until she was only about twenty yards away from the driveway where she laid down in a large clump of wild grass that was about waist high. There, she was completely invisible to anyone from the house. They would have to step on her before they would discover that she was there.

If she didn't show up as scheduled, the policeman would surely leave the cabin and go looking for her. If her mom was there with the laptop, they would think she was a hundred yards away, behind the cabin, and might even just call out for her. If neither happened, then something bad was going on. The gunshots had already signaled that the latter was most likely true.

If nothing happens by lunchtime, I am going to disappear into the woods for good, Sandra thought. *If my mom is still alive, she'll send out the army to find me. Then, I'll know that it's safe to be discovered. I think there are enough empty vacation homes around here that I can get plenty of supplies to last at least a month without needing to go back into town.*

Sandra remained perfectly still and completely hidden. She had practiced doing that over the years that she had spent in the woods alone. She wasn't sure why. She just liked feeling as if she had been absorbed by a force much greater than her. She was now, once again, one with her surroundings. And she waited.

CHAPTER SIXTY-NINE

Quinn could hear them yelling. *Obviously, something wasn't going according to plan.* Then there were the gunshots. *It's my dad,* Quinn thought. *I knew that he'd come for me.* Quinn heard some commotion, then silence. It felt like the silence lasted forever. *What was happening? Why weren't they rescuing me?*

Finally, he heard a door open again, and footsteps. A lot of footsteps and more voices. Next, Quinn heard the cellar door open, and light from above flooded the darkness below it. *Is it my rescuers or my killers?*

The first person he saw was that cop, the one who had questioned him. He fell forward down the stairs and landed on his face, just like Quinn had the night before. His hands were also bound behind his body. When he rolled to his knees, he looked up, and his eyes met Quinn's.

"What are you doing here?" he said, obviously surprised to see Quinn bound in chains.

Quinn didn't respond. *Clearly, these are not my dad's men. The cop had just meddled too far.*

Next came an elderly woman that climbed down the stairs backwards. They had untied her hands, but her mouth was gagged. She could just stand upright in the cellar and stood aside as a third person climbed down the stairs holding an AR-15. When he got to the bottom, he pointed his gun at the woman first. "Over there," motioning toward where Quinn was chained to the floor. She complied and walked over to Quinn, her eyes widening a little when she saw him, recognizing him as the man on Sandra's phone.

"Sit down," the man with the gun commanded. Susan obeyed and sat a few feet away from Quinn.

"You too, Peters," Atkins said. "Get over there by the others."

"Why are you doing this, Atkins? You were supposed to be one of the good guys. How much did Frank have to pay you to get you to flip?" Chuck asked.

Atkins started laughing. "Pay me? Frank didn't pay me. No, sir. I don't work for Frank. I'm taking his place."

At this, Quinn piped up. "Who are you? Where's Wesley?"

Atkins laughed again, "You think that you have to worry about Wesley? Wesley is dead. I shot him myself. The thing is, criminals have no loyalty. They will just work for whoever pays them the most. Wesley's guys are now my guys, and they brought him right to me. Of course, he begged me to let him work for me, but I don't need guys like him. He wanted to be boss. I would never have been able to trust him. Gary helped tremendously. He really is a fine actor. Without Gary, Wesley never would have come to Whitefish."

Quinn seethed. Gary had betrayed him all right but not at all how he had thought.

"I have been preparing for this day since that first trial back in Chicago. You weren't even born yet, Quinn. No, but Chuck here knows. He was the cop that altered evidence which led to the conviction of three innocent young men. It was so easy, wasn't it Chuck? If only your guilt hadn't got the best of you, your mother and sister might still be alive. And who knows, we could have been partners. Anyway, no matter. It's just funny how life seems to always come full circle, isn't it? After that trial, I kept digging and learned all about your dad's business, how he made so much money, how he never got caught. Well, I know how to do it better. I can do it best right from inside the FBI. But you know what that means? It means you all are going to die. I can't leave any witnesses, can I? Chuck, you deserve it. Quinn, you're the heir. You can't be lingering around. The only truly innocent one is the lady here. I'm truly sorry you got caught up in this. You seem like a very nice person. But every war has collateral damage."

Susan's face turned red, and tears started falling.

"There is only one person that we're missing before we can start the party. Your lovely and brave daughter. Chuck, here, told me all about her. It's a truly remarkable story. I am very sorry that no one else will ever hear it. It would have been a good movie, you know," Atkins grinned. "Anyway, shouldn't be long now. My guys are tracking her down. Who knew that you would just give me the tool to make it so easy to find her? You handed her right to me!" Atkins laughed again. He let out a sharp whistle with his tongue, and one of his goons came down the stairs and bound Chuck's and Susan's legs with a rope that he then secured to the same chain that was holding Quinn's shackles. "I should have planned better," Atkins said light-heartedly. "I only had shackles for one. But that'll do. Won't be long now anyway."

Atkins and his goon climbed up the stairs and shut the trapdoor, and the cellar once again was dark except for the cracks of light from the floorboards that left stripes on the hard pack dirt floor.

CHAPTER SEVENTY

Sandra laid still in the grass for a full hour without moving. She could hear voices inside the house and occasionally saw movement through the window, but none of the voices were her mother's. She wasn't sure what to do. Her main question was still unanswered. *Was my mother still alive?*

She decided that she needed to go back, back to where she could see the deck. Maybe there would be more action there. That is where they would expect her to come. So, she slowly inched backward, staying hidden in the grass until she was behind a tree where she could stand up and still be obscured from view.

She then retraced her steps, back across the road, circling again close to where she started. As she approached the cabin from behind, she could see a man with a gun standing on the deck. She froze and blended into the shadows. After a few more minutes, two other men with guns emerged from the woods. One of them was holding her backpack in one arm. They went up the stairs and laid the backpack down on the deck. Then one of them reached into a pocket and pulled out her watch.

"We found this," the man said. "And her backpack, but no trace of the girl. She must suspect something."

"Go get the old woman," the original man from the deck said. "We'll use her as bait. The girl will eventually come looking for her. Plus, we now have all her stuff. How long could a disabled girl stay out in the woods by herself anyway? She'll be here before you know it."

One of the men from the woods went into the cabin and after a few minutes, Sandra saw her mom being led out onto the deck, her mouth gagged, and her hands tied. They pushed her down on a bench, and the man who seemed to be the leader approached her.

"Okay, Susan, you have a job to do. It's not a hard job, but if you fail, I will shoot you. All you need to do is sit here and look natural. When your daughter comes, you smile and wave at her to come and join you. Okay? That's it."

Susan looked hard into the man's eyes but didn't make any other expression of agreement.

"Take off the gag and untie her hands," the leader told the other men who complied. "Now if you scream or run, you are dead. Do you understand? If you're good, maybe I'll let you live."

Susan wiped her mouth with her hands and licked her lips. She looked again at the leader and then started screaming at the top of her lungs, "Sandra! Run! Don't come close! Run!"

That is all she could get out before the man who had untied her clamped his hand over her mouth. Susan bit down hard, drawing blood, and causing the man to drop his hand and curse in pain.

"Run, Sandra!"

The other man grabbed the gag and again forced it into Susan's mouth, keeping his own hands clear. He tied it tightly and then wrenched her hands behind her back and bound them. The leader angrily pointed at the door, and she was again forced inside the cabin, followed by the three men.

Sandra took a slow deep breath. She had forgotten to breathe in fear that she was going to witness her mother being shot right in front of her while she was trying to warn Sandra to stay away. When Sandra regained her composure, she started to make a plan. Her mother was there, inside the cabin with at least three men with guns, and was still alive, for now. But it didn't seem like there was much time. She would need to draw them out into the woods. She didn't stand a chance anywhere else.

Sandra felt strangely calm and focused. She couldn't remember having ever felt this way before to this degree. Her soul was clearly in charge now, and her mind was being obedient. It is like it knew that now was not the time for playing around. She could feel the ground beneath her feet almost vibrating, like the woods, her woods, were full of nervous energy, ready to help her and keep her safe. They were going to protect her. She was a part of them.

As Sandra breathed in and out, filling her lungs with the pine-scented mountain air, her mind filled with a plan, almost traced in a gold blueprint of where to go and what to do. She smiled and took two steps forward. Then another two and another, until she was two steps into the clearing behind the deck. She then let out an ear-splitting, air-piercing scream. She kept screaming until the three men spilled outside of the back door of the cabin and saw her. Within another second, before they could even raise their guns, she was gone.

CHAPTER SEVENTY-ONE

"Go get her! What are you waiting for?" Atkins yelled at his two companions.

The two men shouldered their guns and ran toward the spot where Sandra had disappeared. Atkins stood on the deck and settled in for what he thought would be a short wait.

When the men reached the woods, they decided to split up until they figured out which way she went. One of them turned left and started looking for broken branches or footprints. He could tell where she had been standing in the clearing but as soon as he entered the woods, all traces of her disappeared. He circled the area deliberately but found nothing. He came upon a hiking trail that looked well-used. He figured she would most likely have jumped on this trail as it was easy-going and maybe familiar to her. So, he started up the trail and headed away from the cabin.

Every few minutes, he paused and listened for any sign of human activity. But all he heard were some angry squirrels scolding him for being near their nest. The trail eventually came to a stream where there were a couple of logs placed purposefully to act as a bridge. Just above that spot, he could hear the rushing sound of a waterfall. He spotted her as soon as he crossed over the bridge. She was up ahead on the trail where it looked like there was a fork that probably led to the waterfall. She didn't seem to notice him as she turned toward the waterfall.

This should be easy enough. The boss would want her alive, he figured. *She was going down a dead-end trail. I'll just follow her and grab her by the water.*

The man reached the fork and followed quietly behind. When he reached the waterfall, he was surprised at how tall it was, at least fifty feet. There wasn't much of a pool at the bottom, mostly just another series of large boulders and fallen trees. Most surprising was that the girl was nowhere to be seen. He looked all around the area at the base of the falls. He could see her footprints, but they seemed to disappear right where the water hit the ground as if she walked directly into the cliff edge. He couldn't see any space behind the water where she could be hiding. Then he looked up just in time to see her legs as she pulled herself up and over the edge.

She just scaled that wall? he thought. It was hard to believe. *I thought this girl was disabled. She climbs like a mountain goat.* He looked around for an easier way up, but the cliff extended for as far as he could see. *She's going to get away if I don't follow her now.* So, he tightened the strap on his gun and started climbing, following the route that Sandra took right next to the falling water. It was hard going. *How did she make it seem so easy?* Initially there were a decent number of ledges in the rock that provided stable foot and hand holds, but as he ascended, things became more precarious. *This was a stupid idea,* he acknowledged, now too high to reverse his course. The rock was slippery from the moss and the mist from the water. He was paralyzed against the side, not able to go up or down. His arms were starting to fatigue, and he knew that he was in trouble.

Just then, something struck him on the top of his head. He looked up, and there she was, looking over the edge about twenty feet above him. She let another one drop, a small rock that hit him directly on the forehead. He let out a yell and started swearing at the cliff in front of him. Another rock, a little bigger one, hit him again on the top of his head, drawing a little blood. This gave him a surge of adrenaline, and he made a few more moves before coming again to a smooth part of the wall. He was now about forty feet in the air, only about ten feet below the top. The girl was still there. She let another rock go, another little one that hit him right below his eye.

"You better stop with the rocks, you little bitch, or I'm going to shoot you as soon as I get up there," he yelled to the sky.

His arms were trembling again, and his hands were going numb. He looked down and saw the sharp edges of the boulders below him. *I am not going to survive that fall. The only way is up.* Just then, the girl appeared again, this time holding a rock that was about the size of a dinner plate. If she let that go, he would surely get knocked off the wall.

He only had one move, and it was all or nothing. Just out of reach was a root from a small pine tree that had somehow found enough space in the rock to grow straight out of its face. For him to reach it, he would have to push off with his legs which meant that he would lose all contact with the wall for a split second. *But what choice do I have?* The girl stood right above him and was lifting the rock to let it go. He leapt up with all his strength and grabbed onto the root firmly. It held. He was almost within reach of the top and of the girl. He found a spot for his foot and gave another tug on the root to pull himself over the edge. As he did so, he saw the girl put down the rock and at the same time, almost in slow motion, felt the root that was supporting his weight pull away from the cliff. His body started falling, and all he could see was a clear blue sky and a pine root grasped firmly in his hand. Then he felt a thump, and all went dark.

. . .

Sandra looked over the edge again and saw his body bent awkwardly over a rock. He wasn't moving and a stream of blood was working its way down the side of the boulder. She took a deep breath, moved away from the stream, and headed the direction that she assumed the other man went. She moved quickly but carefully along the top of the ledge, keeping her eyes and ears trained on the forest floor well below her. The man would probably turn around before he came up to her level unless he had reason to believe that she had come this far. She knew of a place where the trail came very close to the ledge. She would wait for him there. He would probably be on his way back to the cabin after giving up the search in that direction.

When she got to the spot, she found a boulder that was about the size of one of her exercise balls that was perched near the edge of the cliff. It was resting on another flat granite surface with a mild slope. It wouldn't take much effort to get it moving. She sat with her back against it and found that her feet had a good grip. And she waited.

. . .

"Joel, come in. Have you seen the girl?" The second man spoke into his two-way radio but received no reply. *That's weird*, he thought, *we should still be well within range. Maybe he turned down the volume because he doesn't want to spook her. He must be on her tail. I'm heading back. There is no sign of her here.*

He turned around and started heading back down the trail at a fast pace. If they lost her, there would be hell to pay. The trail took a few turns and minor switchbacks as it descended. It led him below the ledge that he had almost finished climbing. He was feeling the extra pounds that he had put on over the last few years after getting out of prison. He could afford them on the outside. Not in prison, though. Appearance of strength is what kept you alive in there.

He stopped for a second and took a breather. He was now next to the cliff, at the bottom of the climb. As he started moving again, he heard something from right above him. *A whistle? Did someone just whistle?* He took a step back and looked up.

He heard it before he saw it, something crashing through some trees. Once he saw it, it was too late: a large rock falling off the edge and heading right for him. There was no time to move.

· · ·

Sandra again looked over the edge. She had hit the mark. The second man lay on the ground below her. His head was crushed on one side. She could see his eyes staring up at the sky. They didn't blink.

She ran along the edge of the cliff until it met the trail and hurried down the switchbacks. When she arrived at the dead man, she grabbed his radio and his AR-15. She kept moving until she was well off the trail and out of sight. Then she examined the rifle carefully. She had never shot a gun before and was afraid of trying. But her mom was being held prisoner, and there was at least one more man who also had a gun that stood in her way. She would have to try to overcome her fear once more.

Slinging the gun around her shoulder, she headed back toward the cabin. She wanted to try shooting it first but wanted to be within earshot so that it might draw him out into the woods.

She approached the cabin cautiously, from a different angle than before. She could see the open and empty grave, where all of this had started. She felt her anxiety increasing and had to pause, to let the woods fill her up again. They had protected her. They would keep protecting her.

She moved a little closer until she could see the deck through the dense underbrush. The man was still out there. He looked angry. He was holding a radio like the one she had and kept yelling into it. She had turned hers off so that it wouldn't make a noise.

She had used a radio before, with her dad. This was how he gradually gave her more space in the woods. They would leave the house together, but then he would send her ahead, staying connected by radio. He would talk to her softly, reassure her, coach her from a distance. Her mom never knew about that, but he was preparing her to be on her own, fostering her independence.

She looked at the radio. With the volume down, she could almost imagine that it was hers and that he was on the other end, still encouraging and coaching. *Just lift the gun against your shoulder, aim the barrel, and pull the trigger.*

She lifted it up, aimed at a tree and squeezed. The gun's kickback wasn't as bad as she expected. She had closed her eyes and missed the target, but she tried again immediately and saw a small chunk of bark fly into the air.

The first shot caught his attention. On the second shot, he stepped off the deck, held his gun out in front of him and began walking directly to where she was hiding.

CHAPTER SEVENTY-TWO

Atkins heard the bullet whistle past him but couldn't tell which direction it was coming from. Then, there was a second shot that hit a tree about 20 yards in front of him. It was far enough away that he knew that he was not the target.

He grabbed his radio and yelled into it, "What the hell are you doing? Are you trying to kill me? Stop shooting in this direction! If you see the girl, we'll surround her. I want her alive!"

After no response, he clipped the radio to his belt and headed toward where he thought the bullet had come from. There had been no radio chatter for quite a while. He figured that they had turned off the radios when they had seen her, so as not to give away their locations. He would have to intercept them physically and make a new plan. Over an hour had passed since they started after her. She must be proving more slippery than any of them had anticipated. She must be close by though if one of them was shooting.

He held his gun out front and covered the open space between the deck and the woods as quickly as possible. When he got to the first layer of trees, he stopped, looked around, and listened for any sign of his guys. He grabbed the radio again, "No more shooting. Meet me at the gravesite. Now!"

Atkins moved through the stand of aspens until he emerged again in the clearing that housed the open pit at its far end. He crossed over the space and looked down into the pit. *Still empty.* But the pile of dirt had been disturbed with fresh footprints. *Small. Definitely female-sized. She was just here,* he thought. *That's why they were shooting.*

The prints led away from the grave and back into the woods. He followed them for about fifty yards until they merged with a trail before disappearing on the more compact dirt. *She's on the trail now,* he figured, and started moving rapidly ahead hoping to catch her before she got much further.

After ten minutes, the trail came near the stream and forked. He wasn't sure which way she would have gone but figured she would stay close to the water, so he turned in that direction and crossed over the river on a bridge of logs. A little further along he could hear the rushing sound of a waterfall. He saw a smaller trail break off and a large boot print heading in that direction. That was one of his guys. He followed the larger set of prints until he could see the waterfall rising from the forest floor. As he approached, he could see something near the base of the cliff. Raising his gun, he moved slowly ahead, but then he recognized him. It was Joel, his back bent unnaturally over a rock. Atkins reached the body and looked into Joel's empty gaze. *Dead. Shit!*

Atkins turned around and started immediately back to the cabin, moving as quickly as he could without risking a fall. He slung his gun over his shoulder to help him keep his balance, his arms unencumbered. When he got closer and could see the cabin deck, he grabbed his gun again and approached cautiously. Everything was quiet and when he had left.

He climbed the steps slowly trying to avoid any creaks, then opened the screen door and slid inside. Everything seemed undisturbed. He turned into the back room and lifted the trap door. Slowly he went down the stairs, his gun held out in front. It took a minute for his eyes to adjust to the dark but when they did, he could see three bodies across the room, still tied together. He let out a sigh and lowered his gun. "Are you all enjoying each other's company?"

As he moved closer, bending his head so that he didn't hit the rafters, he could see Quinn staring angrily back at him. He shifted his gaze to Susan, who smiled at him. *No gag.* Next to her sat a pretty, young woman, holding her mother's hand and avoiding eye contact. In the split second that it took him to process what was going on, he felt the barrel of a gun against his back. "Drop it, now, Atkins! And I mean now!"

Chuck waited for Atkins to drop his gun and then kicked it out of reach. He grabbed Atkins' arm and wrenched it behind his back while chopping his knees so that he fell hard to the floor. Chuck pushed Atkins forward with all his weight and further twisted his wrist so that any further movement by either of them would snap his bones.

"Sandra, can you bring me some of that rope, please?"

Sandra grabbed the coil of rope that she had cut from her mom's arms and legs. It was still long enough. She brought it over to Chuck who secured it around Atkins' wrists and then tied them to his ankles.

"That should do it," Chuck said. "Susan, I need you to watch these two long enough for me to go upstairs and call for help. Can you do that?" He handed her the gun. "If they move, shoot them."

"Gladly," Susan said, with a look of fierce determination on her face. She pointed the gun at Atkins' head, "You don't think I could do it? You messed with my daughter. I would not even think twice. Do you really want to try me?"

Sandra got up and moved closer to Quinn. The light from upstairs was shining exactly right to highlight his eyes. She stayed just out of reach as she stared into them. Deeply. She could see it all: his fake bravado, his pain from growing up in a family without love. Mostly she saw fear and regret. Those eyes would never haunt her dreams again.

CHAPTER SEVENTY-THREE

At the police station, Chuck began working on all the paperwork that was required to process the arrests of Agent Atkins and Quinn, as well as the deaths of the three men who had been with Atkins at Slater's cabin. The murder of the officer at the Madison residence was seemingly not directly connected to Atkins, and Atkins told them that Wesley was dead, though they had not yet found his body. Gary, also, was nowhere to be found. The three boys who were being held in the Kalispel facility were released to their parents' supervision until the trial for Slater's murder but would surely be acquitted after the jury heard the testimony against Quinn and Atkins. It was very likely that the two of them would spend the next several decades, at a minimum, in prison.

Chuck stared at the computer screen in front of him and the stack of files that now cluttered his desk. He could see his reflection staring back at him from the screen. He had been prepared to sacrifice everything to save Sandra and her mother. In the end, it was Sandra that saved him. He had been given a second chance in life, and he knew it.

"Kathy," he said, after hitting the intercom button on his phone, "please get the FBI on the phone. Thank you ... "

"Yes, sir."

"And Kathy?"

"Sir?"

"Thank you."

"For what, Chief?"

"Just call me Chuck, okay?"

A few minutes later, Chuck spoke again into the phone receiver. "Yes ... This is Chuck Peters, the current chief of police in Whitefish, Montana ... Yes. That's the one ... I'm happy to have been able to help, and I'm glad we caught him before he caused more damage. Anyway, I'm calling to confess my own sins. Can you please connect me to someone in the Chicago violent crimes division? Thank you."

While he waited on hold, Chuck took off his gun belt and laid it on the desk. He then removed his badge and held it in his hand for a moment. That badge used to be his life, all he had left. Now, it had lost its power for him. He was ready to make amends and then to face what was leftover with a different perspective, hopefully a little wiser, a little kinder, and with a lot better understanding of what it meant to be a hero. Yes, Sandra and her mother had taught him that, too.

CHAPTER SEVENTY-FOUR

Susan sat in silence at her dining room table, next to Sandra who was trying to type something on her laptop. Sandra had already started multiple times. A string of letters filled several lines on the document but were unintelligible as words. After several minutes, Sandra got frustrated, deleted everything, and started over. Susan could see Sandra's body stiffening, and her breathing becoming more rapid.

It had now been almost a week since the arrest of Agent Atkins and Quinn, and Sandra had spent most of that time recovering, sleeping mostly. After the mental firepower that it took for Sandra to do what she did, her body kind of shut down for a while. But, that evening, she had come out of her room holding her laptop. She sat at the table and motioned for Susan to join her.

As she watched Sandra struggle and her anxiety build, Susan resisted her maternal instinct to jump in and save her from the conflict. Sandra had already proven that she didn't need to be rescued.

"Sandra, just take your time, sweetheart. We've got all evening. Or tomorrow. Or the day after that. Thanks to you, that is."

Sandra looked up from the computer briefly and acknowledged her mother, but she had something that she really needed to say, and her brain was blocking her again.

Ever since she had returned to her mother's house from the ordeal in the woods, her soul had been strangely quiet. She couldn't understand why that was the case. Hadn't her soul proven its strength, its dominance over her brain? Why would it go back into hiding now?

Sandra had figured that everything would be easier now and that her life would be transformed. But here she was, craving a conversation with her mother, and now she had lost her ability to find the stupid letters on the keyboard.

Sandra slammed down the screen on the laptop as she felt her anxiety heating to a boil. She started heading toward her sensory room when her mother grabbed her arm and stopped her.

"You are going the wrong way, honey."

Susan redirected Sandra outside on the deck and sat her down on a swinging bench that looked out over the woods. She sat with her for about fifteen minutes without speaking as they rocked gently back and forth. They listened to the rustle of the aspen leaves and the music of the birds. A squirrel ran along the edge of the metal railing that bordered the deck and chattered at some unseen irritant in the woods below. The sun was warm but pleasant, and the smell of pine was fresh in the air.

Susan could feel the tension releasing from Sandra's body as they sat there together. Why had she never done that with her before? It was always her father that loved the woods. Susan was more of a city girl. She had agreed to move to Montana after he retired, mostly to get away from doctors and therapists and crowded grocery stores where Sandra was more likely to have a meltdown. But she had never appreciated where she lived like she did now, sitting here with her incredible daughter.

When Sandra had completely relaxed, Susan got up and went back into the house. Moments later, she came out holding Sandra's laptop in one hand and a brochure in the other. The brochure was folded so that Sandra couldn't see what was printed on it.

Susan opened the laptop, put it on the outdoor dining table, and motioned for Sandra to come over. Sandra did and sat next to her on a bench. Susan opened a word document and began typing with the screen positioned in such a way that they could both read it.

Dear Sandra,

I am going to type this conversation. I don't know if that will help you or not, but I'm suspecting now that it is easier for you to process language this way.

First, I want you to know that I have dreamed of this day for more years than you have been mine—for the day that I could sit down with my adult daughter and have a real heart-to-heart. You came into my life like a shining star and have changed me forever. I knew you were special from the day I first laid my eyes on you.

We have had quite a journey together, haven't we? Lots of challenging moments for sure. Sometimes I think I may have lost sight of you in the midst of it all. But I've never stopped loving you and hoping that, someday, your life would be filled with everything that you deserve.

Thank you, Sandra, for saving me. And I'm not talking about what happened in that root cellar. I'm talking about who I am because of you. You made me stronger, kinder, more patient, less judgmental of others. I am better because of you, and I am grateful.

Sandra grabbed the laptop and typed without mistake. *Mom, I love you.*

Susan responded aloud. "I have something to show you. You have given us more time together; I'm not sure how much more time, but I don't want to waste a minute of it."

She opened the brochure and laid it flat on the table in front of Sandra. It was a real estate brochure with a picture of a house on a private lake. Susan pulled up the listing on the laptop and scrolled through the pictures. The house had an open floor plan with the outdoor living space spilling inside, separated only by a retractable wall of windows between the great room and an even larger covered deck. There was a tree growing through the deck and out of the roof like it was a support post. The deck had multiple levels that cascaded down to the lake where there was a dock for kayaks and canoes. The house was made of all wood and stone that blended in beautifully with the surroundings, like it was built by Mother Nature herself.

Sandra scrolled through the pictures several times and smiled brightly. She opened the word document again and typed, *It's beautiful.*

Susan pulled up another page which showed a signed contract. "It's ours if we want it," she said.

Sandra started typing something but stopped in mid-sentence. She looked at her mom. Deeply. She stared for minutes without looking away, each of them absorbing each other's desires, touching each other's souls.

Sandra broke eye contact first and grabbed the brochure. She touched the keyboard once more and paused. She closed her eyes, taking in the sounds of the woods and filling her soul with energy. She then started typing.

Yes. A home in the woods. A new life. A daughter and a mother. Long lost conversations. Walks in the forest. Home.

AUTHOR'S NOTE

In the story, there was a moment where Sandra saw her words immortalized outside of her brain for the first time. I have had that experience, and, in fact, completing this novel is another moment like that for me. Like Sandra, I have autism. Like Sandra, my language is limited. And like Sandra, I know what it feels like to be trapped in your own mind.

My journey has paralleled hers in some ways, although the details are mostly different. I did grow up without a way to communicate what I was thinking inside my head. I spent many years doing Applied Behavioral Analysis and many more years in the special education system, though neither of them gave me what I wanted the most—a way to truly unlock my potential. I knew that I was smart enough but that I had emotional intelligence as well, something that most autism experts would not assume is possible. I just couldn't express it, so no one else knew. And life became very dark and hopeless for me.

When I was fifteen, I started working with a woman named Soma Mukhopadhyay who had developed a method for helping nonverbal or limited verbal people with autism break out of their shells and to express what she knew was in there. I won't go into details about how she does it, but here is her website if you want more information. www.halo-soma.org. I took those early skills and, more importantly, the confidence that she gave me, and translated them to an iPad. And that is how I wrote this novel.

I have heard from other authors that, once started, the story takes on a life of its own and the characters are born on the screen. That is definitely how it was for me. Before starting, I had a few basic ideas about the story and the main character, Sandra, but she came to life for me as I went along.

Some readers are undoubtedly wondering if she is me, just fictionalized. I would say yes and no. I definitely understand Sandra on a deeper level than anyone who has not experienced her challenges. I do feel the daily battle between what I want to achieve and believe I have the intellectual capacity to accomplish and my other challenges that keep holding me back. I, too, struggle with sometimes debilitating anxiety and have had to devise ways to deal with that internally. Some of my methods are the same as Sandra's and some are different. I do have an important relationship with nature, and being outside is where I can best think and focus and plan. In the mountains, in particular, I feel less autistic. But Sandra is her own person, and in many ways, she has become my hero. I aspire for her courage and independence and persistence.

In the story, I also touched somewhat on the subject of human trafficking. It was a much larger part of my first draft of this story, but it felt like it was adding too much complication to the storyline, so I changed it on the rewrite. That said, as I researched the problem, I was astounded about how prevalent it is in our country and throughout the world. I still wanted to leave it in as part of this version because those victims have some parallels with what Sandra experienced. Like people with disabilities, they are also marginalized, trapped and voiceless.

Sandra can be their champion, too. Who knows—maybe that is what drives her in the next phase of her life?

Thank you for reading. I hope that this story helps the readers to pause when they meet someone who is labeled as "disabled," whether it be through physical, emotional, or intellectual challenges, and consider instead their strengths, their abilities, their capacities and yes, even their power to change the world around them for the better.

Aaron Jepson

ACKNOWLEDGMENTS

I have many people to thank for helping me complete this project. First, I thank God for giving me a way to break out of my shell. I have proposed that the commonly used symbol for autism of a puzzle piece be replaced by an acorn. The acorn is small, unimpressive in and of itself, but inside, carries everything needed to transform into a great tree. All it needs is the right environment to unlock this potential. God has blessed me with this environment, and I am indebted.

I thank my parents for planting me in rich soil and watering me daily, although it was many years before I sprouted. This dedication and perseverance made all the difference.

I thank my many teachers and therapists over the years who were all so kind and always did their best for me. I thank Soma Mukhopadhyay for developing a communication system that worked for me and helped me to envision the possibilities.

This book was a several-year effort and included a full revision. My dad sat by my side for every word. I never could have stuck with it without him. My mom is my biggest cheerleader and helped me so much in character development and bringing Sandra to life. Thanks to my proofreaders including my grandparents Don and Carolyn Jepson, my brother Ben, and his fiancé, Becky.

I need to thank my brothers Ben and Austin. Ben is the oldest in our family and is not autistic. He had to put up with a lot growing up with a brother with my challenges but did so with patience and grace. I will always look up to him. My younger brother, Austin, joined our family when he was seven. Unlike me, his early life was not conducive to the sprouting of his acorn. His challenges definitely exceed my own, but he was the first of us to start spelling out his thoughts. The things that he writes are so beautiful that it inspires me to try harder. He has a book of poetry called *Passing by the Moon* that is available on Amazon. I encourage you all to check it out.

I also want to acknowledge all the people out there who work so hard to break down barriers for people with all kinds of disabilities. Your efforts are noticed and so appreciated.

Finally, thanks to all my peers who the world labels disabled but who get up every day determined to prove that the world has it wrong. You are the true heroes of this story and inspire me to never quit trying to overcome my own obstacles. Thank you.

Aaron Jepson

ABOUT THE AUTHOR

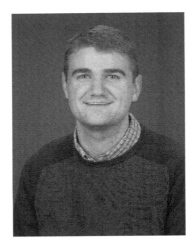

Aaron Jepson lives in Monument, Colorado with his family. Besides writing, he loves to spend time in the outdoors. His favorite place is his family cabin in Grand Lake, Colorado, near Rocky Mountain National Park. The setting in this novel of Whitefish, Montana is a similar kind of place, so it felt natural. Aaron also loves running and has completed five marathons at the time of this publication. He has also learned how to mountain bike, cross-country ski, and downhill ski and has climbed eight 14,000-foot peaks, so far. Aaron is diagnosed with autism and has limited verbal language. This is his first novel. You can follow him on his blog at www.aaronjepson.com.

Made in the USA
Middletown, DE
09 July 2023

34176371R00203